DEADLY OBSESSION

by

Shirley B. Garrett

Positive Directions LLC
Huntsville, Alabama

This is a work of fiction. All of the characters, organizations, and events portrayed in this novel are either products of the author's imagination or are used fictitiously.

DEADLY OBSESSION

ISBN: 978-1-943065-05-9

Published by Positive Directions LLC, Huntsville, AL.

Cover design by Dan Thompson and Shirley B. Garrett

PREVIOUS BOOKS IN THE

CHARLIE STONE CRIME THRILLER SERIES

Deadly Compulsion

Deadly Lessons

Also by Shirley B. Garrett,

the Phoenix O'Leary Hot Flash series

Hot Flash Divas

Hot Flash Desires

Hot Flash Decisions

DEDICATION

This book is dedicated to all the innocent victims of gun violence.

ACKNOWLEDGMENTS

Many people have helped me with the writing of this book. My gratitude to the following writer's critique groups for your guidance, constructive criticism, and encouragement: North Alabama Mystery Writers, The Huntsville Literary Association, and Coffee and Critique.

The following beta readers offered their valuable time and expertise to help me improve this novel: Edie Peterson, Bonita McCoy, and F.E. Anderson.

Special thanks to Larry's Pistol and Pawn in Huntsville, Alabama, for helping me to choose the weapons for this book and for the training and opportunity to fire the weapons for my research.

Glenn Grady served as my weapons expert beta reader and helped me to correct many of the details I had wrong. Without him, the book would be less authentic.

Without the support of my family and friends, my writing life would be much more difficult. Thanks for having my back.

My appreciation to my editor, Lisa Prince, whose diligent efforts made my manuscript better.

My highest gratitude goes to my husband, Bob, who supports me in so many ways while I struggle to achieve literary success.

Table of Contents

Table of Contents, continued

CHAPTER 1

The Marksman swiped the stinging sweat out of his eyes with the back of his hand and thought, *If this August heat don't kill me, nothing else will. It's almost September. When will this heat wave break?* A swarm of gnats circled his face trying to sneak up his nose and ears. With a discreet wave of his hand, he once again shooed them away, for all the good it would do.

The neighborhood over Chapman Mountain in Huntsville, Alabama was perfect for his needs with plenty of trees and shrubbery. He lay hidden under a thin camouflage sheet, nestled between several large azaleas. The occasional smell of dog urine wafted past.

Some mutt probably marked his territory.

Most of the homeowners were at work, and the rest were hibernating during the heat of the day in their air-conditioned houses, except the old man who kept moving his sprinkler. His bandy legs poked out of wrinkled khaki shorts, topped by a grey tee shirt stretched to capacity by his bulging gut.

The gut's an interesting target.

His grandfather's truck was parked one street over, a quick jog away between two houses. He'd placed stolen magnetic lawn care signs on the trucks doors and put a push mower and weed eater in the bed of the truck for camouflage.

After the Marksman first settled in place, he'd used his laser rangefinder to determine the distance to the planned kill zone. It was a hundred and twenty yards away. With this information, he adjusted his scope the way his grandfather had taught him.

A postal truck worked its way, its engine revving and slowing, box-by-box toward a special painted one. When he sighted down his

1

scope, the Marksman noticed the heat waves rising off the white hood. He mumbled, "Grumps would say it's hotter than Hades."

The Marksman shifted his focus to the driver in time to see a bead of sweat trickle down the side of his dark, shiny face. The guy's graying curls glistened in the unrelenting sun. *At least I'm not suffering alone.*

The old man came out and moved the sprinkler again. It made the classic repetitive sound the Marksman associated with summer. An occasional breeze wafted the clean, fresh scent of water his way, offering a brief respite from the baking heat and the odor of dog urine.

He sighted on the retreating back of the balding old man, who disappeared behind a red door.

The Marksman glanced at his watch. *He'll be back in twenty minutes to move that damned sprinkler again.*

He focused back on the postal worker, who was sorting a large rubber-banded wad of mail. The worker's hands had gnarled, arthritic knuckles like his grandfather's. *A big bundle like that would've given Grumps a fit.* After, flexing his neck and shoulders, the Marksman decided the guy looked a few years short of retirement. *Too bad he won't get to enjoy his benefits.*

The Alabama sun and the cloak of humidity drained the Marksman's reserves like an energy-sucking vampire. Sweat tickled his scalp. He paused to wipe his face and head with his handkerchief and to shoo away more of the pesky gnats.

His Grump's voice spoke in his head. *"Be patient, boy. A little sweat and a few gnats don't hurt nobody."*

During the week he did his surveillance. The old man had watered his yard like clockwork and the mailman always took longer at this particular box. His typical pattern in this neighborhood was to shove envelopes inside the boxes and drive to the next. He treated this custom-painted one with care.

People with mailboxes this fancy were picky. Hell, maybe he has a supervisor riding his ass like a cowboy on a bull, just waiting for him to screw up. If so, that worry is about to disappear.

The homeowner had placed large square boulders of limestone around the mailbox to protect it. The Marksman had noticed at least ten damaged boxes. *A damn wide road and the idiots in this neighborhood can't miss a mailbox?*

The Marksman shouldered his rifle.

The rocks forced the postman to release his seatbelt so he could lean further out to open the box. He winced while he yanked on the door.

Time to put you out of your misery. He squeezed the trigger.

The postman was still tugging on the door when the bullet pierced his skull. He jerked. Brains from the exit wound exploded across the white mail truck. Slumping, he slid out of the vehicle. It idled down the road until it entered a nearby yard, where it came to an abrupt halt. The front end wedged against the slope of a drainage ditch.

The body lay crumpled in front of the box painted with a pleasant mountain scene. A bizarre death marker.

The Marksman pumped his fist. *A one shot kill! Grumps will be proud.*

"Get your ass outa here, boy. Time to celebrate later."

CHAPTER 2

Dr. Charlene Stone stood under the funeral tent lost in her own thoughts while the minister droned words of comfort. She hadn't known the two people being interred. She was there to support her patient, Rose Maynard. The double funeral was for Rose's mother, who died from a stroke the day Rose escaped her abusive home at the age of eighteen, and Rose's infant daughter, who'd been murdered by her father and eldest brother, to cover up the incest occurring in her home. The bodies had recently been found on the old family homestead during a criminal investigation.

Furious that the two most important people in her life had been buried behind her family home like dogs, Rose had told Charlie she wanted them to have a proper burial with gravestones.

Charlie's friend and business partner, Marti Hathoway, stood next to her. She and Marti shared a private practice and were members of the Huntsville Police Department's new Sexual Assault Task Force or SATF for short.

Since Rose was a patient in the sexual abuse therapy group that Charlie and Marti supervised, several of the group members had attended the service to offer support.

The minister was reaching the end of his diatribe, when Detective Ryan Roberts, homicide division, entered the shade of the tent. He moved close to Charlie and took her hand.

Charlie smiled at him, tears glistening in her eyes.

He gave her hand a squeeze.

Ryan had been present when Rose's relatives were discovered; along with other, yet to be identified victims. Rose was so grateful that he'd located her mom and daughter's remains, that she insisted he attend the burial.

After the funeral, two white doves were released. Each spiraled higher into the cerulean blue sky. Rose's fellow group members surrounded her for a group hug. When they'd finished, Rose walked to the three waiting professionals.

"Detective Ryan, so glad you could make it."

Ryan extended a hand and Rose took it, smiling up into his face.

"I told you I'd try my best."

Rose released Ryan's hand and turned to Charlie. "Dr. Stone, wasn't it a beautiful ceremony?"

"Lovely and meaningful," Charlie said.

"Ms. Marti, I appreciate you coming, too."

Marti nodded.

Rose shifted her purse to her other shoulder and looked over to where her fellow group members were standing. "I need to run. We're going to lunch."

Charlie nodded and turned to leave. She treaded her way between gravestones to her car. As she neared her Honda, a flapping note under her windshield wiper caught her attention. Curious, she lifted the wiper to retrieve it.

Charlie stopped for a moment looking back. Ryan and Marti weren't behind her. They were still by the funeral tent talking. Squinting, she shaded her eyes with her hand, hoping to catch a final glimpse of the doves. They were gone.

A dizzy spell caused her to stumble. She shook her head hoping to disperse the feeling while she pulled the car keys from her purse. *Must be the heat. I hope September will be cooler.*

Opening the car door, she tossed her purse in to the passenger seat. While she waited for the enclosed heat to seep from the car, she opened the folded paper.

The note read, "YOU WILL BE MINE OR YOU WILL DIE."

Her hands shook, causing the paper to rattle. Her insides seemed to quiver as she sank into the driver's seat. She reread the note.

The SATF had recently captured the Trainer, a serial kidnapper, rapist, and murderer. Charlie had felt a measure of closure on that case —at least until now. She looked out over the miles of flat headstones dotted with vases of fake flowers. *Crap! Did that controlling, sadistic maniac escape?*

Charlie's mind raced back to his attempt to kidnap her, so he could brainwash her to become his perfect wife.

Marti stepped off the curb and approached her car. "Hey, Charlie, now that the funeral's over I was thinking we could go get pizza. Ryan wants to go. Do you…." Her voice trailed away when she rounded the hood of the car and saw Charlie.

Charlie looked up.

"Ryan! Come quick," Marti yelled as she dropped to one knee in front of her friend and placed a hand on her forehead. "You look pale. Are you sick?"

Ryan jogged over.

Marti stood and shifted to the side. "She feels clammy."

Ryan knelt in front of Charlie and pried the note from her fingers. His concerned expression morphed to anger. "Where did you find this?" Ryan placed a hand on each shoulder and gave her a gentle shake. "Charlie, answer me."

"On the windshield." Charlie met his gaze and read the worry in his eyes.

Marti stood on tiptoe to peek around Ryan's shoulder so she could read the note. "What the hell! Has the Trainer escaped? Is he threatening Charlie again?"

Ryan pulled his phone from his pocket and called Detective Werner Griffin, the head of the SATF.

"Griffin, this is Roberts. I'm checking on the Trainer. He's still in Taylor Hardin Hospital? Right? No transfers, or anything like that?" Ryan pressed his phone to his ear listening.

Charlie bit her lip as she thought about Taylor Hardin and the fact that it was only a mere two hours away in Tuscaloosa. Her stomach cramped. *Too close.*

"Well, you need to check. Someone left a note on Charlie's car threatening to kill her. If it's not the Trainer, we need to find out who, and pronto." Ryan ended the call and looked at the two women. "Werner will phone to verify that he's still in custody."

After shoving his phone into his pocket, Ryan pulled Charlie into his arms. He held her tight, murmuring words of comfort into her ear.

"I feel shaky and faint. I think I need to eat. I skipped breakfast."

Ryan said, "I'll drive to the restaurant."

On the way to eat, Charlie wondered, *If it's not the Trainer, who? Is it one of my former patients?*

CHAPTER 3

Charlie eyed the garlic bread in her oven while she half listened to Ryan's rant about his current murder case in North-East Huntsville. Murder wasn't her favorite dinner topic but she could see this recent case had bothered Ryan and he needed to discuss it.

Ryan paced the kitchen. "I tell you, Charlie, Tyson Jones was delivering the mail on his route like he has for years, and someone shot him." Ryan held up two fingers. "The guy was two years away from retirement."

Charlie pulled the bread out, flooding the kitchen with the aroma of butter and zesty garlic.

Ryan froze mid-step and sniffed.

She placed the slices on the stove. "Poor guy." Turning, she walked to the fridge and pulled out two bowls of salad.

"It was a clean shot to the head. Not a pretty sight." Ryan reached to take the bowls from her before transporting them to the small table nestled in the breakfast nook.

"Was it close or a distance shot?" Charlie dug in the fridge for the salad dressing.

"Distance. We'll know more about the weapon when we get the report back on the bullet. We found where the shooter hid under some bushes but didn't find a shell casing. It's one of those neighborhoods where most folks work, so our door-to-doors weren't helpful. There was one older gentleman who said he was in and out moving his sprinkler. He didn't see or hear anything. He's hard of hearing."

Charlie handed Ryan the dressing bottles before returning to the stove to stir her sauce. The steam from the spaghetti noodles made her face feel hot. After fishing out a strand, she blew to cool it, and gave it a test nibble. She smiled. *Perfect.*

Ryan placed the dressing on the table. "The woman who owned the mailbox freaked out when she came home and found the police, paramedics, and a coroner's van parked around her house."

"I imagine discovering your postman dead at your mailbox would be a shock." Charlie pulled off her scrunchy and shook her blonde locks until they fell in a curtain down her back. "My heart goes out to the poor soul who was shot." She frowned. "His family must be devastated. I can't imagine what I'd do if someone came to my door to tell me you were killed, and we're only dating."

In truth, she thought about this possibility quite often. Now she had even more to worry about since she had received the threatening note. The good news was Detective Werner had confirmed the Trainer was still secure at Taylor Harden Hospital for the criminally insane. The bad news: they still had no idea who wrote the note.

Ryan interrupted her musings. "Joe and I told his wife. You know how I hate that part of my job. I wish they'd add informing victim's families about deaths to your consulting duties."

Charlie held up both hands as if warding off a curse. "Oh, no you don't, Ryan. I have enough on my plate with the profiling, SATF, and my private practice. Besides, I wouldn't want that job anyway. I'd be crying with them. Don't you dare hint such an idea to Captain Strouper."

She stirred her meat sauce. "Was it bad? Telling his wife?"

Ryan looked down. "Mrs. Jones covered her face and wailed. She swayed a little and dropped to the floor with a thud. She was out. Joe and I were standing there like two fools."

"Bless her heart. I hope you called the paramedics after she fainted." Charlie filled two glasses with sweet iced tea and placed them on the table.

"We did. It took four of us to get Mrs. Jones on the gurney. She was a lotta woman." Ryan ran both hands through his dark, wavy hair. "Must have been a combination of the shock and the heat. You know how hot it was yesterday. We were all drenched with sweat within minutes of arriving on the scene. I swear I felt like I was inhaling a lungful of steam."

Ryan walked around the table and wrapped Charlie in his arms. "This case has really bothered me for some reason. I couldn't wait to get here tonight. When we're together things seem more tolerable." He nuzzled her neck.

"That tickles." She wiggled out of his grip and walked to the stove. You've got me curious. "How was Mr. Jones discovered?" She slid the hot bread into a towel-lined basket.

"He fell out of the truck in front of the mailbox." Ryan ran his hands through his hair again. "No telling how long it was before the old guy across the street found him. He admitted to the reporting officer that he'd fallen asleep while watching The Weather Channel. After his nap, he came out to move his sprinkler and noticed the mail truck. It was still running and stuck in the drainage ditch. Curious, he walked over to check it out and saw all the blood. The report said he went back inside and called 911."

Ryan walked over and put an arm around her waist. "The reason I'm telling you all this, is because I suggested to Joe that we should have you do a profile. Joe's not opposed to the idea but wants to run with it a bit first."

Charlie nodded. "What time of day was the victim found?" She turned on the cold water, placed the colander in the sink, and pointed toward the large pot on the stove.

"We're estimating the hottest part of the day, around two." Ryan hefted the large pot of boiling pasta and poured the steaming contents into the colander to drain. "He was beginning to stink and the flies were all over him."

"Thanks, Ryan. I really needed to hear those details before a meal." Charlie gave her meat sauce a final stir and poured it into a blue bowl.

"Sorry." Ryan shook the colander a few times and poured the steaming pasta into a large matching blue bowl sitting on the counter, before carrying it to the table.

They each took their seats at the small table for two in the breakfast nook.

Charlie's beagle, Spanky trotted over and sat next to her. The year-old pup placed her head on Charlie's shoe and sighed. Charlie looked down and smiled.

"I wonder if the Post Office will put the vehicle out of service?" Ryan opened his bottle of dressing and drizzled it onto his salad.

"Why?" Charlie covered her spaghetti with the red meat sauce.

"You know."

Charlie looked into Ryan's eyes and down at the blood red sauce that covered her plate. Her stomach tumbled. She imagined for a moment she'd picked up a whiff of the coppery scent of blood. As an FBI-trained psychological profiler, she knew the smell all too well. Several past bloody murder scenes flashed through her mind. She pushed the pasta away and pulled the salad in front of her.

"Let's discuss something less gruesome."

"Good idea."

Charlie stabbed a slice of carrot with her fork. "Our new Office Mommy is working out great."

"What's her name again?"

"Deloris Monk."

"I'm glad it's working out. I'll feel better knowing there's someone else there to dial 911 if needed." Ryan speared lettuce on his fork and gave her an earnest look. "This whole thing with the threatening note on your car and now this shooting has me worried. We don't know if this shooting was personal or if we have some nut out there with a gun doing target practice."

"Remember, Werner said the Trainer is still locked away. He's no threat to me."

"True, but we don't know who sent the note. The only prints we've found were yours and mine," said Ryan. "So I've been thinking…"

"About what?" Charlie picked up her knife to cut up a large leaf of lettuce.

"That you should move in with me…on a permanent basis."

Charlie's knife clattered to the table.

CHAPTER 4

The Marksman squatted behind a shield of scrub bush on an undeveloped lot across the street from the Happy Days Retirement Home. He'd spent an entire week of research before choosing this site, this prey, this day.

He unzipped his last birthday present from Grumps, a backpack for his rifle. Grumps never scrimped when it came to his gifts of firearms and accessories.

The Marksman released his rifle from its Velcro strap and gave it a quick caress. It was a beauty: a Remington 700 Action with a 16-inch barrel and a custom-built AICS 2.0 short action stock. He remembered his excitement when he'd opened it on Christmas morning two years ago.

He folded out the stock, attached his quick-mount locking Vortex Viper PST scope using the levers, and made sure everything was secure. He peered through the scope to satisfy himself that it was clean enough.

Grumps said, *"If you take care of your equipment, it'll take care of you."*

He pulled the quick-detach bipod from a pocket in the backpack and attached it to the rifle.

A vehicle stopped. He shifted forward to peer between branches. A UPS driver jumped from the truck carrying a package toward the front entrance of the facility. Five minutes later he returned to the truck and left.

Satisfied all was clear, the Marksman reached for the AAC SDM 6 Suppressor and screwed it onto the barrel. He then inserted several

.308 subsonic rounds into the magazine, pushed the bolt forward and rotated the bolt handle down.

It's September and it's already hotter than Hades.

"Quit your whining, boy. If you're going to be a man you need to buck up," Grumps said.

He whispered, "Yes, sir."

Sweat trickled down his forehead He pulled out a sweatband, and placed it on his head to keep his eyes free of the stinging perspiration.

He squinted across the street. *Not yet.*

"Better get moving, boy."

The Marksman secured the rifle in place before pulling out his camouflage sheet. He shoved the black backpack out of sight under a nearby bush.

After scooting between the bushes, he adjusted the placement of the rifle and pulled the sheet over his back to hide him. He was early, but he understood from experience prey could be unpredictable. A mosquito hovered near his face. He slapped at his cheek, his hand coming away bloody. *Got that little bloodsucker.*

Grumps said, *"Mosquitoes are the least of your worries. Stay sharp!"*

He'd checked the range on a previous reconnaissance, so all he had to do was adjust his scope for one hundred and thirty-five yards. He peered through it and smiled when the crosshairs lined up on one of the three rockers on the porch of the facility. *Excellent. Now all I have to do is wait.*

Thirty minutes passed. The Marksman shifted his position.

Grumps said, *Quit squirming. You gotta learn discipline.*

The door opened. The Marksman stiffened, preparing to shoot. A woman in her twenties came out the door of the facility. She wore a long white tee shirt that displayed the word BABY with an arrow pointing to her rounded belly. He scoped the bump of her protruding belly button. *Interesting. It's almost like a bull's eye. A twofer.*

His grandfather's voice rang clear in his mind. *"You've got to stay on track, kid. Don't get distracted by every squirrel that crosses your path. Choose your prey and wait it out."*

The woman was in her car now, backing out of the space. Her black SUV disappeared down the street.

A slight breeze fluttered the leaves. *No more than four miles an hour*, he estimated. *I'll take that into account.* He settled down and waited.

The door opened, again.

Grumps said, *"Look lively, boy."*

A hunched woman with a cap of tight, white curls pushed her walker to the chair on the far left. The golden yellow tennis balls that covered the front feet of her walker came into sharp focus through the scope. She aligned her walker against the rail and eased herself into the chair like a piece of fragile crystal.

The Marksman rolled his shoulders to ease his stiffness. *Not yet.*

A man with a headful of thick, iron-grey hair shuffled out leaning on a four-pronged cane. His eyes remained focused on the cement porch in front of his feet. He turned to sit and began the slow descent until he fell the rest of the way into the rocker next to the woman.

Come on. The Marksman wiped his nose with his sleeve.

Grumps's voice said, *"You can't hunt, boy, if you're not patient."*

Several minutes passed before a frail, spindly-legged Asian man walked with careful deliberation onto the porch. Wire-rimmed spectacles perched on his wrinkled face. He tottered over to the woman and handed her a pair of glasses.

She smiled and took them, offering a nod.

He made it back to the empty rocker and lowered himself into the seat. Once settled, he laid his head against the high back of the chair, closed his eyes, and smiled.

All three seemed content to sit and enjoy the peaceful sunny morning.

The Marksman adjusted the crosshairs on his target. The wind had died down. He was ready.

"Be patient," Grumps' voice reminded him. *"Line up your shot and squeeze the trigger."*

He took a deep breath and squeezed the trigger on his exhale.

The Asian man jerked. The bullet entered the center of his forehead, and his face collapsed. He was dead before the man and woman sitting on the porch could hear the muffled pop of the silenced rifle shot.

The Marksman pocketed the casing and scooted backward out from under the sheet. He folded it and pulled the rifle toward him. He pulled out his backpack from under the bushes and began disassembling his rifle.

He heard a woman scream and scream and scream.

"Do it faster, boy. As many times as we practiced this you should be quicker," Grumps said.

With trembling hands, he put things away and zipped up the backpack, before slipping away from the screams through the brush. His body still zinged with adrenaline when he entered a clearing near the road and stood upright.

Once he donned the backpack, he looked like any other student wearing jeans and a tee shirt. He looked both ways, crossed the deserted road, and walked to his car parked by the curb.

The woman's screams still echoed through the area. His lips curled as he placed the backpack in the trunk.

Grumps voice said, *"You hear those screams? You done good. Go on home."*

CHAPTER 5

Charlie received Ryan's call on the way to her private practice office. Adrenaline shot through her veins when she heard it was another shooting victim. She turned around in a nearby parking lot, and drove toward the scene of the murder.

Once there, she parked on the street behind the State of Alabama crime scene van. She texted Marti: *"Working a case for Ryan. Won't be in until this afternoon. Tell you about it later."* Charlie didn't want her partner to worry.

She grabbed the lavaliere that held her Huntsville Police Department consultant badge out of the glove box and pulled it over her head before sliding out of her seat. After locking her purse out of sight in the trunk of her Honda, she stuffed her keys into the pocket of her conservative navy suit. Charlie shielded her blue eyes from the glare as she visually swept the entire area.

The area buzzed with activity like a productive hive of forensic bees. The police had cordoned off the front porch of the assisted living facility with yellow crime scene tape.

The wide porch with a white railing and filigree decorations on either side of the white support posts reminded her of a Victorian mansion. It looked like a safe, protected place to live out the end of a lifetime.

After sweeping the scene once more, her attention focused on the elderly man slumped in the rocker closest to the door His collapsed visage chilled her.

Ryan looked up from his notepad. When he spotted her, his furrowed brow smoothed. His eyes crinkled when he smiled. She relaxed with relief. Things had been a bit awkward between them last night after she'd told him she didn't want to move into his house. *It's not that I don't love you*, she thought. Charlie had only had her home for two years and preferred to maintain her independence. *It's too soon to move in together. Besides, it's for all the wrong reasons.* She returned his welcoming smile and began working her way up the ramp, dodging the personnel who were coming and going.

Her gaze slid back over to the crumpled form of victim. The smell of blood, urine, and feces assaulted her sensitive nose. *Copper, ammonia, and shit—what a combination.* Bile inched its way up her throat forcing her to swallow hard. Her smile vanished. "What've we got?"

He cocked his head toward the victim. "Li Chang, an eighty-year-old retired tailor. A single, fatal shot to the head." He pointed with his pen. "Two residents occupied the other rockers at the time of the shooting. They're pretty upset. Joe and I waited to interview them until you arrived."

Charlie raised a brow and began to put on gloves.

"Since we've determined it was a long distance shot, there's no need to put on a Tyvek suit yet. We've identified the trajectory." Ryan pointed across the road to a wooded area where officers were busy stringing more crime scene tape. "The shot originated over there. I'll take you over there after the interviews."

"Can you believe Joe waited for me to show up before interviewing?"

Ryan ran a hand through his dark hair. "The female witness was hysterical when we arrived."

"I see." Charlie tried to control the smirk creeping onto her face. "We both know Joe doesn't like hysterical women. He should give the lady a break. Residents of nursing homes don't generally get shot after breakfast."

Charlie's first profiling case with the Huntsville Police Department had been with Ryan and his misogynist partner, Lieutenant Joe Sparks. She had profiled a murder, which had turned into a spree perpetrated by a female serial killer who called herself the Huntress. Joe had taken an instant dislike to Charlie. Toward the end of the case, he'd accused her of being the Huntress and removed her from the investigation, pending DNA analysis. It had all worked out in the end. She'd earned a medal of commendation for her work on the case, as well as a part-time position on the newly formed Sexual Assault Task Force. Somewhere along the way she'd gained Joe's grudging respect.

Holding her breath, she walked over to the body. Jason, the police photographer, nodded a greeting while sliding past her. The coroner and his assistant moved forward to place the body in a bag for transport.

"Hi Walter," Charlie said, shooing a buzzing fly from her face.

Not only was Walter Dodd the elected coroner of Madison County, he was also the funeral director who had made the arrangements for both of Charlie's parents, after cancer had claimed first her mother and then her father.

He nodded at her. "Doesn't take those flies long to find a dead body. Doc, what's this world coming to when people start shooting the elderly in their rocking chairs?" He pulled the body forward, and Jason's camera flashed as he took photos of the back of the victim's head. A splatter of brains and blood covered the chair. The mess dribbled down the back.

Charlie grimaced then turned away. "Not good."

"I tell you, it's going to hell in a hand basket, that's what," Dodd said.

Charlie walked away, trying to swallow the bile inching up her throat. She mentally recited a quick prayer for Mr. Chang and his family.

Joe stuck his head out the door. "Where the hell is she? That wo —"

Charlie interrupted his complaint. "I'm here waiting on you."

"Oh! Hi, Doc. We're ready if you are." He ran a finger inside the collar of his white shirt muttering, "Damn starch. I swear this shirt will stand in the corner by itself when I take it off tonight."

Charlie stifled a grin. Joe's wife, Sarah, had confided to Charlie that she kept asking for starch at the cleaners despite his requests. He had thwarted most of Sarah's efforts to keep him looking spiffy, but it didn't keep her from trying. Sarah's task was made more difficult because Joe looked like a lumpy concrete block with a buzz cut.

"We're using their conference room," Joe said.

Charlie noticed a smear of powdered sugar on his navy pants. "Does Sarah know you've been eating doughnuts? I thought you were on a diet for high blood pressure."

"No, she doesn't know and don't you go telling her, either." He squinted at her. "How'd you figure it out?"

"Powdered sugar on your left pants leg."

He looked down. "Damn." He swiped at the white smear and shook his head. "I'll get that later."

Charlie walked into the living room-like lobby of the facility and blinked several times as she waited for her vision to adjust to the dim interior. "Why is this place so gloomy? People with poor vision need brighter lights."

The dark wooden end tables combined with the burgundy and navy over-stuffed furniture contributed to the dismal appearance. The smell of bacon filled the air.

She followed Joe into a conference room flooded by bright fluorescent lights. A stooped man was already seated at the long table with a cane hooked over the chair next to him. Joe took the seat across from him. Ryan and Charlie took seats on either side of Joe. Ryan turned on the recorder and gave the date and time, and stated the full names of those present.

Joe looked at Charlie. "This is Harold Loggerstein who was in the rocker next to Li Chang when the shooting occurred." He jutted a thumb in Charlie's direction. "This is our consultant, Dr. Stone."

"What'd you say?" The older man cupped his ear.

Joe repeated what he said, but louder. A high-pitched whine filled the quiet room while Mr. Loggerstein adjusted his hearing aids.

"I'm sorry about the loss of your friend," yelled Charlie, trying to be heard.

"No need to yell at me, young lady, I can hear you just fine." He jutted his chin forward. "That man wasn't my friend. I hardly knew him. He only moved in two weeks ago."

More squealing occurred while he readjusted his hearing aids.

Loggerstein's sagging jowls reminded Charlie of a hound dog. His thick, gray hair looked like he'd skipped a few haircuts. Stooped shoulders forced him to peer from under bushy brows. His ears sprouted tufts of hair, adding to his canine appearance.

"Can you tell us what happened?" asked Joe.

"I wanted some fresh air after breakfast. Joyce Littlejohn peed her pants again. Hell, I didn't want to suck in piss fumes until they could get her cleaned up." He turned to look at Charlie. "Don't get old, young lady. It's a crappy existence."

"Go on, Mr. Loggerstein," Joe said, frowning.

"Gladys Templeton beat me out the door, the old biddy." He shook his head. "I tell you, knowing I could have gotten my head shot off shook me up. Made me think about missed opportunities." He looked Charlie up and down and grinned, donning a hopeful expression. "These old women around here don't put out. Do you? I have some Viagra in my room. Ordered it off the Internet."

"No." Charlie slapped him with a fierce glare that wiped the lecherous grin from his face. "Continue with your story."

Joe coughed a laugh into his hand. Ryan's hard look shifted from the old man to Joe.

"Too bad," said Mr. Loggerstein. "You're quite shapely. Anyway, Gladys beat me to the first rocker. I made it into the second one. Damn, I swear they're making them lower to the ground nowadays. That woman started jabbering in my ear, so I turned off my hearing aids." He shook his head. "That's when that Chinese guy came out and claimed the other rocker. He was the quiet sort. Didn't talk much.

"Did you see anyone with a gun?" asked Joe.

"Nope. I had my eyes closed until that fool woman started screaming like a banshee and shaking my arm. I looked over and his head was blown apart. It was horrible. Hell, it could've been me." He rubbed his chin.

Charlie noticed the tremor in his hand.

"I looked around to see if I saw someone, but I've got cataracts—all those years of working as a truck driver. I have my first surgery next week."

After a few more questions, they released Loggerstein to return to his room. He shuffled close to Charlie and tried to touch her. She was too nimble for him and moved out of reach, grimacing at the smell of his unwashed hair.

"Getting too damn old. At this rate, I'll never get to use that Viagra," he mumbled, as he made his way out the door.

Charlie looked toward Ryan. "I hope Gladys Templeton is a more helpful witness."

CHAPTER 6

Marti opened the outer office door and turned on the lights. *I wonder what's keeping Charlie? She's usually here by now.*

She walked down the hall and unlocked the door to the business office. Her phone jingled with the tone assigned to Charlie's texts. She slipped it from the pocket of her blazer and thumb-printed it on.

"Working a case for Ryan. Won't be in until this afternoon. Tell you about it later."

Marti rolled her eyes. "Well, that explains just enough to leave me guessing." She stuffed her phone back into her pocket.

Since Charlie would be in late, she backtracked and fed the goldfish in the fifty-five-gallon tank sitting in the lobby. The fish flitted about when she approached. *Goldy used to get excited about being fed, too.* The memory of the pet goldfish she'd had as a child brought a smile to her face.

She returned to the business office and unlocked the file cabinets, with the intention of pulling her charts for the day. She found their new part-time office manager, Deloris Monk, had already pulled them and banded them together with a note on the front with her name.

Impressive, Marti thought. *She's been on the job for a mere two weeks, and already she has this entire office more organized.*

Marti returned to her therapy room to thumb through her charts before her new client arrived. She glanced around her office admiring the simple lines of her furniture. The creams, tans, and blues of her color scheme filled her with a sense of calm and peace. *I hope it does the same for my clients.*

This room was so different from her partner's. Charlie's room gleamed with jewel-toned colors and tended toward the traditional.

Marti finished reviewing her charts and slid them into a nearby oak file, before grabbing two bottles of water from the small fridge in an adjacent room. She returned and placed one on a coaster next to her chair and the other on the glass-topped coffee table for her new client.

Marti heard someone coming up the stairs and stepped out of the office onto the landing to see whom it was.

Joyce Martin trudged up the stairs carrying a briefcase and an armful of yard signs. She owned the real estate business across the hall from Charlie and Marti's office.

"Looks like you ordered new real estate advertisements," Marti said.

Joyce adjusted her grip on the slipping signs. "I wouldn't have to order as many if people would stop running over them with lawnmowers." She huffed up the final step and leaned the signs against the wall while she searched her huge purse for her door key. "How do you like your new office manager? I met her the other day."

"Deloris is great."

Joyce opened her door and dropped her purse on the nearest chair. She returned for the signs. "Deloris reminds me of a petite Mrs. Doubtfire. You know, the character played by Robin Williams. What does Charlie think of her?"

Marti smiled. "She calls her 'Office Mom Extraordinaire.'"

Joyce slipped the signs inside the office. "Where *is* Charlie? I didn't see her car. She's usually gets here before me."

Marti sighed. "Off working another case."

Joyce scrutinized her with narrowed eyes. "You ever wish you'd gotten the profiling job instead of her? You're just as good as she is, maybe better."

Marti's face grew hot with embarrassment. She'd never admitted to anyone that Charlie being chosen for the position had irked her. "Well, sometimes yes, but most of the time, no. Don't get me wrong, I love Charlie like a sister, it's just that she's..."

"Larger than life?" Joyce nodded her understanding. "Do you ever get tired of playing Midge to her Super Hero Barbie?"

Marti sputtered, "Midge!"

Joyce patted Marti on the shoulder. "Don't worry, you're far from Barbie's frumpy friend Midge. Heck, I'd love to have your thick mane of brown hair."

Marti's hands moved to the strands on her shoulder. "Thanks but I'm not a—"

"Blond bombshell?" Joyce rolled her eyes. "I swear, if Charlie isn't in the news, she's winning commendations from the mayor."

Marti bristled. "It's not as though she wants the publicity, Joyce."

Joyce crossed her arms. "You sure? She sure seems like a publicity hound to me."

"You don't understand her. Charlie can't stop herself from helping people. She cares way too much and agonizes over decisions that affect others." Marti raised her chin. "She's a combination of a curious cat and a rescue dog."

Joyce leaned against the doorframe and cackled. "What does that mean?"

"If there's an unturned stone, Charlie will get a pry bar and flip it over. If someone's in danger, she throws herself into the fray without even thinking about it."

Joyce raised a brow. "You make her sound fearless."

Marti tamped down the irritation stirring in her. "No way. I've seen her scared out of her wits." She leaned closer and lowered her voice. "She even has nightmares about stuff that's happened to her. You were around when she was working the Huntress and Trainer cases. Imagine living in fear every day. We were both terrified. Who wants that kind of horror?"

Joyce fluffed her hair. "Well, I'm glad that's over."

Marti nodded. "Me, too."

Joyce glanced at her watch. "Oh, my. I have a property to show in thirty minutes." She closed her office door and locked it. "See you later."

Marti watched Joyce clunk down the stairs in her three-inch heels. Aggravation washed over her.

Fuming, Marti locked herself into the restroom on the landing until she had calmed down. Joyce managed to upset her nearly every time they talked. *That woman loves to stir the pot.*

Back on an even keel, Marti returned to the business office.

Five minutes later, the doorbell rang. She greeted her new patient.

"I'm Lorraine Springle." The woman wore a Waffle House uniform. "I hope it's okay that I wore my work clothes. I have a shift after this appointment."

"That's fine," Marti said.

She seated Lorraine in the lobby and had her fill out the initial paperwork. Ten minutes later they were sitting in Marti's office.

She eyed the room with apparent interest.

"What brings you in?" Marti asked.

Lorraine looked at the floor and sighed. "My father died several months ago."

Marti nodded. "I'm sorry to hear that."

Lorraine looked up, her face a mask of anger. "I'm not. He was a crazy sonofabitch and I'm glad he's gone."

Startled by the sudden change in attitude, Marti sat back, and waited for Lorraine to tell her story.

CHAPTER 7

When Charlie returned from the ladies' room, Gladys Templeton sat in the chair formerly occupied by Mr. Loggerstein, clutching several tissues in her gnarled hands.

Charlie sniffed and smiled. The odor of unwashed hair had been replaced by the scent of L'Air du Temps.

Charlie joined Joe and Ryan at the table. Looking irritated at the delay, Joe huffed and started the tape recorder.

After introductions, Joe asked, "Mrs. Templeton, can you please tell us what you witnessed today?"

Her lower lip trembled. "I'd gone out to the porch after breakfast. I was talking to Harold when I heard a pop." Her hands trembled, and tears welled in her eyes. "All that blood."

She paused to wipe her eyes and honked into the tissue. She reached into the pocket of her pink sweater and pulled out a fresh one.

Joe asked, "Did you see the shooter?"

She sniffled and wiped her nose. "All I could look at was the blood. The killer shot him in the head, you know. His entire face…it, it… collapsed." She shook her head and focused on her blue-veined hands. "I'm so ashamed of myself."

"Why?' asked Charlie.

Mrs. Templeton didn't raise her eyes. "I threw up my breakfast. Then I couldn't stop screaming."

After a few additional questions that confirmed she hadn't seen the shooter, Joe ended the interview. Mrs. Templeton stood, steadied herself, and pushed her walker out of the room.

Moments later, someone screamed. Charlie beat Joe and Ryan out the door.

Mrs. Templeton lay in a stupor on the floor. A nurse knelt next to her taking her pulse.

Charlie knelt, too. "Anything I can do to help?"

"Find me a Coke or juice. She's diabetic. This has been way too much for her."

Charlie rose and spotted a table with a container of orange juice and plastic glasses. She filled one halfway with juice and carried it back to the nurse.

"Sip a little of this, Ms. Gladys. You let your blood sugar get too low." The nurse helped her to sit.

Charlie stood off to the side with a small group of residents, waiting.

After Ms. Gladys sipped the orange juice, she seemed to come to herself. "Goodness, did I faint? I didn't mean to cause such a fuss."

Feeling a bit like a wrung-out- sponge, Charlie decided to grab a breath mint from her purse before going to see where the shooter took the shot. She needed to be on her game.

She told Ryan, "I'll meet you across the street. I need something from my purse."

On her way out, she spotted Loggerstein heading toward her. She hurried out the door and down the steps. He was persistent, but she had speed.

Charlie pulled her keys from her pocket and opened the Accord's trunk. She dug through her purse, found the tin of Altoids, and popped one into her mouth. Snagging her phone from a side pocket, she checked for messages. None. After shoving the phone into her blazer pocket, she slammed the trunk shut.

Through the back window, she noticed something white pinned in place by her wiper blade. Fear squeezed her throat and set her heart racing.

The scrape of a shoe sent a warning zing down her spine. She whirled to find Ryan walking her way, looking at his phone.

She croaked, "Ryan!"

He looked up. "What?"

She pointed. "There's another note."

"Shit! Did you touch it?"

She shook her head.

Ryan walked around to the driver's side and leaned over to peer at the paper without touching anything.

"Doesn't appear to be an advertisement. It's folded so I can't tell what it says." He backed away from the car. "I'll get the techs over here."

Jason was the first to arrive.

"Charlie, is this another note from your whacko?" he asked, checking his camera.

She shrugged. "We don't know, Ryan's being cautious."

He took shots of the note pinned under the wiper from various angles.

She gripped her elbows and tried to calm her nerves.

After Jason finished, the techs extracted the note with tweezers and slid it open into a clear evidence bag.

"YOUR TIME IS COMING."

Charlie's heart hammered like timpani drums in her chest. Ryan slipped his arm around her waist.

"What's going on here?" Joe groused.

"Someone put another threatening note on Doc's car," said Jenny, one of the techs.

"Well, hell!" Joe barreled through to take a look. "Do you have any idea who this might be?"

Charlie shook her head.

Joe looped his thumbs in his belt. "Is one of those wackos you see in your practice gunning for you?"

Charlie saw the concern in his face. "No, I don't think so."

"How about the guy who threatened you when you worked for the treatment center? He still in jail?"

Charlie rubbed her arms. "I don't know."

"I'll check with his P.O.," Ryan said.

Jason took a few photos of the open note. He winked when he finished. "Watch your back."

Charlie gave a weak smile. "I'll try."

Ryan tapped her shoulder.

She turned.

"What's your plan for the rest of the day?"

"I plan to go home. My first patient isn't until after lunch."

"You can't leave until they finish fingerprinting your car," Ryan said, one hand resting on his gun. "I'll call Scott."

"Why?" Charlie asked.

"To make sure you get home safe." Ryan pulled his phone from his jacket.

FBI Special Agent Scott Horner was Charlie's next-door neighbor. He'd worked with the SATF on the recent Trainer case.

The techs had finished and returned to the murder scene by the time Scott pulled up.

He rolled down the window of his silver BMW. "I'm ready to follow Charlie home."

Ryan leaned down. "Where's your truck?"

"At the dealership getting an oil change."

Ryan hugged Charlie close. "Lock up when you get there. I'll come to your house tonight as soon as I can."

"I'm sure I'll be fine."

He held her by the shoulders, his brow furrowed. "If nothing else, it'll ease my mind."

Charlie doubted it would ease hers.

CHAPTER 8

Charlie's hands had stopped shaking by the time she steered her green Accord into the driveway of her home. In her rearview mirror, she saw Scott pulling in behind her.

She fumbled to find her garage door opener. "Where is it?" She spotted it between the seats. Cramming her hand into the tight space, she felt around until her fingers grasped the device.

Scott rapped on her window, causing her to jump. He motioned for her to lower the window.

He held out his hand, palm up. "Give me your keys. I want to clear the house before you enter."

Charlie turned off the engine and handed him the key to the door. "It's this one."

With his Glock down by his side, Scott moved with athletic grace toward her front door.

Minutes stretched like salt-water taffy while she remembered the Trainer's thwarted attempt to break into her house.

The house alarm blared.

She jerked to attention. "I forgot the alarm."

She shoved the car door open and sprinted toward the open front door. She plastered herself against the wall to make a smaller target in case anyone wanted to shoot her. She sidled over and punched in her code.

The racket ceased.

She inhaled several deep breaths to slow her pounding heart.

A hand touched her shoulder.

She shied away and turned, her heart racing like a thoroughbred after a steeplechase.

Scott backed off, one hand raised. He still held his Glock in the other hand, pointed down by his side. "That alarm scared the shit out of me. Maybe you should give me the code for next time." He shoved his Glock into his holster.

Charlie's hand covered her pounding heart. *Oh heck, I wet my panties.* "I'm hoping there won't be a next time."

"Me, too." He stepped closer, reached around, and started massaging her neck. "You're so tense."

She stiffened and moved away.

Ignoring her silent protest, he pulled her into an embrace and rocked her from side to side. He murmured, "It's all right. The house is secure."

Charlie pushed against his chest. "I appreciate your concern but I'm fine now."

A whine broke the silence.

"Spanky! Where's Spanky?"

"Calm down, I closed her into the bedroom until I cleared the rest of the house."

Charlie slammed the front door shut, locked it, and beelined to her bedroom. When she opened the door, Spanky yipped and wagged her tail with delight.

Charlie dropped to her knees and hugged her. "Are you okay, Sweetie?"

Spanky kissed her nose, wiggled from her grasp and rushed toward the kitchen. Charlie followed in her tail-swinging wake. She tossed Spanky a treat and turned to find Scott leaning against the doorframe. He looked concerned.

"We need to talk." He walked over to the breakfast nook table and pulled out a chair. After he settled his long frame into the seat, he gestured for her to sit across from him.

Too antsy to perch yet, she asked, "Do you want coffee?"

"That'd be good."

"Do you still have my keys?"

He shifted in his seat and pulled them from the pocket of his dark blue suit. "Right here."

She leaned her hip against the counter and crossed her arms. "Would you please pull my car into the garage and close the door while I make the coffee?"

"Good idea."

While Scott moved the car, Charlie busied her hands making coffee. Her mind whirled with thoughts. *Who is sending me these notes? Is it one of my patients?* No one new came to mind. *If anyone can figure this out, it's Ryan and Scott.*

She heard the rattle of the garage door's descent. Seconds later, Scott came through the door into the kitchen. He covered the distance between them in three long strides.

"You okay?" He rested a warm hand on her waist. At six-two, he made her slender, five-seven frame feel small. While Ryan was lean and muscular, weightlifting had added bulk to Scott.

She nodded. "The coffee should be ready soon. If you'll get the cups down from the cabinet next to the stove," she pointed, "I'll be back in a sec." She stopped mid-stride. "My keys, please."

Scott pulled them from his pocket and tossed them to her.

She deftly caught them. "Thanks."

Once in her bedroom, she closed the door, walked to the dresser across from her bed, and slid open her underwear drawer. She snatched a pair of black bikini panties and hipped the drawer closed. She took three strides toward the bathroom and stopped. An uneasy tingle ran down her spine. She pivoted and walked back to the dresser. Yanking open the drawer, she examined the contents. She did laundry yesterday, so she thought she'd remembered putting her red lace thong on the left side of the drawer. *It's gone.* She shook her head, not sure if her memory was correct. She'd been in a hurry to leave for work. *I'm losing it. Almost killed by the Trainer, and now all these notes...*

After changing into dry underwear, she dropped the other pair in the laundry hamper and joined Scott in the kitchen.

He sat with two mugs of coffee, ready to begin their discussion. Charlie retrieved the fat-free half and half from the fridge. Once settled, she started doctoring her coffee with stevia and cream. For some reason, this ritual always calmed her. She glanced up and saw

Scott sipping from his steaming cup. *He drinks his coffee black, like Ryan. It must be a law enforcement thing?*

Scott locked gazes with her over the top of his mug. Lowering it, he said, "Tell me everything."

Charlie summarized the situation. Scott's gaze never left her face. Uncomfortable under his scrutiny, she looked away and sipped her coffee.

He sat straighter in his seat, rested his forearms on the table, and cupped his mug in his large hands. "You sure you don't know who's doing this? Maybe a whacked-out patient from your past?"

"The only one I'd consider a possibility is still in jail. Ryan checked."

He frowned and rubbed his face with his hand. "This is so strange. First, the Trainer stalked you, now some nut's leaving you threatening notes. You should work on being less desirable."

She ignored the compliment. "Who said the note writer is male?"

He shrugged. "Good point. I shouldn't assume. What about that bombshell, Janet something, that Joe Sparks told me about? Wasn't she a suspect on one of your previous cases?"

"I've thought about her. I spoke to my former boss last week. She's currently in a thirty-day treatment program."

He blew out a breath.

"I've been wracking my brain trying to figure this out." She ran both hands through her hair. "It's driving me batty and keeping me awake at night." She gripped her cup to control her trembling hands.

He reached across the small table and pried one of Charlie's hands from her coffee cup and held it.

She felt her shoulders stiffen as she looked into his eyes. His expression was earnest.

"You know I won't let anything happen to you. I'll do whatever's necessary to keep you safe." He chuckled. "Besides, Marti would have my hide if something happened to you."

Charlie pulled her hand from Scott's. "Marti's a good friend. Excuse me."

Scott stood and pulled out his phone. "I'll call Ryan and let him know you're home and safe."

She stood and swayed as first a hot flush rush over her, followed by a cold one. *What is wrong with me?*

Charlie left the kitchen and closed the bedroom door before phoning Marti. A wave of dizziness hit her. *That's it. I'm canceling today's appointments.*

"What's up, Charlie?" Marti sounded distracted.

"Is this a bad time?"

"Nope. I finished my new assessment. She may make a good addition to our women's group someday. Pray for me, I'm about to start the paperwork. You know how much I *love* paperwork." Sarcasm dripped from Marti's words.

"The crime scene Ryan called me to assess was about the sniper. When I came out of the assisted living facility, I found another note."

"What did it say?"

Charlie rubbed her stomach. "Your time is coming."

"This is getting scary," Marti said.

"Getting? It's already scary for me. Ryan called Scott and asked him to escort me home."

"Convenient, since he lives next door." Marti's tone brightened. "He asked me out to a movie this weekend. I can't wait to get my hands on Agent Marble Butt again."

"Some friend you are. I'm getting threatening notes, and you're fantasizing about Agent Marble, um, Scott. Is Deloris there?"

"She came in thirty minutes ago. Why?"

"Ask Deloris to cancel and reschedule my appointments this afternoon. I'm not feeling well."

"Will do. Let me know what you find out about the note writer."

Charlie hung her suit in the closet and changed into a comfortable t-shirt, shorts, and sandals. She stopped long enough to brush her long hair into a ponytail that she secured with a scrunchy. *Why am I feeling so hot and dizzy? I'm too young for hot flashes.* She steadied herself by holding onto the counter.

When the wave of dizziness passed, she wondered if Scott had gone home.

When she entered the living room, she discovered that Scott had made himself comfortable on the sofa. Two china plates sat on top of the pizza box that took up most of the coffee table. He raised one of Ryan's Yuengling beers in a toast.

"Have a seat. Damn, are you okay? You look pale. Sit down and eat something." He gestured toward her clothes. "I thought you were going back to your office?"

"I'm not feeling well so I canceled this afternoon's appointments. I've decided to stay home and take a nap. I haven't slept well the last couple of nights. Maybe sleep deprivation is catching up with me."

Ryan's not going to like that Scott helped himself to one of his beers.

"I'll be back." He rose and shot out the door.

"What now?" She was tempted to lock the door and go take a nap, but it would be rude.

Within minutes, Scott bounded back in the door and closed it. He locked up and held up a DVD case. "I brought a movie over from my house. White House Down. It's action-packed and ought to take your mind off things."

I doubt it. "Don't you have to go back to work?"

Scott shook his head. "I called in and took the rest of the day off. Nothing much happening today."

"I appreciate all this, but I only want to grab a bite of this pizza and go to bed and forget this day ever happened."

"Bad idea." Scott shook his head with conviction. "You'll lie in there and ruminate. You won't be able to unhinge your brain after something like this. Better to keep your mind busy. Believe me, I know."

Charlie had to admit he was right about the ruminating. She was the queen of dissecting events in her mind. She glanced over at the glass of red wine sitting on a coaster and felt a prickle of unease ripple down her spine. *Wine at lunch? Isn't it too early to be drinking?*

Charlie decided to be polite the way her southern-born mother had taught her. "Hey, you didn't have to do all this. I'll be fine."

He lifted the lid of the box.

The fragrant pizza steam assailed her nose making her mouth water. *Jeez, that smells good.*

Scott pointed at the food. "Eat. You won't regret it."

Charlie shrugged. "Maybe you're right. I am hungry." She pulled out a large slice and draped the hanging cheese string back onto the slice. "I wish I knew what I did that was so awful. I keep asking myself why someone would send me those notes?"

"Sometimes people don't behave logically."

True, she thought, as she nibbled the pointy end of her pizza. "Mmm. Delicious."

"Nothing's too good for my new neighbor."

"Where did you live before you came to Huntsville?"

He wiped his mouth and swallowed. "Virginia. I was doing some special training at Quantico. I was there for several years."

"Quantico was where I did my community-profiler training. I'd love to work at the BAU. It seemed like an interesting place to work."

"How long were you there?"

"I was only there for three months. We may have been there at the same time." She looked at him and smiled.

He shrugged. "Law enforcement is a small world."

She pushed a sliding piece of sausage back in place and licked her finger. "Shirley McClain says 'the world's a golf ball.' With airplanes and the Internet, the world has shrunk."

Scott took a swallow of his beer. "I wish all that new technology meant we caught more of the bad guys."

"I thought we are catching more criminals," said Charlie. "Perhaps they're breeding faster than the good guys can catch them—like a science fiction movie plot." She wiped her hands on a napkin and looked at him.

He arched a brow as he reached for another slice of pizza. "Not enough for me. Despite everything, it feels like the Bureau is always behind. The rise in international and domestic terrorism doesn't help."

"Did you ask for the transfer, or were you assigned here? It must be hard being at the whim of an organization that can transfer you anywhere at any time. If I worked for the Bureau that would be a downfall for me."

"You'd get used to it." He took a bite and waved his hand in front of his mouth and gulped some beer. "I asked to go south. Got tired of the cold and the traffic."

"Did you have someone special there?" Charlie wanted to make sure the way was clear for Marti who hadn't dated much since her break up a year ago. Marti seemed to like Scott—a lot.

He sat back to look at her. "There was someone special. Unfortunately, I never made a blip on her radar. She was too focused on her training. You know how it goes."

"Sorry that happened to you." *Yeah, I know. Lately, Ryan seems to be working day and night.*

He picked up the remote. "You ready to start the movie?"

"Um, sure."

Scott glanced at her glass. "Here, let me get you some more wine. Mission number one...relax...with booze."

"Just fill it with water," she said, as she finished the last sip.

"Don't think so. Trust me." He took the glass from her and turned toward the kitchen.

Mama always told me not to trust any man who tells you to trust him. Although he was right, I do feel better now that I've eaten.

A little over an hour later, only one slice of the pizza remained, and the movie approached the ending. Charlie could barely keep her eyes open. Italian food always lured her into a warm, drowsy, satisfied state. Only the fast-paced film kept her from falling completely asleep. During one of her mini catnaps, Scott had gone to the restroom and upon his return sat a bit closer to her. He'd draped his arm across the back of the sofa. The scent of beer drifted her way.

Charlie knew she should move, but she felt glued to the cushion. *Too much wine and pizza. Why is it so hot in here?*

Her stomach roiled, leaving a feeling of uneasiness behind. Her hand automatically covered it.

The front door swung open.

Charlie looked over the back of the couch. Ryan stood in the foyer. Spanky streaked in his direction and whined a greeting at his feet.

Scott stood, holding one of Ryan's pilfered beers.

Charlie ran her hand down her face but couldn't seem to move yet. Her stomach rumbled.

A broad grin creased Scott's face. "Hi, Ryan. You missed the movie, but there's one slice of pizza left."

Ryan's brow furrowed. "What's going on here? I asked you to make sure Charlie got home safe—not wine and dine her."

"Hey man, she was upset." Scott spread his arms wide. "I was only trying to take her mind off things."

"Looks like you're trying to help take her mind off me," Ryan said his tone acidic.

Charlie managed with some effort to push herself to her feet and swayed. *How many glasses of wine did I have? Two? Three?* She steadied herself by grasping the back of the sofa.

Ryan glared at her. "Are you drunk?"

Feeling dizzy, Charlie walked around so she could improve her hold. Her stomach lurched a protest at the movement. "I'm going to be sick!"

She threw her hand over her mouth and stumbled toward the bathroom. She slammed the door and dropped to her knees on the cold tile. She groaned before revisiting her pizza. She sank back on her heels. Acid burned her throat.

Ryan and Scott yelled at each other in the living room.

She clasped her cramping stomach with both hands and rocked, wondering if the two men would come to blows. The disgusting sight and smell triggered her to be sick again.

The front door slammed, shaking the house. She didn't know who'd left.

She pulled herself to her feet and flushed the toilet. Turning on the cold water, she splashed her flushed face and rinsed the sour taste from her mouth. She doubled over in pain. Her insides spasmed like her intestines were being wrung out. Tears welled in her eyes and her reflection looked both pale and feverish.

There was a tap on the door.

"Charlie? Are you all right?"

She opened the door. Red splotches dotted Ryan's cheeks. His eyes held deep concern.

"What's wrong? Are you sick?"

Ryan was reaching for her when the world went black.

CHAPTER 9

Marti stood by Charlie's bed. They'd been in a cubicle in the ER at Huntsville Hospital for fifteen minutes.

Charlie moaned and held up her hand to block the bright overhead light.

Marti smiled, feeling relieved. "She's awake."

"Wha..." Charlie licked her lips and swallowed. "What happened?"

Ryan smoothed Charlie's hair off her forehead. "You fainted in the bathroom and hit your head on the edge of the tub. I called 911."

"My head hurts."

Marti took her hand and squeezed. "You may have a mild concussion."

Charlie turned to look in her direction and appeared to regret the movement. "Water."

Marti reached for a cup and spoon. "You can only have ice chips so you won't get sick again. They started an IV. Ryan said you vomited before you fainted." She spooned some chips in Charlie's mouth. "I called Kate. She may stop by later after her shift ends."

Kate O'Cleary, a police officer who also served on the Sexual Assault Task Force had become fast friends with Charlie and Marti.

Charlie groaned. "Pizza! I got sick after eating pizza. Do I have..." She paused and licked her dry lips again. "Food poisoning?"

Marti glanced over at Ryan.

Charlie touched the bump on the back of her head and winced. "What's going on?"

Marti spooned more ice chips into her mouth. "We're not sure yet. We're waiting for test results, and you're scheduled for a CT scan."

Scott shouldered open the door. "Is Charlie all right? Kate called and told me she'd fainted. I swear she only had three glasses of wine."

Marti pursed her lips. "Charlie's a one-glass-of-anything person. She doesn't drink much."

His brow furrowed. "Hey, don't blame me. I didn't force it down her throat!"

Marti took a step back, surprised by his aggressive tone.

Ryan closed in on Scott, his eyes like blue glass marbles.

Marti frowned. *What's going on?*

"What're you doing here?" He poked his finger into Scott's chest.

Scott batted it aside. "She's my friend and neighbor. I have every right to be here."

Marti noticed the yelling had caused Charlie to place a hand on her forehead.

"Stop it! You're upsetting Charlie."

A nurse looked in the door. Her gaze narrowed onto the two men. "This is a hospital." She pointed at the guys. "Take it outside." Inclining her head toward Marti, she said, "You can stay."

Like chastised children, Ryan and Scott walked toward the door, their faces flushed with emotion.

After the door closed, Marti leaned close and asked, "Did Scott do anything to you? Ryan's really pissed at him."

"I remember Scott bought a pizza and produced a movie. I didn't feel well and only wanted to go to bed. I had a hard time staying awake. My stomach felt.... unsettled." She closed her eyes as if trying to recall the events of the afternoon. "Ryan came in. When he saw Scott there, he accused him of wining and dining me. They were yelling at each other. I ran to the bathroom because I felt sick."

"Anything else?" Marti took her hand and squeezed.

At that moment, Officer Kate O'Cleary pushed into the room. "What in God's green earth is going on?" Her copper curls bounced with each step. She stopped next to the bed, spread her feet, and placed her thumbs in her utility belt.

"What do you mean?" Marti turned to face her but didn't release Charlie's hand.

"Ryan and Scott are close to blows in the parking garage. He's accusing Scott of drugging you with Rohypnol. Sam broke it up," Kate said.

Sam, Kate's partner, was a six-foot-seven former offensive tackle for Auburn University and quite capable of handling the two men.

"Roofies?" Charlie said.

"We'll know soon. The doctor is running a drug screen," said Marti. "I sure hope Ryan's wrong."

A well-muscled guy wearing blue scrubs stuck his head in the door. "Time for your glamour shots."

Marti and Kate waved as he rolled her out the door.

Thirty minutes later, Marti, Ryan, and Kate were sitting on any available surface when the hunky guy rolled Charlie back into the room. Charlie didn't ask about Scott's absence.

Ryan looked half angry and half worried when he stood to greet her.

The nurse walked in and glared at Ryan. "Y'all can stay, but she needs quiet and time to rest." She pointed a finger at him. "No shenanigans."

Ryan scowled but kept quiet.

Charlie settled back on the pillow and closed her eyes.

Kate whispered, "I'll be back in a jiffy. I need a cup of coffee. There's a Starbuck's in the lobby."

After she left, Ryan motioned for Marti to join him outside the room.

Marti closed the curtain and leaned against the wall in the hallway. "Ryan, what the heck is going on?"

Ryan ran his hands through his hair. "Things were going okay until Charlie found the note." He explained what he knew of the sequence of events.

* * *

Two hours later, a doctor strode into the room with a nurse in his wake.

Marti patted Charlie's arm. "Wake up."

Charlie frowned and rubbed her face with her hands. She glanced around the room. "Kate's gone?"

"For now," Ryan said.

The doctor strode forward. "I'm Dr. Chasen. I hope you're feeling better."

Marti helped Charlie to push herself upright in the bed.

"The CT scan shows only a mild concussion, so that's good news. Your drug screen came back clean. However…." He gave Charlie a hard look. "Your blood alcohol level was 0.25. You were legally intoxicated."

"I'm not surprised," said Charlie. "I'm a lightweight when it comes to alcohol, and I heard I had three glasses of wine."

The doctor cocked a brow and looked at Marti and Ryan, who both nodded agreement.

"Ms. Stone, you're running a low-grade temperature because you caught a mild case of the twenty-four-hour bug that's going around."

"So that's why my stomach feels like a washing machine on spin cycle?"

Marti looked at Ryan. They both backed away from the bed.

"The combination of the alcohol and the virus is what caused you to faint. We'll be keeping you overnight, due to the concussion and because you need fluids. I'll release you before noon tomorrow if all goes well."

After the doctor and nurse left the room, Ryan crossed his arms. "That's it, you're moving in with me."

Marti glanced over at Charlie. *What's she going to do?*

Determination flashed in Charlie's eyes. "That's not your decision to make—it's mine. How many times have we had this discussion? I'm not ready. I'm enjoying my house."

Feeling like a voyeur, Marti backed into a corner.

"Be reasonable, Charlie. You've had two threatening notes and now this." Ryan rocked back on his heels. "It's clear to me you can't figure out when a man is coming on to you. Scott liquored you up and was ready to pounce."

Stunned, Marti took a step forward before she burst into tears.

Ryan looked first at her and then Charlie.

"Now you've done it!" Charlie gestured toward her.

Spreading his arms wide, palms up, he asked, "What'd I do this time?"

Charlie angled her chin up, defiant. "Scott is taking Marti to the movies on Saturday. They're dating."

Ryan ran his hand through his hair. "How was I to know? I show up, and you're drunk. Scott's all cozy with his arm around you."

Marti's heart lurched. *What?*

Charlie looked over at her. "His arm was on the back of the sofa, not around me." She returned her gaze to Ryan. "Yes, I admit I drank more than usual, but I was also freaked out about today, and sick to boot."

Ryan's face turned red. "What am I supposed to think? Wine, dinner, and a movie with him drinking *my beer*."

Marti's hand covered her mouth. *Good, God! He's upset about the beer?*

Charlie sat up straighter in the bed. "You're jealous!"

He put both hands up in a stop gesture. After a deep breath, he looked down and shook his head. "We're not getting anywhere. I'm beat and you have a concussion. Besides, I have a meeting at eight in the morning. Call me when you get released, and I'll drive you home."

He moved closer to give her a kiss and stopped. "Forgot. You're sick." He blew her a kiss instead.

After Ryan left, Marti said, "You look ready to explode, or else your fever just shot up. He seems convinced that Scott's interested in you." *Is he?*

Charlie rubbed her temples. "How do you disprove something you didn't do?"

"It's hard." She looked down twiddling her hair. "I've been thinking. Ever since the Trainer tried to get into your house, Ryan has tried to get you to move in with him."

Charlie shrugged. "Yeah, I guess."

Marti sank into a chair by the bed. "Think about it, who was around when both notes were found?"

"Me, Ryan, and the mystery person."

Marti looked up. "This is hard for me to say, but could Ryan be leaving the notes so you'll get scared and move in with him?"

CHAPTER 10

The next afternoon Ryan drove Charlie home from the hospital. The oppressive silence made the twenty-minute trip seem like an hour. Charlie was still trying to determine which scenario was true. Was Scott trying to create problems between them, or was Ryan sending her the threatening notes to get her to move in with him? On some level, the scariest scenario was some unknown maniac stalking her. Since Charlie liked to think the people in her life were trustworthy, she didn't want to believe the first two.

Charlie noticed Ryan's grip on the steering wheel tighten and his jaw flex as they drove past Scott's house. Once in the door, Spanky did her welcome dance, her long beagle tail whipping about.

Charlie bent to stroke her ears. "I know, sweetie, I missed you, too."

"I stopped by last night and this morning to feed her." Ryan reached out a hand to steady Charlie when she wavered while straightening.

"Thanks." Charlie rested her hand on the table in the foyer. She felt a flush of heat and wondered if her fever had returned. Despite the IV she still felt weak.

"Why don't we sit?" He pointed toward the living room. "We need to talk." Ryan walked over, sat on the couch and patted the cushion beside him.

Famous last words. Charlie took the seat but left a space between them. She folded her hands in her lap and waited.

"I don't know where to begin."

She sat in silence and waited.

"I can see you're not going to make this easy. You know how I feel about you."

Charlie held up her hand to stop him. "Ryan, you've never told me how you feel about me. When we first began dating, you told me once you were crazy about me. Since then…"

He ran a hand over his face and exhaled. He moved closer and placed his hand on her thigh. "You know I-I….love you." He cleared his throat. "I know I haven't said the 'L' word before, but I thought we understood each other."

Charlie smiled and shifted to be closer. "I'm glad to hear you say it. You show you care in many ways, but caring and love can be different. I need to hear the words."

He draped his arm across her shoulders and kissed her tenderly.

She reached over and placed a hand over his. "I love you, too. Why are you so bent out of shape about Scott? He's dating Marti now."

Ryan shifted to see her face better. He stroked her hand. "I think he wants to break us up, so he can date you."

Charlie shook her head. "I think he's trying to be a friend and good neighbor. He moved here and didn't know many folks. I know he has some boundary issues, but he doesn't have many friends yet. I'll have to be more firm with him."

"I've seen how he looks at you when he thinks no one is looking."

She heaved a sigh of exasperation. "How does Scott look at me?"

"Like the big, bad wolf." Ryan's phone rang. It was Joe's ringtone.

"What now?" Charlie ran her hand through her hair and frowned.

"Sorry, I need to get this. Joe and I are up for the next case." He answered and frowned. After shaking his head, he ended the call. "Two idiots had a shoot-out at a gas station on University Drive. One guy is DOA at Huntsville Hospital. Gotta go." He leaned over to kiss her forehead.

She winked. "So you don't love me enough to risk catching the stomach bug?"

He laughed and held up his index fingers to form a cross as if warding off evil. Then he dropped his arms, and a serious expression cloaked his face. "I'll lock the door on the way out. You look like you could use a nap."

After he left, she felt even more confused. She sent a text to Marti. *I'm home. Plan to take a nap and a shower.* Next, she called her answering service to check for important messages and to let them know she'd return to work tomorrow. Satisfied her life was more on track, she slumped into her recliner, snuggled under the soft throw draped across the arm, and elevated her feet. Spanky jumped up to join her, wiggling to create a space by her side.

Charlie closed her eyes, but her mind kept whirling with questions. Had any cars stopped near her Honda at the cemetery? She tried to think through each step of the funeral, but her attention had been on the event and the release of the doves. *Ryan came late. He could have placed the note. There had been several funerals in progress that day. So many cars drove past. No help there. What about the crime scene?* She'd been inside the facility when someone placed the note on her car. *Was Ryan with me the whole time?* She struggled to remember. *He'd gone to find the men's room, so there was an opportunity.*

She turned her mind to Scott's intrusions into her relationship with Ryan. She had to admit there were times he made her feel uncomfortable, but she'd attributed this to his loneliness and poor boundaries. *I need to stop feeling sorry for the guy.*

A mild headache pounded her temples. She drifted off to an uneasy sleep with a multitude of unanswered questions whirling in her mind.

CHAPTER 11

The Marksman wiped away the sweat that trickled down his face with the back of his hand. He shifted position, swearing under his breath. To avoid detection by the neighbors, he'd hidden in the shrubbery of a house where three newspapers lay on the driveway. Despite being in the shade, the heat prickled his skin, making him itch all over. The camp sheet made it feel even hotter.

He amused himself while waiting by watching a line of ants parade past him inside the stone border surrounding the landscaping that concealed him.

If the woman followed her usual routine, she'd round the corner at any minute pushing her stroller. Her habit the last four days was to stop under the shade of the oak tree across the street, to check the baby, and drink some water.

The rangefinder verified the distance to be one hundred and twenty-three feet to the tree. He'd set his scope and was locked and loaded. After wiping a drip of sweat from his nose, he pulled his water bottle from his utility belt and chugged it. Some sloshed down his chin. *Hell, it's not even ten o'clock yet, and it's miserable. Isn't it supposed to get cooler in September? Damn global warming.*

He could hear Grumps's voice in his head, raspy and impatient. *"Damn boy, huntin's never easy. Quit your whinin'. You're beginning to sound like your sniveling bitch of a mother."*

The Marksman didn't want to sound like his mother. He'd do anything to make his Grumps proud.

The ticking sound of a sprinkler worried him. An old man had come out fifteen minutes earlier and placed the sprinkler on a section of new sod. *Hope he doesn't check it anytime soon. What is it with these old guys and their sprinklers?* He glanced at his watch. *Almost time.* Shifting further down into the dirt, he looked around for witnesses. The kids were in school, all the garage doors were closed, and only two cars had driven by in the last hour.

His escape route wound through a dense thicket of trees, coming out one street over. If necessary, he could skulk through the bushes and exit further down. He visualized the group of bushes where he'd crouch and disassemble his rifle, before stowing it in the backpack. Afterward, he'd calmly walk over to the park across the street where he'd parked the car.

He checked the leaves on the trees. *No wind. That's why it's so damn hot.* He nestled the butt tight against his shoulder.

A Latina woman in her twenties rounded the corner at a brisk pace, pushing a three-wheeled stroller. Purple earbuds protruded from her ears, and her head bobbed to an unheard tune.

He focused his scope on her. She'd pulled her dark hair back into a ponytail that swished back and forth with each step. Perspiration glistened on her smooth brown skin. The swells of her large breasts jiggled as they strained against the confines of her white tank top.

Fantasies of what he could do with her if the circumstances were different flooded his mind and aroused him.

Grumps's voice filled his head. *"Keep your mind out of the gutter, boy! Stay focused."*

He wiped his face with his sleeve. *I've got to relax.* He filled his lungs with air that felt as dense as water, before wiggling his shoulders a bit. Less tense now, he put the rifle snug against his shoulder.

"It's a powerful feeling, ain't it?" Grumps said.

The woman stopped in the shade and reached for the bottle of water nestled in the holder.

He shifted the scope to the baby and centered the crosshairs on its blue-clad chest. The infant smiled and kicked his chubby legs and bare feet.

You won't be smiling much longer, little man.

CHAPTER 12

Another one-shot kill, the Marksman thought. His hands trembled while he stored everything in his trunk.

You did good, boy, Grumps said.

Adrenaline pumped through the Marksman's body. He turned on the air conditioner and smiled as the cold air blew across his sweaty face. It was past his usual lunchtime. He ordered a Coke, Whopper, and fries at a Burger King drive-thru on the way home. The smell of the hot salty fries permeated the inside of the car.

He'd finished the last of the fries by the time he pulled into the gravel drive where the single-wide trailer once owned by his grandfather squatted. Small rocks pinged off the underside of the car as his tires crunched their way past the overhanging oaks and towering pines that surrounded the clearing. He parked beside his grandfather's old truck.

A stroke had claimed Grumps three months earlier. The old man had willed the trailer and the truck to him.

The trailer wasn't much. The exterior was white, spotted with rust. Part of the rippled metal skirt sagged away from the right side, under the kitchen. Three concrete steps led to a cheap metal door. A wooden shed with weeds growing along the outside walls hunkered to the left of the mobile home.

His mother, Lorraine, a waitress at a nearby Waffle House, still lived with him. Her car was gone. *She must be at work.*

* * *

The Marksman slid out of the car gripping his Coke and burger. He shifted the bag to a secure position under his elbow while he walked up the steps. He put the key in the lock.

The door flew open.

"Fuck!" His keys were ripped from his hand. He almost fell while scrambling back down the steps.

"You know I don't like smut-mouth language!" Lorraine stood with her hands on her blue-jean-clad hips. "Where have you been? My car wouldn't start." She glared at him like it was his fault. "I had to get Jerry at the repair shop to come and pick it up. You won't give me a copy of the keys to Dad's old truck, so I was stuck here."

"What's wrong with the car?" he asked.

"Jerry said it's a starter solenoid. Now I've missed my shift, and I'll need that money to pay for the repairs." She crossed her arms and gave him a squinty-eyed glare. "Answer me! Where've you been?"

Grumps growled in his head. *"You gonna let that bitch of a mother talk to you that way, boy?"*

"None of your damn business," the Marksman said. He pushed past her.

Lorraine grabbed him by the shirt.

He dropped the bag holding the burger, rounded on her, and smashed his fist into her face. Blood splattered her shirt.

Lorraine's hands flew to her face. She pulled them away looking shocked at the blood. She stared wide-eyed at him. "You're just like him." She spat out the words. "The sonofabitch!"

Fury flamed along his nerve endings. Like a man possessed, he backhanded his mother to the floor. Sneering, he said, "In more ways than you know."

The white bag crinkled when he grabbed it off the floor. "It's a good thing you didn't make me spill my Coke." He turned and stomped down the hall, slamming the door to his room. The entire structure shook from the force.

CHAPTER 13

Charlie eased out of the courtroom door and sighed. She'd finished her testimony in a child abuse case as a witness for the Alabama Department of Human Resources. She hoped her testimony would make a difference.

She'd started down the hall when her phone pinged. A text from Ryan said, *Come ASAP.* Ryan offered no explanations, which sent her imagination into overdrive. *Is it the Marksman again? Dear Lord, who did he shoot this time?* The very thought made her stomach burn.

She tightened her grip on the locked carry case that held her patient's chart and slung her purse onto her shoulder. She was walking down the stairs when the next text pinged. She checked her phone. It was an address.

She squeezed past a man talking to a guard in the security line and rushed down the front steps of the courthouse. Once she was on the square, she headed toward the parking garage.

Fifteen minutes later, Charlie tooled through a neighborhood nestled in a middle-class section of southeast Huntsville. She admired the well-tended lawns and mature trees while following the directions on her GPS. She pulled to a stop behind a blue-and-white. Looping her consultant's badge over her head, she popped the trunk and slid out of her vehicle. She placed her purse and suit jacket alongside her secure carrycase and closed the lid.

Charlie perked up when she spotted the barrel-chested officer with the bulldog face guarding the entrance to the crime scene. Frank Dennison was always a welcome sight.

"Hey, Dennison," she lowered her voice and winked, "Where's No-Neck?"

He jerked his thumb over his shoulder. "He's over there gawking, as usual."

"Let's hope he doesn't throw up his guts again." Sweat trickled down her back. She scribbled her name on the sign-in sheet and checked her watch before entering the time.

Dennison chuckled while taking the clipboard. "Ain't that the truth? Last time he pulled that stunt, I had to finish a shift with him stinking to high heaven. Should've kicked him to the curb."

Charlie laughed. "Uncle George told me you two are getting together for a few beers next week."

Dennison's grin crinkled his eyes. "Yep, we'll be telling cop tales and bragging about our kids."

Charlie cocked her head. "Uncle George and Aunt Evie don't have any children."

He reached out and patted her on the shoulder. "You know he thinks of you as his kid. He's really proud of you."

Charlie smiled. "So what have we got? Ryan didn't give me any details when he texted me the address."

Dennison shook his head. "You're not going to like it." He handed her all the gear she'd have to put on to enter the crime scene area.

"I didn't have to wear all this last time."

He shrugged. "They told me to have everyone suit up until they tell me otherwise."

She zipped up the Tyvek suit and put on the booties.

"Charlie. Over here." Ryan signaled her over.

She waved back and pulled on her gloves. "Gotta go. See you later, Dennison."

Charlie walked up to Ryan and Joe. The tightly packed crowd of workers blocked her view. A flash told her Jason, the department's forensic photographer, hadn't finished his work.

Joe nudged Dennison's young, muscle-bound partner. "Get out of here, Jackson. The Doc's here."

Jackson frowned at her and walked off.

She slid into the spot he'd vacated between Joe and Ryan. The coppery smell of blood, evacuated bowels, and male sweat assaulted her sensitive nose. She thought she might gag until relief arrived on a water-scented breeze. The sound of a sprinkler ticked a rhythm in the background.

A jogging stroller lay toppled on its side.

Charlie sucked in a breath when she saw the blood and brains sprayed on it and the sidewalk. She'd dissected human brains in her classes but had never before seen them scattered and steaming on a blazing hot sidewalk.

Holy Mother of God! She swallowed and said a silent prayer for the deceased.

A baby whimpered to her right. She searched until she spotted the baby, and then returned her focus to the young Latina mother sprawled on the grass. The woman wore a white tank top, black workout shorts, and multi-colored jogging shoes. An open water bottle lay close by. Her upper face had collapsed. She suspected the exit wound at the back of her skull might be worse.

Charlie's heart raced like a car taking laps at the Talladega Raceway. "It looks like she was out walking trying to stay healthy. All her efforts were for naught."

The infant's whimpers escalated to a full-blown wail.

Joe turned. "Can't you shut that kid up?" He glared at a young patrolman.

"I don't know what to do with him," he said, holding the baby out at arm's length.

Charlie rolled her eyes, walked over, and took the baby. "Good grief, you don't hold a child like a sack of garbage." She propped the child on her hip and swayed from side to side. The little boy stuck his thumb in his mouth and stared up at her with beguiling brown eyes. She moved the child's head close to her chest, thwarting his attempts to see his mother while she evaluated the crime scene.

Glancing over she said, "Ryan, is our victim the baby's mother?"

"No ID yet," he said.

"Who found her?" Charlie asked.

"The neighbor across the street came out to move his sprinkler. Said he heard the tyke crying and saw the stroller was on its side. He came over to investigate and saw her." Ryan nodded toward the victim.

"It looks like the same MO to me," Charlie said.

Joe belched. "Yep, a precise headshot. We'll know more when ballistics tells us if it's the same caliber bullet. So far they haven't found any shell casings." He pounded on his chest with his fist. "Damn heartburn." Pointing over to a house across the street, he said, "The techs think he took the shot from the bushes."

Charlie took a circuitous route for a closer look so the baby wouldn't see his mother. She wasn't sure if it mattered, but she didn't want to leave a traumatizing visual image on his brain. Being careful to avoid contaminating the crime scene, she watched an officer string crime-scene tape to block off a bed of shrubbery. She glanced around. "He picked a house which seems to be unoccupied."

"Why do you say that, Doc?" Joe asked, wiping his face with a handkerchief.

"There's three papers on the drive."

Ryan came up beside her and offered the little guy an index finger. The baby grabbed it and looked up at him.

Ryan grinned.

Charlie pointed. "So he hid out in bushes again?"

"Looks that way. Hid in bushes at all the crime scenes," Ryan said.

She rubbed circles on the baby's back. "At least he's consistent."

The child put two fingers in his mouth and sucked.

Charlie grinned at the tyke and asked, "Anything found in the bushes?"

"Scrape marks and indentations on the ground," Ryan said.

"Indentations?"

"Where he set his rifle. We suspect he left that way." Ryan pointed to someone's backyard. "There's a park one street over. He could've parked there."

"I feel so bad about this. If I knew what was driving this guy, y'all could have caught him before this child's mother was killed."

56

"How do you think Joe and I feel? Both of us are losing sleep over this one," Ryan said running his hand though his hair.

A woman headed toward them as if she had an internal tracking device.

Charlie switched the child to her other hip. "Must be the social worker."

"I'm Tamiki Smith with the Department of Human Resources." She showed Charlie her ID. "I've come to pick up the baby." She grinned and held out her hands. "Hello, little man. Let's see if we can get you cleaned up and give you something to eat."

The child cried as Charlie handed him over. Charlie tweaked the baby's toes. "Shush, sweetie. She'll take good care of you until they find your daddy."

Tamiki bounced him with vigor on her hip to calm him. Without warning, the baby spat up on her dress.

"Whew!" Tamiki waved her hand in front of her face.

"Better you than me," said Charlie, trying not to chuckle at the woman's scrunched facial expression.

"This"— Tamiki gestured toward the mess—"is why I keep spare clothes at the office."

"I sure hope he's going to be all right," said Charlie. "Poor kid can't even walk yet, and he's lost his mom."

Ryan said, "If you've seen everything you need to see here, Joe will supervise the scene." He winked. "We can go to the diner down the street to discuss it and get out of this heat."

Charlie knew he was trying to raise her spirits, but it wasn't helping.

"Besides, Joe wants us to bring him a large Coke with lots of ice."

She shook her head with disapproval. "Sarah won't like it if she finds out. She's trying to get Joe to cut back on sugar and caffeine."

"Do you want to tell Joe he can't have a Coke in this heat?"

"Not me. I'm not married to the man." *Thank God.*

CHAPTER 14

After Charlie drank half a glass of iced tea, she asked, "Are there any other cases with a similar MO?"

Ryan shook his head.

She sighed. "Okay, let's go over what we know since I didn't see the first scene and only part of the second one."

"We have a shooter who likes precise headshots," Ryan said.

Charlie nodded. "So, he's an expert of some kind. Former military, current military, hunter, gun enthusiast, maybe the sniper competes or —"

Ryan interrupted. "Joe's that angle. He said the International Shooting Sports Federation controls most of the shooting competitions in this area. Although, there are others. He's mining his sources."

"Does that mean he's flashing around his NRA membership card?" Charlie asked.

Ryan shrugged. "I wouldn't put it past him."

She sipped her tea and thought for a moment. "I hate to ask. Could it be a cop or ex-cop?"

"Hell, I hope not." Ryan ran his hand through his dark hair. He glanced around the restaurant. "With all the bad publicity and people taking pot shots at police officers, that's all we need."

Charlie drank some more tea. The condensation from the glass spotted her blouse and ran between her breasts. "Crap." She frowned and snatched a paper napkin from the dispenser. She looked up to find Ryan's gaze following her every move.

"I hope it's not a cop, too." Charlie snatched another napkin. "Do we know what kind of gun the sniper used?"

"Can't tell at this point. Joe's the oracle on guns, and his guess is a high-powered sniper's rifle with a suppressor," Ryan said. "He theorizes a suppressor because no one's heard a rifle shot."

"I thought suppressors were for handguns?" Charlie plopped a napkin under the sweating glass.

"Nope. They have them for rifles."

"Do they work well?" Charlie asked.

Ryan rested both elbows on the table. "Pretty well. It's not silent, but with subsonic ammo it would only sound like a pop."

"Wow. I didn't realize it would be so quiet." She twiddled with her earring. "Since Joe is our gun...what did you call him? Oracle? Let's focus on the victims. There's a black, male postal worker in his...."

"Sixties."

"A retired eighty-year-old Asian man who was a ..."

"Tailor. Owned his own shop."

"Now a young, Latina mother," Charlie said.

"I don't see a pattern." Ryan loosened his tie and stretched his neck.

"Oh, there's a pattern. So far, the sniper has killed minorities. Could be a hate crime." She tapped her index finger on her lips. "We just haven't found the complete pattern yet. The fact he's so organized and repeats his kill methodology shows he likes patterns. I hope the door-to-doors offer something helpful, like a neighbor who saw some guy crouched in the bushes with a rifle."

"That hasn't happened so far." Ryan cocked his head. "We think this perp's a guy. What about you?"

"According to my new firearms instructor, Jack, only the Air Force encourages sniper training for women, not that other branches of the Armed Forces haven't trained a few women here and there in the US."

Ryan leaned forward. "And how do you know this?"

"Jack was a sniper in the Marines. He said on a technical level, women would make better snipers because they tend to be steadier when holding a gun."

"Do *you* believe women would make better snipers?" He raised both brows.

"I think in general, men are more psychologically suited. They find it easier to compartmentalize different areas of their lives."

"What do you mean?" he asked.

"Think of a chest of drawers, and each drawer holds a different aspect of life."

Ryan nodded. "Like one drawer for work, another for family, and so on?"

"Exactly." Charlie rewarded him with a smile. "Men tend to open one drawer at a time and close it before opening another. Women have most of the drawers open to some degree or another most of the time. This gives them a better overall view of their lives, but it makes it easier to be overwhelmed and harder to seal off the bad stuff."

Ryan sat back in his seat. "I'll have to think that over. So, when did you start firearms training?" He ran his fingers over the sweating glass. "You never mentioned it."

Charlie looked down. "After I found the first note. I was tired of feeling like a sitting duck. Somehow mace didn't seem to be enough."

"Why didn't you ask me? I would have trained you."

"You're so damn busy all the time. Besides, I don't want to spend what little time we have together at a firing range."

Ryan nodded and reached across to squeeze her hand. "I'm glad you did. It'll make me feel better." He leaned back. "So, what's your take on this case?"

"I need to do some research, and look at my notes from the academy." She lifted her glass to her lips, sorting through her thoughts as she drank some more tea. "This case isn't like the Beltway Snipers. This guy's well trained, and I suspect he's a lone wolf. One thing I'm confident about. The only way he'll stop, short of death, is if we stop him."

CHAPTER 15

Charlie left the diner and decided to pick up a few things at the grocery near Five Points. She was approaching the intersection when she noticed the Mystery Spy Shop in a strip mall to the right. She swerved and managed a quick turn into the parking lot without ticking off any nearby drivers.

She turned off the motor and hesitated. *Do I really want to do this?* She looked out at the small establishment's plate-glass windows and saw the image of the young mother with her brains splattered all over the sidewalk. This prodded her into action.

Charlie got out of the car, squared her shoulders, and strode toward the door. An attractive woman with mocha skin greeted her when she entered.

"I wondered if you'd make it in the door, Sugar. Most women hesitate before coming inside. A few even leave." She winked. "What do you need? A stun gun? Pepper spray? Maybe you want me to check on your husband to make sure he's where he's supposed to be?"

The woman tapped one long bejeweled nail on the glass. Her royal blue top hung long over black leggings.

Only one descriptor popped into Charlie's mind, *brick house*. "I need some surveillance. A stun gun and pepper spray doesn't sound bad, either."

"Well, Sugar, you came to the right place." She adjusted a curl on her short, dark hair. "Mystery Jones. I own this here joint, such as it is." She offered her hand over the counter.

Mystery's hand was warm and the handshake firm.

"I'm Charlie Stone."

Mystery leaned back as if to see Charlie better. "You the Dr. Stone who works over at the treatment center?"

Surprised, Charlie blinked. "I did, but I've started a psychology practice."

"You're the one who got my niece, Monique, straightened out. She's married now and has a baby boy."

Charlie had a dilemma. She wanted to say, "I'm so happy to hear she's doing well." Standards of confidentiality demanded that she not acknowledge that Monique was a former patient.

Before she could respond, Mystery said, "I know all that patient-doctor stuff is hush-hush, but she talks about you *all the time*. She still has that book you gave her and has read it twice."

Charlie nodded and tried to remember what book she'd given the young woman.

Mystery reached under the counter, pulled out a sizeable lavender purse, and plopped it on top. From the clunk it made, Charlie suspected it was a concealed-carry bag.

"You like this purse? We have a whole display of 'em over there in a variety of sizes and colors."

"I may need to come back and purchase one after I get my license to carry a concealed weapon."

"Sugar, I don't go anywhere without multiple layers of protection."

Charlie was afraid to ask what "multiple layers of protection" meant.

Mystery continued to dig around inside her purse. "Here it is." She pulled out her phone, and after several taps and swipes held up a photo of her niece holding a smiling baby up for Charlie to see.

Charlie grinned. Monique looked happy and healthy. "That's one good-looking little boy."

"Damn tootin'." Mystery pushed the purse back under the counter. "What do you need?"

Charlie explained about the threatening notes.

"Let me get this straight." Mystery leaned on the counter, exposing what seemed like a canyon of chocolate cleavage. "Some dickhead is stalking you and leaving notes to rattle your cage. Have you told the cops?"

"I'm dating a homicide detective, and my next-door neighbor is an FBI agent."

"And this stalker is still messing with you?" She shook her head. "Any thoughts about who it might be?"

Charlie shifted her weight and looked down. She felt guilty for even thinking the thought.

"Girlfriend, you tell Mystery what you suspect."

"It's not me, but my friend, Marti, thinks it's Ryan. He's the guy I'm dating."

"Why does she think your man is trying to scare the bejeezus out of you?"

"He's brought up several times that we should move in together."

Mystery stood straight. "I don't get it? Why don't you want to move in with him, and why does this Marti think your guy is sending the notes?"

"I'm not ready to move in with anyone. I haven't been divorced but two years. I don't want to be pushed into something as serious as a live-in relationship. Marti thinks Ryan is trying to scare me so I'll decide to stay with him for safety reasons."

Mystery nodded. "Are the notes being mailed to you or what?"

Charlie explained about the cemetery and the murder scene at the assisted living facility.

"Was this Ryan-guy at both places?"

Charlie nodded.

"And you need me to help you catch him or whoever is doing this?"

Charlie pulled out her credit card. "How much?"

"No charge to you, Sugar."

"I can't let you do that. How much?"

"Why not?" Mystery asked, frowning.

"There are ethical standards in my profession."

"I won't tell anyone." Mystery winked.

"I would know." Charlie knew from years of counseling others that once a person began the slide down the slippery slope of ethics, the waters of right and wrong became muddy.

Sighing, Mystery planted a fist on a curvy hip. "I need to think about this some more and consult with my technician, but I do have one idea for your car." She walked to a nearby counter and waved Charlie closer.

CHAPTER 16

Receiving scary notes and knowing some nut can shoot your brains out, puts a different perspective on life, Charlie decided. *The next moment has no guarantees.*

With those sobering thoughts running through her mind, Charlie unlocked the door to her office and put away her purse. She talked about her conclusions with her fish while sprinkling food into her aquarium.

"What's going on?" Marti asked over her shoulder while walking toward the business office to stow her purse.

Charlie raised her voice to be heard down the hall. "I'm thinking about how short life can be and what I've been missing."

Marti came back into the lobby and plopped into the chair opposite Charlie. "Serious thoughts. When I deep-sea dive into my gray matter, I start thinking about my bucket list. So, what's on your list?"

Charlie chewed her bottom lip and looked at the ceiling.

Marti looked up, too. "Is the answer up there?"

Charlie chuckled. "I wish. Let's see…I've always wanted to own a red convertible."

"So why don't you?"

"I can't afford another vehicle right now. Besides it's not a practical car."

Marti shifted in her seat and slung a leg over one arm. "What do you want to do that you can afford?"

"Take dance lessons."

Marti sat straighter and grinned. "What kind of dancing?"

Charlie leaned forward. "Ballroom dancing."

"So what's keeping you from doing it?" asked Marti. "Group lessons are affordable."

"How do you know?"

Marti's face lit up. "I started taking lessons at Southern Elegance Dance Studio last month. It's loads of fun and great exercise. I've already lost five pounds. They have a dance party every Friday night with a group lesson included in the price."

Charlie thought about the suggestion. "It sounds fun but I don't have a partner."

Marti rolled her eyes. "Neither do I, but single guys come and dance with everyone. Besides, wouldn't Ryan be the obvious choice?"

Charlie shrugged. "You know how unpredictable his schedule can be."

"Ask him. Call him right now."

Catching Marti's enthusiasm, Charlie pulled out her phone and tapped in his number.

Ryan answered. "Roberts."

"Um, Ryan, I've been talking to Marti about her dance class. I was thinking about taking ballroom dance lessons. Are you interested?"

Silence.

When she thought maybe they'd become disconnected, Ryan said, "Did you say dance lessons?"

"Yeah. What do you think?" she asked.

"I'll think about it. Gotta go, I'm running late for a meeting."

Charlie frowned at the phone in her hand.

Marti took her leg off the arm of the chair and leaned forward. "Well? From the look on your face, I'm guessing his answer wasn't a resounding, *yes*."

"He said he'd think about it. He was on his way to a meeting."

Marti grimaced. "I figured he'd let you down. That, my dear, is a slow no."

"Huh?"

"We both know dance lessons will exit Ryan's head once the meeting begins, if not sooner. This means you'll wait for an answer because you don't like to be pushy. One of several things will happen."

"Oh?" Charlie crossed her arms interested in hearing her friends take on the situation.

Marti counted the options on her fingers. "You'll forget you ever asked, he'll tell you he's too busy, or you'll give up and never learn to dance. Either way, the outcome is a slow no."

"You're right." Charlie sighed. "You want to meet me at Southern Elegance tomorrow night?"

Marti stood and stretched. "Sure. Let's go out to eat first and make a girls' night of it."

"Deal!"

On Friday night, Charlie and Marti changed into cute dresses at the office, before going to the Cajun Steamer Bar and Grill located at Twickenham Square, not far from Huntsville Hospital.

They were lucky and found parking in front of Another Broken Egg across the street.

Charlie dropped her keys in her purse and said, "I've heard lots of good things about this place, but I haven't eaten here yet."

"I tried it last week." Marti rubbed her tummy. "It was great."

They looked both ways and crossed the street. Charlie opened the door and was blasted with Cajun music. A bar hunkered to the left, and the rest of the seating consisted of booths and tables with chairs. Once the hostess placed them in a booth, Charlie looked at the photos on the walls and tables. Every scene depicted run-down houses and people with gap-toothed grins. It appeared everyone was shucking oysters with a knife.

Charlie tapped a photo under the glass on their table. "If this is what the state of Louisiana looks like, I'm not sure I want to visit."

"I'll admit, I thought the same thing when I ate here last week," Marti said. "I'm sure the whole state doesn't look this way. Surely they do something beside shucking oysters."

Charlie perused the menu. Red beans and rice, shrimp and grits, gumbo…. An item caught her eye. "I think I'll try the crawfish enchiladas."

Marti, hidden behind her menu said, "I'm going to try the voodoo chicken." She lowered the menu and smiled. "Well, look who walked in the door."

Charlie turned.

Scott stood next to the hostess stand. The young hostess looked up at him with a big smile while throwing her shoulders back to emphasize her upper assets.

When Charlie turned back around, Marti didn't look pleased.

"I guess we better save him from Miss Perky Boobs." Marti raised her hand and waved. Within seconds, Scott stood beside their table, the pouty hostess standing behind him with a menu.

Charlie maintained her central position on her side of the booth.

Marti scooted over to make room next to her.

Scott took the offered space. "Some of the guys at the office told me about this place but suggested I come early, or I'd have to wait for a table." He glanced at the menu. "I know what I want. A shrimp po-boy."

As if by magic, the waitress appeared to take their orders. She left, backside swaying for Scott's benefit.

"What are you two lovely ladies up to tonight?"

All smiles, Marti touched his arm. "We're going ballroom dancing."

Scott reared back, eyes wide. "You're kidding me. I went ballroom dancing all the time in DC. Where do you dance around here?"

"Southern Elegance. You should come with us. The studio is doing a waltz lesson before the dance party."

So much for girl's night out, Charlie thought.

"Sounds like fun." Scott looked at Charlie. "Where's Ryan?"

She grimaced. "Working."

Scott grinned. "I guess I'm a lucky man tonight. Two dance partners."

Charlie focused on stirring her tea. *Ryan won't like this at all.*

The dance studio was on the upper floor of another business. Charlie could feel it grow warmer as they walked up the stairs. The studio walls were covered with mirrors. An oak dance floor covered most of the space. A small carpeted section toward the front windows held round tables, which seated four.

They walked to the seating area and claimed chairs. Charlie glanced around while putting on the new shoes Marti had helped her purchase at Blooms, a local dance apparel store.

The instructor called everyone to the floor. "Guys on one side and ladies on the other."

Twenty-one people were taking the lesson. The instructor asked a lady in a glittering black top over black pants to help him. First, he showed the step with his partner. Then he went over the pattern with the men. When satisfied, he demonstrated the steps for the ladies. To Charlie's surprise, she could replicate the dance patterns, a significant feat since she was known to be a klutz.

When the instructor asked them to pair up, she found she was looking up at a tall, dark-haired man with a mustache.

After several opportunities to dance the pattern, the instructor yelled, "Ladies, switch to the man on your left."

A smiling Indian man introduced himself. "I am Reyansh Kapoor."

"Hi, I'm Charlie Stone."

"You are new?"

"Yes, my first lesson."

They danced the pattern several times. Reyansh led well, and she found him more comfortable to follow than her last partner.

The instructor yelled for them to switch partners again.

A red-haired man told her, "You dance well for a beginner."

Charlie blushed. "Thanks."

This continued until each lady had danced with each potential partner. Then the instructor added an additional section to the pattern and the process began again.

When the practice lessons were done, Marti led Charlie toward a table that contained snacks, water, and sodas.

"How'd it go?" Marti asked.

"Good. Some of the men danced better than others."

The tables were packed. Everyone rested and ate a snack before the music for the dance party began.

Reyansh was seated at their table with his wife, Anaya.

Scott managed to wedge himself at the table for four. After introducing himself, he asked, "So what do you do?"

"I'm a professor of aerospace engineering at UAH. And you?"

"FBI."

Reyansh raised a brow and then turned to Charlie. "What made you decide to start ballroom dancing?"

Anaya leaned forward to hear her answer over the noisy chatter from nearby tables.

Charlie thought, *death*, but instead said, "It was on my bucket list."

The music started, signaling the beginning of the dance. The first song was the Tennessee Waltz.

Scott took Charlie's hand and pulled her to her feet. "Shall we dance?"

She looked over at Marti, who was no help because the instructor was escorting her to the floor.

Scott took her in his arms, grinned down at her, and winked. "It's a shame Ryan doesn't know what he has in you."

"Ryan appreciates me," Charlie couldn't keep the defensive tone out of her voice.

Scott changed directions to avoid a collision with a slower couple. "I live next door. Seems to me he neglects you."

"He's a homicide cop. It's not his fault people keep shooting each other."

Scott shrugged. "Hey, I'm not judging him. I just hate to see you sad and lonely."

"If you want to do something to help a lonely woman, take care of Marti. She likes you, Scott."

Scott's jaw flexed. "You know if Ryan screws you over, I'm here for you, right?"

"I know."

The song ended, and she was grateful when the kind engineering professor claimed her for the next dance.

CHAPTER 17

The Marksman knew this kill would be a challenge. He'd waited for a night when the new moon would help his chance for escape. The parking lot in front of the club was well lit, but there was only one light over the rear stage door.

The wooded area across from it offered the cover he needed. It was dark, and the bright interior lights of the club would temporarily blind anyone exiting the door. He'd watched his target for several days and knew this was the last show for the club's current review.

Grumps's voice echoed in his head. *"Make sure you plan everything, boy. Especially the escape. You can be the best sniper in the world, but if you don't have a plan to save your ass, it don't matter how well you shoot. You're one dead sniper."*

He's right. The Marksman ran through his plan once more while he waited. After he took the shot, he'd run down the path through the woods, hop into his car, and drive onto the ramp to Interstate 565. After he put some distance between him and the crime scene, he'd head home and clean his rifle.

His target's stage name was Clarisse LeBeau. The Marksman had made his choice when he attended the show the first night of the review. Due to the slight stature, expert makeup, and high voice, at first he'd thought Clarisse was a female singer.

The whole experience made him uncomfortable. The bawdy song and flirtatious gestures left him both aroused and disgusted. The shouts and whistles of the crowd had made him cringe, but he wanted *this target*. It would be an excellent addition to his collection.

The Marksman shivered when he thought of the names Grumps's would've called him if he had known he'd been aroused. On the positive side, this would be a four-fer—a Caucasian, gay, cross-dressing, male.

He exhaled and tried to get comfortable as he leaned against the trunk of a nearby tree.

"Better get your ass ready," Grumps said.

The Marksman leveled his rifle for the shot by shifting the dirt around. The laser rangefinder danced across the back door of the club. *One hundred and thirty yards.* He adjusted his scope.

The humid night was much too sticky for late September. A faint breeze was the only relief.

The Marksman lay down and made adjustments until he was comfortable, practicing the stealth his grandfather had taught him.

Grumps said, *"Boy, a noisy sniper is a dead sniper."*

He peered through the scope, careful to avoid the light above the door. *Don't want to lose my night vision.* Moths attracted to the light swerved and dived into the scope's view. *I'll have to adjust for the upward trajectory.*

Minutes later, loud voices and raucous laughter broke the stillness. Couples and small groups exited from the front of the club. They shuffled and stumbled toward their cars parked in the side lot.

Most of the customers had left by the time the back door of the club opened. Chatter flowed through the air in waves as the cast congratulated each other while they came down the three steps to the parking area.

"It was a good run," said a tall man wearing a long red wig.

"I thought that crazy dude was gonna come on stage there at the end," said a shorter man, wiping makeup off his face with a white cloth.

More laughter. The two men stopped to chat behind the building.

Moments later, two more people exited, still wearing their stage makeup. He waited, rifle tight against his shoulder.

There he is! His heart hammered as he prepared to squeeze the trigger.

Someone shoved past the target, pushing him to the side. The Marksman cursed under his breath.

"Steady," said his grandfather's voice in his head.

The way cleared.

He squeezed the trigger.

The gun recoiled.

The suppressed shot was a mere pop in the night.

Clarissa LeBeau's blood and brains splattered the heavily made-up face of the man behind him. His lifeless body slid to the bottom of the stairs.

Hysterical screams and shouts covered any noise he made when he grabbed his backpack and rifle and ran. Two hundred feet down the trail, he tripped over a tree root and fell hard.

"Get your ass up and moving," Grumps growled.

Winded by the fall, the Marksman tried to force his lungs to breathe. He staggered to his feet and almost fell again, but steadied himself against a pine tree.

"Get going," his grandfather yelled in his head.

He stumbled along until he spotted his car. He threw his rifle strap over his shoulder, ready to sprint to the vehicle.

Blue lights bounced off the tree trunks around him.

He dropped to the ground and lay flat among some bushes.

A patrol car raced past without slowing to check his car.

Guess he's going to the club. Stupid wanna-be.

He jogged to the trunk, opened it, and placed the rifle and backpack inside. After a quick glance to ensure he was alone, he unlocked the door, slid inside, and drove away.

Blue lights blinded him sending his heart racing with fear.

"They found me!" His foot pressed the gas pedal. He resisted the urge to speed away.

The police SUV raced past him.

The Marksman exhaled his relief while he watched the police car turn the corner in his rearview mirror.

"You done good, boy. You didn't spook," Grumps said.

The Marksman nodded before turning on a local country station with a shaking hand.

The Marksman pulled onto the gravel drive. His tires crunched, announcing his arrival. Grumps said, *"Your sniveling, bitch mother left the light on for you. Isn't that sweet? If it were me, I'd strip her down and take my belt to her for wasting the energy."*

The Marksman shook his head to clear it. He stepped out of the vehicle and went to the trunk to get his rifle. He shouldered the case and slammed the trunk closed.

The rusted hinge on the trailer door squeaked when Lorraine opened it. Looking uncertain, she clasped the collar of her robe shut with her free hand.

He walked toward the mobile home with his insides jumping. The first wooden step creaked under his weight.

"Where were you, Son?"

"None of your damn business."

She flinched and backed away.

The savory smell of meatloaf filled the room. "I saved your dinner. It's in the fridge. Do you want me to pop it in the microwave?" Lorraine asked.

"Not hungry." In truth, his shaking insides made him feel sick. It was always this way after a kill.

The inside of the mobile home was paneled with cheap, blond plywood. The furniture was old, but the inside was clean. His mom had tried to make it more livable since his grandfather's death by picking up paintings she liked from a local thrift store. Even when she used to drink, she'd kept him and Grumps well fed and the place clean. Grumps would have beaten her if she hadn't.

"There's been another shooting. I saw it on the news." Her gaze shifted from his face to the gun case he carried toward his room.

He shouldered past her without replying.

"You sure you don't want me to heat up your dinner?" she asked. "It's your favorite."

He shook his head, walked into his bedroom, and slammed the door.

Grumps told him, *"She's probably out there wringing her hands. She won't tell. She's too damned scared."*

The Marksman turned on the television in his room before he opened the closet and took out his gun cleaning kit.

CHAPTER 18

Fueled by pure adrenaline, Charlie crossed the Governor's Drive overpass and exited onto University Drive. She parked on the street under a tunnel of overhanging trees and walked to the crime scene entrance.

After signing in with her buddy, Officer Dennison, Charlie gave a resigned sigh. *Time to boil in a suit.* She put on a Tyvek suit and shoved her hair into a cap. She was balancing on one foot pulling on a bootie when she said, "I thought you switched to days, Dennison. Hasn't your shift ended, or are you working day and night shift now?"

"I switched with another guy. One of his daughters is tying the knot tonight. Don't know why he's so happy. This wedding is costing him a bundle." He handed her gloves.

Charlie pulled them on, fiddling with them until they were comfortable. "Maybe she was costing him more than the wedding. Now she's someone else's responsibility."

Dennison said, "Who knows. We had all boys. Sparks will be glad you're here."

Charlie looked up, puzzled. "Why would Joe be happy to see me?"

"I hear they have a hysterical witness down there."

Charlie wiggled her shoulders, trying to adjust the suit to a more comfortable fit. "I'll do what I can." She walked down the taped path feeling like she was ready for a moonwalk. The Tyvek material made a swishing noise as her thighs brushed against each other. The suit didn't breathe, and she knew she'd be soaked with sweat soon. When she spotted Ryan, she lifted a hand to catch his attention.

Ryan met her part way and whispered, "This whole scene is batshit crazy right now."

"Tell me what happened." Charlie gave his arm a discreet squeeze.

"Tonight was the final night of a cross-dressing musical revue. According to the manager, they had a full house. The performers were going out the back door when someone shot a guy named..." Ryan pulled out his phone and checked his notes. "Clarisse LeBeau. His real name was Clarence Barnsmith. He was an accountant who lived across the border in Tennessee."

Charlie's stomach flipped. "A shot to the head?"

"Yep, a clean kill."

When they arrived at the rear of the club, they found Lieutenant Joe Sparks squatting near the body, a sour look on his face. He eased his way up as they approached. "Damn knees. Don't get old, Doc."

Charlie gestured toward the body, "My only other option doesn't look like fun, Joe."

"True." He tilted his head toward the corpse. "What do ya think?"

"Give me a minute to look at things, or do you want me to do divination?" Charlie asked.

Joe laughed. "No, I'd rather stick to the facts. This one's weird enough already."

Despite a rough start, she and Joe had managed to come to a truce, which pleased her. According to Joe's wife, Sarah, he respected Charlie, but he'd cut off his left nut rather than admit it.

Charlie rubbed her right knee as she squatted near the body. "What do you know, Joe?"

"Well, the vic was coming down the stairs after the show when the perp shot her, um, him, in the center of his forehead." Joe jerked his thumb to the left. "The hysterical guy over there was behind him and caught the blowback."

Charlie's gaze skittered to where he indicated. A man sat with a blond wig in his lap, crying while he wiped Clarence's brains and blood from his face with a white towel. The thick stage makeup and gore created a grotesque mask, smearing with every swipe.

The man blubbered as he looked up at an officer taking his statement. "It was a great show. I was trying to leave when all this shit hit me. Stinks to high heaven."

A paramedic knelt on one knee, taking his blood pressure.

Charlie closed her eyes a moment, trying to erase the horrible image. "If it's the Marksman, this is his first night shot."

Joe shook his head. "Doc, this doesn't make sense. A Black postal employee, an Oriental—"

"Asian," Charlie corrected.

"Whatever! A retired *Asian* tailor, a young Hispanic mother, and now a Caucasian whatever he was? Doc, there's no pattern here that I can see."

"There's a pattern, Joe. I'll bet the bullets are the same caliber. Right?"

Joe nodded.

"The killing headshots are consistent. Only the motive and victim choice are still unclear." Charlie stood and tapped her lip with her index finger while she studied the man's body sprawled on the steps. *Why? Why you? What made you the target?* She took a moment to say a silent prayer for him and his family.

An hour later, Charlie had calmed most of the witnesses and had passed out cards for therapists in the area who treated this type of trauma. Her exhaustion made the uphill walk back to Dennison's station seemed like forever. Once there, she peeled off her gloves and elastic cap before she began the ordeal of peeling off the sweat-soaked Tyvek jumpsuit. Sweat trickled down her sides, and the suit clung to her damp arms like paste. *A long, hot shower will seem like Heaven after sweltering in this getup.*

Dennison held open the garbage bag while she stuffed the protective clothing inside. As a contract profiler, she was off the clock and could go home. Joe and Ryan would be here several more hours.

"I forgot to ask, where's your partner, Officer No-Neck, I mean Jackson?" Charlie asked with a sly wink.

Dennison chuckled. "He's on vacation down in Florida flexing his muscles and hoping to get lucky."

Charlie laughed. The vision of No–Neck flexing his massive biceps at one female sunbather after another helped to shove away the image of the horror she'd seen.

"You think he's wearing a Speedo?"

Dennison laughed. "Shit, I hope not. By the way, I had a beer with George last week."

"That's great. Uncle George mentioned it when I had dinner with him and Aunt Sadie a couple of days ago. He's enjoying the guy's night out." Charlie leaned closer. "It gets him away from Aunt Sadie." She waved goodbye, happy to be heading home.

No streetlights penetrated the canopy of the giant oak trees, which cast Charlie's Honda into deep shadow. Once in her car, she leaned her head against the backrest and closed her eyes. *It's there, on the edges of my mind. Why can't I figure out the pattern?*

She opened her eyes and put her hand on the key in the ignition. The flutter of a note trapped under a wiper caught her attention. "Not again!"

Before she did anything else, she removed her motion-sensitive spy camera from her visor. Her fingers shook as she slipped it into her purse. *I'll hook it up and download the data at home.* Mystery Jones had told her to use the larger screen on a desktop computer. It would offer better clarity.

Feeling vulnerable, she locked the doors and called Joe Sparks.

"Sparks."

"Joe, this is Charlie. I got inside my car and noticed another note on my windshield."

"Hot damn! Did you touch it?"

"No."

"Where are you?" Joe asked.

Charlie gave him the directions.

"Don't move. Like we don't fucking have enough going on right now," Joe grumbled.

"Hey! I didn't ask to get threatening notes," Charlie snapped.

"I know, I know. This Marksman case is bugging the crap out of me," Joe said. "I'll grab some techs and be there in a jiffy."

Charlie hung up. *Everything bugs the crap out of you. I wonder how Sarah puts up with you.*

Charlie got out of the car but made sure not to touch anything while she waited.

As promised, Joe appeared out of the darkness with two techs in his wake.

Holly grinned. "Charlie, you are one popular woman. First the Trainer, now 'the Writer.'" She made quote marks with her fingers.

Charlie ran her hands through her damp hair. "What can I say, I'm a good catch." She tried to sound flippant, but her insides felt like a milkshake, whirled at high speed.

Holly's assistant pulled out a camera and took flash photos. Charlie raised her hand to block the bright light but still had to blink away the spots.

After Holly had removed the note with tweezers, her assistant began dusting the wiper for prints.

Joe pulled on his reading glasses. "What does it say, Holly?"

They crowded around the paper.

YOU NEED TO MAKE A DECISION—OR ELSE!

"Or else what?" asked the assistant.

"What do you think?" Joe yanked off his glasses.

"What's going on?" yelled Ryan as he walked toward the group. "I saw flashes, and one of the guys told me you were up here with Holly."

When Ryan was close enough to see the car, he rushed forward. "What's happened? Where's Charlie?"

Charlie stepped around Joe. "I'm here."

"Thank goodness." His eyes met hers. "What's happened here?"

Holly stepped forward and extended the note clad in a protective evidence bag. "The Writer left Charlie another note."

Ryan strode forward, grabbed it, and read. He looked up. "Why didn't you call me?"

Charlie raised both hands, palms up. "You were busy."

Ryan crossed his arms. "Joe was busy, too."

Heat crept up Charlie's neck. She hadn't called Ryan for several reasons. The biggest one being she wanted to prove to Marti that Ryan wasn't the person producing the scary notes. She also knew if Joe was in charge of the scene, Ryan couldn't mess with the forensics. She wanted to believe he was innocent, but the tiny part of her mind that harbored doubt knew she'd made the right choice.

"That's it, you're moving in with me so I can protect you," Ryan said.

Charlie stiffened. *Your reaction is another reason I didn't call you.* She stepped forward to close the distance between them and placed her hand on his arm. "Ryan, with my alarm system, new locks, Spanky, and Scott next door, I feel safe when you're not there. Your house doesn't even have an alarm system."

"So Scott makes you feel safer than I do?" Ryan flicked away her hand, whirled, and stomped off mumbling to himself.

She called after him. "That's not what I said."

Joe shook his head and looked at his feet. Everyone was silent while they watched Ryan disappear into the darkness.

Once he'd gone from sight, Holly and her assistant busied themselves with gathering their few pieces of equipment.

Joe reached out and gave Charlie an awkward pat on the shoulder. "He'll come around, Charlie. He's just upset."

"So am I," said Charlie. "So am I."

The further Charlie drove, the more her fear morphed into anger. By the time she pulled into her garage, she was fuming. She stopped the car, hit the remote to close the door, and slammed the car door. She stomped into the house grumbling.

Spanky ran toward Charlie with a tongue-lolling doggie smile. She skidded to a stop, turned around, and scampered with a lowered tail into the bedroom.

Good idea, Spanky. Seething, Charlie dug the small camera from her purse. "All right, Mr. Mystery Man, it's time to reveal your identity. I've had it!"

She stomped into her home office and turned on her computer. "Come on. Why is this taking so long?" When the machine booted, she hooked up the camera. After a few clicks and growls, a file came up. She clicked on it, and a man's head almost came into focus.

"Damn!"

Charlie could tell the person had short hair. The image was anything but recognizable due to the near total darkness where she'd parked. *Note to self: Park in good light.* She enlarged the picture. *The nose is large enough to be a guy. There's something familiar about him. His hair is short like Ryan's. Damn, if it weren't so dark I could tell the hair color. Dear Lord, don't let it be Ryan.* Charlie squinted and moved closer to the screen, and then backed away for a different perspective. She slumped into her desk chair feeling frustrated and defeated.

"I'll have to try again. I'll catch the guy next time." *If he doesn't kill me first.*

CHAPTER 19

The latest murder had peppered Charlie's sleep with nightmares of threatening notes left by snipers. Refusing to be a victim, she decided a little target practice was what she needed. If whoever was leaving her notes came after her, she wanted to be ready.

She showed up at the local pistol and pawnshop to use their indoor shooting range. In the range's prep room, she zipped herself into a Tyvek suit, put paper booties over her shoes, and raised the hood. Her instructor, a former Marine sniper trainer, had warned her during their practice sessions about the dangers of lead poisoning. Before that, she'd never thought about how much lead from the ammo floated in the air, and coated her and all the surfaces.

A guy in his mid-twenties, wearing jeans and a wife-beater shirt eyed her. "You goin' on a moonwalk or do you plan to shoot?" He smirked at her "Are you one of those germaphobes?"

The heat rose in her cheeks. "I know this seems a bit extreme, but I did a little research. Folks who shoot or work at indoor ranges have blood levels of lead that are much higher than the general public."

The guy looked at her like she'd sprouted antlers. "So?"

Charlie slipped on her protective glasses. "A day or two of shooting can cause lead to linger in your body for months."

"So?"

"Lead poisoning can cause tremors, high blood pressure, heart disease, and decreased kidney function. It's even worse for kids because it affects the development of their brains." She pulled on her paper mask to shield her nose and mouth.

He ran his hand through his short, sandy hair. "Been shootin' since I was old enough to hold a rifle. Nothin's wrong with me." He put on his ear protection, picked up his scoped rifle, and pulled the door open to the shooting range.

The brief leakage of noise assaulted Charlie's ears until the door closed. Her instructor had also told her gunfire was a significant factor in both hearing loss and tinnitus, so she put in her earplugs and placed ear protection muffs over her hooded ears. She donned surgical gloves before picking up her pistol and ammo. When she entered the range, most of the shooters stopped to stare. Several of the men guffawed and pointed at her.

Let them laugh. Just because these guys can't see the lead floating in the air and coating everything doesn't mean it's not there. She placed her target paper on the clip and sent it back to position. Opening the cylinder, she loaded her Charter Arm's five-shot revolver and clicked it shut. Jack's instructions ran through her mind. Assuming the correct stance, she sighted down the barrel and squeezed off her first shot.

It pierced a hole on the edge of the center circle.

Charlie made the necessary adjustment, sighted, and fired. The process took her entire attention. Twenty-five minutes later, she'd finished her box of ammo. She wiggled her shoulders to loosen the muscles while considering another box of rounds but changed her mind. *If I walk into the store area looking like this, I'll cause a stampede or get shot.* She chuckled and emptied her gun of casings.

"You gonna recycle those? If not, can I have 'em?"

Startled, Charlie turned to find the man in the wife-beater shirt standing behind her. "You can have them."

He nodded toward her target. "Damn good shootin' for a girl."

Charlie decided to let the "for a girl" pass. She flipped the switch to pull in her target.

He moved against her as he reached to take it off the clip. He pointed at the one hole that was on edge of the center circle. "This your first un?"

"Yes." Charlie took the large sheet of paper from him. She crumbled it for disposal and picked up her empty pistol.

Back in the prep room, Charlie sat and sealed her protective glasses in a plastic bag. She'd rinse them at home. She then stood and peeled off her protective gear except for her booties and gloves, and threw it and the target in the trash.

The guy who wanted her casings pushed through the door followed by booming gunfire. He disassembled his rifle and placed it in his case. Eying her, he zipped up the plastic bag full of her casings. "You're right purty, now that you've stripped off all that space garb."

Charlie avoided his gaze and focused on wiping down her pistol before removing her gloves.

"I was thinkin' about getting a burger for lunch," he said.

Charlie threw away the paper towel and shoved her gun in the slot of her concealed-carry purse.

"You wanna come?"

Charlie looked up into steel-blue eyes. They had a disturbing glint to them. Her danger radar pinged. "I'm flattered, but I don't know you. A girl's got to be careful these days."

He grinned and held out a callused hand. "I'm Jared."

With reluctance, she shook it. *Yuk! Creepy.* She pulled her hand back. Sensitive to people's personal energy, she shuddered as she took several steps closer to her purse on the bench.

His eyes narrowed. "You really are a germaphobe."

Putting on a conciliatory smile, she said, "Thanks for the offer, but I'm seeing someone." She grabbed her purse and headed for the door. Once outside the room, she pulled off her gloves and booties and dumped them in the trash without looking back. She scrambled to her car, locked the door, and rushed from the parking lot. She shuddered. *That guy is major creepy.*

Charlie drove straight to the Waffle House near her home. *I need comfort food.* After finding a parking space in the almost-full lot, she entered the restaurant.

"Hey, Charlie, have you caught that nut who's shooting people yet?" a waitress asked.

Charlie strolled to the far end of the place and sat in a small booth near the front window. "Cinda, I'm a part-time profiler, not a detective. I can't arrest a soul."

A waitress she hadn't seen before was filling a napkin holder on the bar. "I'm afraid to go from my house to my car. My neighbors think I've gone berserk because I run instead of walking."

The cook laughed. "Nivess, what makes you think you're a worthy target?"

She popped her fisted hands on her hips. "This Marksman guy is clearly a racist."

The cook rolled his eyes and turned to fill a waffle iron with batter. "What makes you think this sniper is racist?"

"The news this morning said he done shot a black guy, an old Chinese man, and a Hispanic woman. Sounds racist to me."

Charlie wasn't surprised Nivess saw this shooting rampage as a string of hate crimes. *Could be, but I'm not convinced.*

The cook plated a meal, handed it to Nivess, and said, "The dude shot a white guy, too."

Nivess tilted her nose in the air and took the plate. "He don't count. The news said he was one of those transgender, transsexual… heck, trans-something folks. Either way, I don't want to get dead."

The cook scattered some hash browns on the grill. "Then I suggest you zigzag while you run. This guy seems to be a crack shot."

Charlie put away her keys and strolled toward the restroom to wash her hands. "What makes you think it's a guy?"

The cook swiveled to face her. He pointed the spatula at her. "It's gotta be a guy. No woman shoots that good."

Charlie rolled her eyes.

When she returned to her table, Cinda placed a coffee, water, and several containers of cream on the table. "The usual?"

Charlie pulled the mug closer. "I need to work on being less predictable."

"Yep." Cinda turned to the cook and yelled, "Pull one bacon, well. Pecan waffle, dark."

Charlie looked up in time to see Jared walk in. The staff exchanged uneasy glances.

Nivess walked past Charlie and muttered, "He gives me the heebie-jeebies."

Charlie thought *Me, too. Did he follow me?* She lowered her head, pulled out her Bluetooth earbuds, and stuffed them in her ears. After thumbing open her phone, she started an audiobook and pulled out a pen and paper to list her errands to run after lunch, which included a doctor's appointment.

A hand waved between her and the paper.

Charlie started and looked up. To her relief, it was Ryan.

"I thought I might find you here. Getting your pecan waffle fix?" Ryan dipped his head to kiss her and then dropped into the seat opposite her.

Jared had stopped near the register, his brow puckered. After a brief hesitation, he turned and strode out the door.

An hour later, Charlie sat on a crinkling sheet of white paper in an examination room in Dr. Markle's office awaiting the results of her annual blood work.

The door opened and the doctor entered, followed by a rotund nurse. His gray eyes twinkled. "How's my favorite headshrinker?"

Charlie smiled. "You tell me. Those folks at the lab drained me almost dry. Are you sure you're not supporting a vampire?"

He chuckled while pulling up her test results on his laptop. He popped on his reading glasses and read. His brows drew together.

"What's the matter?"

"Your glucose is high. You fasted, right?"

Charlie nodded, gripping the sides of the examination table.

"Your A1C is also a bit high as well as your triglycerides."

"So what are you telling me?"

He put down the laptop and pushed his glasses up on his head. "Lie down." He palpitated her stomach. "Does that hurt?"

"No."

The doctor took her hand and helped her to sit. He probed her back and chest with an icy stethoscope.

"Yikes. Do you stick those in the freezer between patients?" Charlie asked.

Dr. Markle winked. "Only for you. Now take some deep breaths."

Charlie complied.

The doctor looped the stethoscope around his neck and sat on a rolling stool facing her. "Charlie, you're a borderline diabetic. Any history of Type 2 diabetes in your family?"

Charlie tapped her lip with a forefinger. "My mom was diagnosed with Type 2 diabetes in her forties, but it was after she'd gained a lot of weight." She looked down at her trim physique. "I'm not overweight."

"No, your weight is fine. Are you getting enough sleep? Poor sleep habits can affect glucose levels."

Charlie felt her heart racing. *Diabetes? This can't be true. I feel fine.* "I don't sleep well if I'm stressed."

"Stress can also affect this problem. I want you to use my five-step system: exercise regularly, watch your diet, cut out sweets, practice good sleep hygiene, and reduce your stress."

She was so shocked, she could only manage a nod.

Dr. Markle stood, reached behind him, picked up some pamphlets, and handed them to her. "These should give you more information." He pointed at a specific pamphlet. "I suggest you set up an appointment with this clinic for diabetes education and for some help with nutritional planning. The receptionist at the checkout desk can set up an appointment for you."

Charlie felt numb. She walked down the hall, past the scheduling clerk, and out the door forgetting to pay her co-pay.

CHAPTER 20

The Marksman's frustration with the woman at the firing range temporarily marred his triumph from the previous night. He wanted her and she was taken. Like his grandfather before him, he didn't like roadblocks or delays to his plans.

His truck slid to a stop on the gravel drive. Grumbling under his breath, he climbed out and slammed the door before clomping up the stairs to the trailer. When he banged open the door, his mother jumped.

"H-hi, Son. I see you're back."

His mother already had on her uniform for work, but her shift didn't start until two. "Where're you goin'?" he asked, propping his rifle backpack in the corner.

"I thought I'd stop by Wal-Mart and grab a few things. You need anything while I'm there?"

He shook his head before picking up the paper. His grandfather always said, *"Boy, you need to keep up with what's going on in the world."*

His mother stood with her hand on the doorknob, staring at the paper in his hand. "There are some leftovers in the fridge."

He grunted again.

She hesitated a second and then left.

He pulled the curtain aside to watch her depart. Once she was out of sight, he fired up his laptop and began researching the news about last night's kill. He needed a pick-me-up to improve his mood.

A warm glow filled him while he read about his killing shot. *I'm feared and respected.* He picked up the paper to learn what the Huntsville Times had to say.

His grandfather's voice rang in his head. *"Boy, get your head out of the clouds. You're only as good as your next shot. Start planning."*

CHAPTER 21

The next day, Charlie and Marti sat in Charlie's therapy room and discussed the Marksman. They had thrown ideas back and forth for over a week. Charlie was ready to write a profile.

Charlie tapped her lip. "I checked with the FBI's Behavioral Analysis Unit. Most of their data is about mass shootings. The Marksman is a serial sniper."

"True." Marti polished her lenses. "Aren't most snipers white males who are trained to become psychopaths?" Marti placed her glasses back on her face.

"Or psychopaths who train to become snipers. I'm sure the majority of military and police snipers aren't true psychopaths. I suspect they believe they're doing the right thing by eliminating a threat to society. That's different from an assassin who's a killer for hire."

"The '007, licensed to kill' idea?" Marti asked.

"Yeah, something like that. My parents had a neighbor who was a sniper during the Vietnam War. He told me every person he shot 'needed shooting' because they were 'bad people.' He also made sure anyone who knew he was a sniper understood it was legal because he was 'under orders' and 'at war.'"

Marti frowned and harrumphed.

Charlie shivered at the memory. "The guy gave me the creeps. He liked my parents, so he watched our place. From the way he talked, if someone had tried to break into our house while we were gone, he'd have shot first, and asked questions later. If the burglar had died, he'd have called it 'streamlined justice.'"

Shaking her head, Marti reached for her hot tea. The mug read, "Everybody is somebody."

Charlie stared at the cup. An insight clicked. She snapped her fingers. "The Marksman wants to be somebody famous or important. He's searching for status through these kills."

Marti sipped more tea, a thoughtful expression on her face. Then she nodded. "Sounds right."

"He's trying to please someone or is trying to live up to someone's expectations. He didn't get this good without someone training him," Charlie added.

Marti put down the mug. "Okay. Let's follow that line of reasoning. What caused him to feel he lost status?"

Charlie counted the points off on her fingers. "Maybe a loss of some kind. Could be the death of someone close, a divorce, or unemployment. All of those events could cause depression expressed through anger." She stood and paced again, needing to move to energize her brain. "Maybe he experienced some form of humiliation."

"The humiliation could be long-term or triggered by a recent event," Marti said.

Charlie nodded. "I suspect both. What else do we know about snipers?"

"They compartmentalize their emotions, boxing parts of their lives into neat little drawers to be pulled out when needed," Marti said.

"That's true," said Charlie as she resumed her seat. "Most snipers spend time following or watching their targets before a kill, which makes the act more intimate." She frowned. "The scope puts them in a position to see the expression on the face of their targets while they die. That may be why it's necessary to either rationalize what they're doing or dehumanize their targets."

Marti sipped her tea and put down her mug. Her face scrunched with distaste. "Speaking of dehumanizing, the Marksman is shooting his victims like they're deer."

Charlie leaped to her feet and threw her hands in the air. "Animals!"

Marti sat straighter. "What? What about animals?"

Charlie paced the floor again. "What do big game hunters do?"

Marti shrugged. "Kill mammals? Where are you going with this, Charlie?"

"Those hunters don't care about the meat so much. They collect trophy animals," explained Charlie. "They slay different types of animals and mount their heads above the fireplace or take their pelts for rugs." Charlie returned to her seat. "This guy is collecting people—different races, genders, and sexual orientations." Charlie gave an involuntary shiver. "That's disgusting."

Marti rubbed her temples. "I agree. The very thought is giving me a headache."

Charlie stood and paced some more. "Serial killers like trophies. So far he hasn't collected any, thank goodness." She tapped her lip. "The media stories are his trophies!"

Marti picked up her mug and held it. "Makes sense. He's collecting stories instead of hanging body parts on his walls. This means he probably has a scrapbook."

"That's why his victim profile is all over the place."

They sat silent again, digesting the current theory.

"Did I ever tell you my shooting instructor, Jack, trained Devil Dog snipers in the Marines?"

"No. In fact, I didn't know you'd bought a gun until the other day."

"I asked Jack about sniper training during my last shooting lesson. The candidates go through Marine Corps Scout Sniper School. They work in pairs: shooters and spotters. When he was in the military, the shooters used M40's. He told me they're trained to take out a man-sized target at a thousand yards or more. Of course, it depends on the conditions."

Marti shivered. "Kinda scary knowing someone could kill me and I'd never know the killer was there until I was shot."

"Jack said the Marines who are allowed into the Scout Sniper School are screened for mental illness. Snipers need to be responsible and levelheaded people, as well as expert shots."

Marti crossed her legs and pulled her skirt down. "I bet they've had a few bad seeds that sneaked into the program."

Charlie nodded. "He did admit on occasion, a psychopath would sneak under the radar and the Corps would discover innocents had been targeted. He called those rogue snipers 'squirrels.'"

Marti frowned. "What happens when the military finds out?"

Charlie shrugged. "Jack didn't say. I got the impression it wasn't advertised." She stretched and reached down to pick up her legal pad. "I'm going to write this profile and email it before I meet Ryan for lunch. Do you want to join us?"

Marti shook her head. "I've got too many errands to run."

Charlie paused.

Marti scrutinized her. "Something else is up. What are you not telling me?"

"I saw Dr. Markle for my physical today and there's a problem."

"Oh, God," Marti said.

Charlie walked into Ol' Heidelberg, a family-owned German restaurant. She blinked as her eyes adjusted to the dim interior. The wood wainscoting and dark green walls didn't help the overall cave-like feel.

She spotted the dessert case. It showcased a decadent display of cakes and treats. Cake was one of her weaknesses and those tasty desserts seemed to beckon her to come view their splendor. She remembered Dr. Markle and turned away. *It's just cake, no biggie.*

A server wearing a dirndl, a traditional German dress with vest and apron, came up to greet her.

"I'm meeting someone here."

"Go peek in the dining room and see if your party is here."

Crimson cloths covered the tables topped with red and white checked over-cloths. Ryan sat in a booth facing the door. He rose when she approached, kissed her lightly on the lips, and waited until she sat before sliding back into the booth.

"Got your profile. So simple. Don't know why we didn't see it before," Ryan said.

Charlie reached for a slice of homemade German bread nestled in a basket. "Because normal folks don't typically kill people to collect them."

"True," he agreed.

The waitress returned and took their order. Charlie ordered a Wiener schnitzel dinner, and Ryan ordered a bratwurst platter. Since he was off the rest of the day, he also ordered a German beer.

"What do you think the next pick will be for our collector?" he asked.

Charlie tapped her lip with her finger. "Hmm. He's collected the categories of African-American, Chinese, Hispanic, Caucasian, male, female, adult, elderly, mother, and cross-dresser. That leaves Indian, Native American, and Vietnamese, to name a few."

"There's also children and infants," Ryan said.

"Let's hope not. The Marksman could've killed the infant, but didn't. What worries me is he may destabilize and go on a rampage."

They ate for a few moments in silence.

"I had my yearly physical yesterday."

Ryan looked up. "Yeah? Everything okay?"

Tears welled in Charlie's eyes.

Ryan dropped his utensils and reached across the table to hold her hands. "You're not dying, are you?"

Charlie chuckled. "Nothing that awful. I'm pre-diabetic. I have to adjust my lifestyle to avoid medication."

Ryan squeezed her hands. "Whatever it requires, we can work it out."

CHAPTER 22

Charlie woke, her mind weighed down with all the unsolved cases in her life. Frustrated, she rubbed her face. *What a night! First nightmares and then waking up paranoid someone will break in and kill me. This can't be good for my health. Something's got to be done. I'm going to set a trap.*

She had the time. A meeting scheduled at the Department of Human Resources had been canceled late yesterday.

After a quick breakfast of cereal for her and dry dog food for Spanky, Charlie set out to solve her problem.

Fifteen minutes later, Charlie pulled into a parking space in front of the Mystery Spy Shop and sat stunned, eyeing the large sheets of plywood that covered the large plate glass window. *Did someone break in or shoot out the window?* She left the car.

Her shoes crunched on small slivers of glass sprinkled on the pavement. She stopped, trying to catch her breath. Her body stiffened as a memory flooded her. She lay on a basement floor, broken shards of glass digging into her flesh. The Trainer was on top of her ready to…

She shook her head to bring herself back to the present. Her racing heart pounded in her ears. Out of breath, she placed a hand on the plywood to steady herself. *Flashback. I need to tell Marti about this.*

Charlie took several deep breaths to control her shaking hands. She stood straight and pulled back her shoulders before reaching for the door of the shop. The bell on the door jingled announcing her arrival.

Mystery walked out of her office near the rear of the store with a tan and white Chihuahua in her arms. "Dr. Stone! Are you ready to let me put cameras around your house?" She placed the wiggling dog on the floor.

The dog pranced over to Charlie with a doggie smile. Her tail whipped so hard, her entire back end swayed.

Charlie dropped to one knee to greet the tiny dog. "Well, hello. Who are you, sweet thing?"

"That's Prissy. You can probably guess how the little rascal got her name. She's my guard dog."

Charlie scooped Prissy into her arms and scratched her ears while the dog licked her wrist. Charlie chuckled. "Guard dog? What does she do, lick the burglars to death?"

"She's one of my layers of protection, a vital role in my defense. That little girl can put up quite a racket. While she distracts the intruder, I disable the threat."

Remembering Mystery's previous remark about "multiple layers of protection," Charlie thought, *I don't want to know what 'disable the threat' means.* She pointed at the plywood. "What happened to your window?"

A curvaceous young woman with dark skin and short hair dyed bright red on top walked in from the back.

"This is my assistant, Jasmine Williams," Mystery patted the top of a nearby glass display case. "Doc, I thought he was going to smash through all my display cases and run over both of us."

Wide-eyed, Jasmine shook her head from side to side. "I saw my life pass right before my eyes."

"Y'all were lucky you didn't get hurt."

Mystery threw both hands up looking exasperated. "The man was eighty-eight and shouldn't have been driving. Heck, he wasn't even my customer. He was going to the Thai restaurant four stores down."

"Do you have insurance?" Charlie asked.

"Oh, yeah."

"The old coot did, too," Jasmine added.

"How long will you have to deal with the plywood?" Charlie leaned against a counter and crossed her arms.

"Until this afternoon. Hopefully, everything will be back to normal by tonight. Now Doc, what can we do for you?"

"I have an idea of how to set a trap, so want cameras around my house, only I don't want them to be visible. The conditions haven't been ideal for catching my note writer with the visor cam."

"Why?" Jasmine asked.

"Too dark."

"Do you have any motion-detector lights on your house?" Jasmine asked.

"No, I never needed any. My life was dull until I started profiling for the Huntsville Police."

Mystery sat on a nearby stool, reached over, and patted the one nearest her. "Have a seat. Let's discuss what you need. Jasmine will follow you to your home to inspect everything and will write up an estimate. If we have the items in stock, we can have them installed within a couple of days."

Charlie sat on the stool, crossed her right leg over her left and bobbed her foot. "Everyone around me works during the day, so it would be best if you came after 8:30 and left before 3:30. I don't want any of my neighbors to know what I'm doing."

"Will you be there?" asked Jasmine. "Zach, our technician will be with me. We'll need to get inside the house to wire things up."

"If you can give me a day's notice, I can clear my schedule. Two days would be better. I'll leave for work as usual and return before 8:30, in case someone's watching."

On the morning of her installation, Charlie waved from her Prius to Scott, as he backed out of his drive. She drove to work, went inside her office, and fed her fish. After she checked the parking lot, she left, drove back to her house, and put her car in the garage. At 8:30, a plain white van pulled into her drive. Charlie pressed the remote for the garage door, and the van pulled inside. She closed the door behind it.

Jasmine jumped out of the passenger side. "Hi, Doc. This is Zach Stanner."

Even with his stoop-shouldered posture, Zach towered over both women. His blond, spiky hair seemed to defy gravity. He said, "We should have this completed by three, no problem."

Spanky barked like a maniac. It sounded like a much larger dog was hidden behind the kitchen door.

Zach took a step back and paled. "Is your dog, um, vicious? You know, does it bite?"

Charlie thought of the Trainer. "Not usually. Let me introduce you to my Spanky girl so she'll calm down. Don't back away. Let her sniff you before you attempt to pet her." Charlie opened the door.

Spanky leaped over the steps and raced toward Zach, whose expression showed round-eyed panic.

Charlie inhaled. *He's going to bolt.*

Zach stiffened and looked left, then right, before climbing on top of Charlie's trunk. He sat with his knees pulled up to his chest.

Charlie placed her hand over her mouth to hide her smile.

Jasmine cackled. "Wait until I tell Mystery about this. A six-foot-five guy terrorized by a beagle."

Spanky stood with her front paws on the bumper, growling and barking.

"If you turn any paler, Zach, we'll have to get you a blood transfusion," Jasmine said.

Charlie performed the hand signal for sit. "Spanky! Sit."

She did. Charlie picked her up, and the pup tried to lick her face. "She's a bit protective. If you stay still, I'll hold her so she can sniff you."

Zach's mouth opened to protest. Spanky sniffed him up one leg and down the other. After exhaling a breath and sneezing, she allowed him to pet her.

Charlie placed her on the ground. She trotted over to greet Jasmine, whom she'd sniffed two days earlier. Jasmine baby-talked to her while scratching behind her ears.

"You're all clear," Charlie said. "Unless you try to hurt me."

With his eyes on Spanky, Zach slid off the back of the car.

They went to work. Zach pulled a ladder out of the van and headed outside with Jasmine, who followed with a toolbox. By eleven, they had installed all the LED motion-sensor lights.

Jasmine mopped sweat from her brow. "We'll be back at noon to install the cameras and monitors."

"Good. Have a good lunch."

"Any suggestions?" asked Jasmine.

"There's a small café down the road on Highway 72 called 3rd Base Grill. It's nothing fancy, but it serves good burgers and hot wings."

"Sounds good to me," Zach said. His spiky hair was drooping from the heat.

Charlie heated a piece of cheese toast in her toaster oven and poured a glass of iced tea. She sat at the small breakfast table and looked down into Spanky's amber eyes. "I sure hope this is worth the trouble and expense, girl."

Spanky woofed.

Charlie remembered her father telling her once, "Peace of mind is affordable at any price."

At noon, Jasmine and Zach returned, looking refreshed and energetic.

He grinned down at Charlie. "Did you know they have fried Twinkies?"

Charlie chuckled. "No, I didn't."

"They were awesome." He grabbed the ladder and headed toward the front porch.

By 2:30, Jasmine was in Charlie's home office giving instructions on how to work the program on her computer, while Zach stored their equipment in the van.

Charlie always kept the office door locked due to confidential material. Ryan never went in there because he knew she sometimes wrote psychological testing reports there.

Jasmine and Zach waved goodbye and backed out of the garage.

"Thank goodness that's over. This asshole is costing me a bundle." Charlie grabbed her purse, set the alarm, and closed the door. She backed out of her drive and drove to work. Once there, she settled down to do some paperwork. At six, she locked the office and drove home.

Scott was at his mailbox when she drove past. He waved and walked into his open garage.

Charlie glanced in the rearview mirror. *I wonder if he noticed anything?*

CHAPTER 23

The Marksman focused the scope of his rifle on the doorway of the Engineering Building located on the University of Alabama, Huntsville campus. His car was parked between a large SUV and a massive dual-wheeled truck. He lay in the shadows under the truck. A thin cloth, which matched the pavement, was draped over him.

A fly buzzed around his face. He twitched his eye to scare it off his cheek. It left but returned to hover before landing on his nose. He scrunched his nose, and it flew away. Then it was back, swooping closer to his face, feeding his frustration.

His grandfather's voice growled in his head. *"Boy, if you sweat, insects will come. Don't let anything take your focus off your target. If there's a distraction, eliminate it."*

The Marksman waited. The fly continued to dive-bomb his face. He struck out and grabbed the fly in his fist. The trapped insect fluttered, tickling the inside of his closed hand. He tightened it until he felt the fly cease its struggle. After he dropped the creature to the ground, he smashed it with the heel of his hand. He glanced at his palm, grimaced, and wiped it on the leg of his jeans. *Damn fly.*

His target on this overcast day was an aerospace professor at the Department of Engineering. He'd seen Dr. Kapoor's photo in the Sunday paper, above an article stating he'd acquired a large research grant. Kapoor had worn a suit and tie, grinning in front of the very building where he would soon die.

The Marksman remembered his grandfather telling him umpteen million times, *"The habits of your prey are important. Do your research, boy."*

He nodded. *I did, Grumps.*

Reconnaissance showed his target exited through the door of the Engineering building three days a week, around six pm. He'd then walk toward his black BMW, get in with his brief case, and drive home. He could've killed his target anywhere, but he knew this location would create more headlines to collect for his scrapbook.

The Marksman was locked and loaded, ready to kill.

The door to the building opened.

He set the crosshairs on the shadow of a person in the doorway ready to shoot.

A young, blonde woman hunched under a backpack turned right and trudged toward the dorms.

He took a deep breath to release his tension and waited.

"*A good sniper can wait for days to get a shot. It's about patience,*" Grumps's voice said in his head.

The door flew open, bouncing back on its hinges.

He stiffened. His finger tightened on the trigger.

A group of three guys piled out, laughing and joking. They stood talking for a few minutes and then parted ways.

The Marksman rolled his shoulders and flexed his right hand before resuming his position. While waiting, he thought through his planned exit. *After I take out this guy, I've gotta get out of here before they lock down the campus, or it's all over. Everyone will assume this is another school shooting spree. Damn incidents are popping up like pimples across the country.* He chuckled softly. *So much for safety in numbers.*

The door eased open.

The professor walked through, carrying a briefcase and looking down at his phone. He started down the steps.

The Marksman followed his progress. "Look up, asshole."

He stopped at the bottom of the stairs, looked up and paused.

The Marksman centered the crosshairs on his forehead.

The professor raised his right foot to step forward.

The Marksman pulled the trigger.

The rifle recoiled.

Kapoor flew backward. He lay sprawled on the concrete stairs, his arms thrown wide. Blood and brains had splattered the area like grotesque abstract art.

The Marksman rolled out from under the truck and looked around. Seeing no one, he ducked back down and pulled his rifle and cloth out. He pulled the magazine out before opening his trunk. He placed his rifle and cloth inside and slammed it shut. After another quick glance around, he jumped into his car and started it. He pulled out of the lot onto Sparkman Drive and soon caught a red light. He wanted to blow through it but didn't want the attention. Seconds stretched like eternity. The light changed. When he drove onto the ramp of Interstate 565, he saw blue lights flashing near the campus.

He smiled as his grandfather told him, "*You done good, boy. Real good.*"

CHAPTER 24

Charlie had turned off her office computer and was looping her purse onto her shoulder when she received the call. "Ryan, I'm leaving the office now. Are we still on for dinner?"

"Afraid, not."

Charlie heard sirens in the background. "Where are you?"

"Outside the Engineering Building at UAH. We have another shooting victim. Can you come?"

"Address?" Charlie asked.

"Come to the Sparkman Drive entrance to the campus," Ryan said.

Marti walked out of her therapy room into the hallway. Her smile faded when she saw Charlie. "Where are you going in such a hurry?"

"Ryan phoned. Our shooter claimed his fourth victim today."

Marti's shoulders drooped. "I sure hope y'all catch him soon. It's enough to make a body paranoid."

Charlie nodded as she pulled her keys from her purse. "It certainly has me looking over my shoulder."

As Charlie drove to the crime scene, she tried to remember where the Engineering Building was located. She felt sure it was close to the lakes and Frisbee golf course near the Sparkman Drive entrance to the campus. She exited Interstate 565 West and turned right onto Sparkman Drive. The University appeared on the right.

The proliferation of blue and white flashing lights clarified the location of the crime. It seemed half of the police force, an ambulance, and the fire department paramedics were all crowded into one parking lot. The presence of the ambulance raised her optimism until she noticed the coroner's van, which eliminated any hope the victim had survived.

She parked as close as possible. After she placed her HPD placard on the dash to avoid a ticket from the zealous campus police, she looped the lanyard with her consultant's badge around her neck. Jumping from the car, she locked her purse in the trunk and placed her keys in a pants pocket. She could see the officer in charge of sign-in and the forensic photographer.

Crime scenes were always a bit frantic with flashing lights, vehicles parked every which way, and personnel scampering from place to place. Onlookers with their cell phones and the press jostling for film footage only added to the chaos.

A Channel 48 reporter pushed past some students and headed toward her.

Charlie sped up, trying to evade the woman.

The reporter yelled, "Dr. Stone! Do you think this is another victim of the Marksman?"

"No comment."

The reporter tried to keep pace with her but stopped short of the police tape.

She strode up to the officer holding the sign-in sheet.

He glanced at her badge before handing her the clipboard and a pen. "Roberts is near the coroner's van."

"Thanks." She accepted the Tyvek suit, booties, and gloves he handed her and suited up.

She didn't have far to walk. The crime scene photographer was taking shots near a spray of blood and brain matter that covered the stairs leading to the glass doors of the building. One officer herded a group of students filming with their cell phones from the area, while another continued to stretch crime scene tape to cordon off a wider swath of the area.

Ryan spotted her and waved her over. "Here she is. Wait a minute before you leave."

Charlie joined him next to a gurney.

Ryan unzipped the body bag to expose the face of the victim. "The victim is Dr. Reyansh Kapoor, who is one of the professors. He's Indian. It seems the Marksman is still collecting."

Charlie's hand flew to her mouth. "No!" She backed away, shaking her head.

"What's wrong?"

Tears sprang to her eyes, blurring her vision. Feeling suddenly dizzy, she swayed. Her stomach churned, causing her to cover her mouth as bile eased its way up her esophagus.

Ryan walked over and took her arm to steady her. "Charlie? What's wrong? You're as white as sugar."

"I-I know him. He's a ballroom dancer who takes lessons where I do at Southern Elegance Dance Studio. I've danced with him when we rotated partners. He's such a nice man." Charlie shook her head again unable to believe what she was seeing.

"I'm so sorry, Charlie." Ryan stepped back and crossed his arms. "When did you start taking dance lessons?"

"Three weeks ago."

Ryan's brow furrowed. "Why didn't you tell me or ask me to go with you?"

"I did ask. You gave me a slow no," Her eyes stayed glued to Reyansh's face.

Joe Sparks harrumphed. "Can you two lovebirds discuss this later?"

Charlie nodded and swiped a tear from her cheek. "I didn't mean to get so upset. Oh, my gosh, he has a wife and two children. What happened here?"

Joe flipped open a little black book and perched his reading glasses on his nose. "No witnesses found yet. The professor exited that door." He pointed with his pen. "Was shot and fell backward onto the steps."

"It was a clean kill shot," Ryan said.

Charlie nodded, but she felt cold and numb. *I can't believe the Marksman shot Reyansh. What could he possibly have done to deserve this?* Charlie knew the answer, but the implication chilled her. *He was collectible.*

CHAPTER 25

Lorraine Springle sat across from Marti, tears welling in her eyes. She dabbed under her lashes with a tissue. "Sorry to be blubbering like this."

"It's okay to cry. It's part of the process of healing. Take your time," Marti said.

"I don't remember much about my father from when I was really young. Mom and I lived in the same mobile home I live in now." She reached for a fresh tissue and blotted under her lashes again. "He came home one day in his uniform. No hug. Told Mom I'd grown like a weed."

"How old were you?' Marti asked.

"Five. Ole Dad pushed me out of the house and locked the door. I didn't know what was happening back then. Now I know he took her to the bedroom and had sex. When I was allowed inside for dinner, he kept eyeing first me, then Mom, looking mean."

Lorraine dropped her head into her hands.

Marti took notes, giving her time to regain control.

Lorraine looked up, blew her nose and took a deep breath. Her face had turned blotchy from the crying.

"Mom put me to bed early that night. I woke when I heard them arguing. He called her a fat pig, before he accused her of having sex with other men. She denied it. He called her a 'lying bitch.'"

Marti leaned forward. You seem to have a very clear memory about this."

"It's burned into my memory. Every time he'd get drunk, he'd tell me to not become a fat pig and lying bitch like my mom."

Lorraine paused to again blow her nose. She reached for another tissue and continued.

"When I heard her cry out, I got out of bed and peeked through a crack in the door." She paused and began to hyperventilate.

Marti feared she'd trigger a panic attack. "Slow your breathing. Deep slow breaths."

Lorraine obeyed.

"Good," Marti said.

When she'd gained control, she looked Marti in the eye. "I saw him kill her."

Marti felt a chill slide down her body. "What happened?"

"He back-handed her around the trailer. She fell back and hit her head on the coffee table. He-he ripped her clothes off and had sex with her. She wasn't moving and blood was trickling out of her ear." Lorraine blew her nose. "Can you believe it? She was probably dying or dead and he banged away inside her like nothing had happened. What kinda person does something like that?"

Marti handed her another tissue, and steeled herself for the rest of the story. She'd heard so many horrific things over the years, yet each one took its toll on her emotions.

"He got off her, zipped his pants and felt her neck. He said, 'Damn bitch.'" Lorraine covered her face with her hands. "He beat her to death and called her, a 'damn bitch,' because she died."

CHAPTER 26

Sweat trickled down Charlie's face as she lugged a box from her bedroom closet to the garage. Relief flooded her body when she dropped the cumbersome box on top of another. She felt sticky, and the desire for a shower was driving her to finish this little project.

"Mom always said, 'Horses sweat, men perspire, and ladies glow.' Or was it glisten? Heck, I'm glowing and glistening." She sighed and wiped the sweat from her forehead with her sleeve.

It was more than a need for relief from her pungent state that pushed Charlie. She wanted closure. *I'm tired of being stalked—tired of feeling afraid.*

For this reason, Charlie needed an excuse to park her car outside of the garage. She had decided to spend Saturday morning cleaning out her closets and garage for charity to prepare for the second stage of her trap.

She held her hair off her neck to take advantage of a light breeze. The tingle across her skin felt delicious. She closed her eyes to relish the moment.

"Hi! What's going on? Need some help?"

Charlie jumped and turned to see Scott grinning, hands on his hips. His biceps bulged. *No wonder Marti has the hots for this guy.*

He held up his hands. "Sorry, didn't mean to startle you."

"No biggie. To be truthful, I'm so exhausted I wasn't paying attention."

"You looked deep in thought," Scott said.

Charlie ignored the comment. "Since you're here, I have a chair in the house that needs to come out to the garage. I could use some muscle to get it out here."

"Lead the way." Scott followed her to the spare bedroom.

She pointed at a cranberry wing-back chair jammed into a corner. It was too large for the space. "That one. I never had a place for it when I moved in, but I couldn't seem to part with it. The poor thing deserves a new home."

"I could use it. I moved from an apartment to a house, so I'm still a bit shy of furniture."

"Take it. It's yours."

Scott grinned and hefted the Clayton Marcus chair with ease.

She followed him out the door into the garage where he placed it on the concrete floor. Charlie realized she'd never been inside Scott's home. He always came to hers. *I wonder if he's messy? I'll ask Marti.*

He ran a hand through his hair. "Speaking of furniture, would you go shopping with me to help pick out some new pieces? I like your taste and could really use some help."

Something prickled at the back of her neck. *If I go shopping with Scott, it will cause an argument with Ryan.* Besides, she hated shopping for furniture.

"Not my thing. Marti loves to shop for furniture and she has excellent taste. Give her a call. She'd *love* to help you."

Scott looked down and shuffled his feet. "I guess you're too busy to help a friend and neighbor."

Ohh, he's good. The old guilt tactic. Not falling for that one, Scott. She smiled and crossed her arms. "I'm so glad you understand."

He looked up frowning, and then glanced around. "Let me pile some of these boxes up so you can pull your car in the garage."

A brief shot of panic moved her forward. "No! I mean, leave them. The truck will be here Monday, and I may add more stuff tomorrow. It won't hurt my car to sit in the drive. It's a safe neighborhood."

"You sure?" He scrunched his nose. "It's a mess out here. I know you're a neatnik."

"It's a garage. No problem." She waved her hand at the boxes. "Besides, it's temporary."

"I don't mind tidying up." He moved closer.

Charlie held out a hand. "You don't want to get any closer. The toxic fumes from my B.O. could knock you unconscious, and then I'd have to call an ambulance."

"You could give me CPR." He winked and took a step closer.

"Back off."

Her tone stopped his progression.

"I'm serious, Scott. I'm ripe. All I want right now is to close my garage door and go take a shower."

"In that case, I'll take my chair and leave." His tone said volumes.

Charlie squelched her desire to smooth over the situation. Scott had boundary issues and could misinterpret her motive.

He snatched up the chair. The moment he exited the garage, Charlie said, "I hope you enjoy it."

He said nothing.

She closed the garage door and headed toward the bathroom. "Fine. Pout if you want."

After her shower, she checked the placement of her car on the monitor of her computer. She chewed at a piece of dead skin on her chapped bottom lip and decided the Honda needed to move a foot to the left. Rather than move her car back and forth in her driveway, she decided to get some spicy chicken and then try to park in the optimum spot.

Ryan and Joe were investigating a murder in north Huntsville, so Charlie had her Saturday night to herself. She mentioned to Ryan that the garage was full. If he caught a break and finished at a decent hour, he'd need to park on the drive next to her. Charlie felt pretty sure he'd have a late night. While she drove, she prayed that Ryan wouldn't be her stalker.

Fifteen minutes later, she returned and did her best to stop in the right place for good camera coverage. She exited the car with her box of chicken and strolled toward the front door. Once inside, she placed the chicken on the counter, out of the reach of Spanky, who danced about whining and sniffing.

"In a minute, Spanky. I want to check the monitor to make sure I parked in the right area."

The car was perfectly placed. The trap was set. "Spanky-girl, let's see if our stalker will take the bait."

* * *

A deep growl rumbled from Spanky's chest, waking Charlie. She sat up in bed, her heart pounding like a bass drum. The bedside clock showed several minutes past midnight. She touched the dog's head and whispered, "What is it, girl?"

The beagle jumped to the floor and trotted out of the room.

A flash of light from the motion detector lights lit her curtains.

Charlie shoved her feet into her moccasins and peeked out.

A figure raced past the bushes outside her window. She could only tell it was a large man. Charlie could hear Spanky barking and scratching at the front door.

She sped to the living room and looked out. A white note fluttered on her windshield, tucked under the wiper.

"Spanky girl, we may have caught us a stalker."

CHAPTER 27

Charlie went outside and inspected the note. The evening news forecast had called for showers during the early morning hours. She hated to wake anyone, but she had no choice if she planned to preserve the evidence. Sighing, she turned and walked back into the house, steeling herself for the phone call she must make.

Joe Sparks sounded more like he was rising from the dead than from a sound sleep.

"Joe, I'm sorry to wake you." Charlie suspected he hadn't been asleep for long.

"Who the hell is this?" He coughed. "It better be good."

"It's Charlie, and it's important."

"What now?"

"Someone placed a note under my windshield wiper a few moments ago."

"Damn, Charlie, couldn't this have waited until the morning? Ow! Stop poking me, Sarah. It was a reasonable question."

Charlie grinned, knowing Joe's wife would take her side. "I would've waited until later to call, but rain is forecast."

"Why aren't you calling Ryan? Ow! Quit it, woman."

Charlie stifled a giggle. "Please keep this between us. Some folks are theorizing that Ryan is writing the notes to scare me into moving in with him. I don't want him involved so he can't be accused of tampering with anything."

Joe harrumphed. "Okay. Makes sense. I'll call the techs. Be there in a jiffy. You'd better have a steaming cup of black coffee waiting for me."

"Will do."

Charlie disconnected, flipped on the outside lights, and rushed to her bedroom to dress, with Spanky in her wake. Then she hurried to the kitchen and pulled a pod of French roast from the cabinet, popped it into her Keurig coffee maker, and placed a large mug underneath.

"Okay Spanky, let's see what the video shows us."

Once she was in her office, she pressed the switch on her new Apple desktop, grateful she didn't have the long wait her old computer had needed.

A few clicks and she was in the app Jasmine had installed. Charlie realized she was holding her breath. *What if it is Ryan? It'll be the end of our relationship. I'll never be able to trust him again.*

She took a gulp of air and clicked her mouse to bring up the video.

A tall figure approached the car. It was clear he was stockier than Ryan. He picked up the wiper blade and placed the note underneath. When the man turned, the camera caught his face.

The shock felt like a basketball slamming into her chest, knocking the air from her lungs. *Oh, no. This is bad.*

The doorbell rang.

Charlie sped to answer the door. Spanky raced alongside her barking.

"Hush!"

Spanky sat and whined.

When she looked out, the peephole framed Joe's sour countenance. *Oh boy, here we go.* She opened the door.

"Where's my coffee?" Joe grumbled.

Sarah pushed her way around her husband and elbowed him. "Joe! Where are your manners?"

"Back home in my warm, cozy bed, where I should be. My manners don't show up until after eight o'clock and three cups of coffee."

Not even then, Charlie thought.

Sarah wrapped Charlie in her arms. "You must be a nervous wreck with some lunatic running around leaving threatening notes."

"Thanks for coming, Sarah." Charlie closed and locked the door. "Let's get Joe his first cup of coffee."

"Now you're talking," Joe said. "It'll be twenty minutes before the techs arrive."

They all headed toward the kitchen while Sarah sweet-talked Spanky.

Joe pulled out a chair in the breakfast area and sat. "Stop chattering at that dog. You're making my head hurt."

Charlie pushed the button, and within minutes, the aroma of brewed coffee filled the room.

Sarah sighed. "I love the smell of coffee." She scrunched her face. "I can't stand the taste."

Charlie placed the mug in front of Joe, who gripped it with both hands like it was a life preserver.

"Have you tried it with cream and sugar?" Charlie asked.

"Only sissies drink it that way," Joe said.

Sarah rolled her eyes. "No."

"Would you like for me to fix you a cup the way I like it?"

"Sure."

"Sissy," Joe mumbled under his breath.

Charlie reached for a pod of light roast and brewed another cup. She added sugar and cream before stirring.

"Try this."

Sarah reached for the cup and tasted it. "This is good. I guess I do like coffee."

The doorbell rang.

Spanky raced into the living room barking like the house was under attack.

Joe pushed himself out of his chair with a grunt. "Must be the techs."

Charlie corralled Spanky in the living room, picked her up, and placed her in the bedroom. When she returned, Joe was outside with the techs looking at the note. Charlie and Sarah stepped out onto the porch and closed the door to keep any bugs attracted by the porch light from flying inside.

A photographer took shots of the folded note from all angles. After the tech put the note in a clear plastic bag, she took more shots of the inside.

Charlie walked closer. "What does it say?"

Joe read in a grave voice, "YOUR TIME IS RUNNING OUT."

She shivered and took a step backward into someone who grabbed her shoulders. She screamed.

"What the hell is going on out here?" Scott asked.

CHAPTER 28

Charlie peeked out her window, waiting for Scott to back out of his garage. She saw him leave and heaved a sigh of relief. She'd already canceled her appointments for the day. Now she rushed to the phone and called Mystery Jones. "Hey, Mystery. It's Charlie Stone."

"Sugar, is that equipment working? Please don't tell me you're having problems."

"Actually, I think I caught the guy on video. Can Jasmine clean it up so we can ID him?"

"Sure. Are you at home? I can have her there in twenty minutes."

"Great. Thanks again."

Charlie called Captain Strouper next. After a lengthy explanation, he agreed to arrange a meeting at one o'clock. Jasmine was at her door a cup of coffee later.

"Mystery told me you caught the asshole on video." Jasmine walked past her and headed straight for Charlie's office, placed her backpack on the floor, and pulled her laptop out. "Lucky for you I finished my program for digital face enhancement."

Twenty minutes later, Jasmine had a better image.

"That looks great, Jasmine. You wrote the program yourself?"

A pleased smile formed on Jasmine's face. "That's why Mystery calls me the 'Queen of the Machine.' Is this the guy you're dating?"

"It's my next door neighbor who happens to be an FBI agent."

"No way!"

Charlie nodded.

"Girl, you need to set your new alarm system every time you leave the house and when you're home."

"I will."

Jasmine pooched out her lip and gave her *the eye.*

Charlie sighed. "I promise." She crossed her heart to show her sincerity.

Ten minutes later, Jasmine had the digital files copied on two CD's and Charlie's thumb drive. Jasmine also made several photo copies of Scott's face.

Charlie waved from her porch as Jasmine left in the store van. After shutting and locking the door, she shoved the two CD's into her purse along with the thumb drive. She patted Spanky on the head before setting the alarm and locking all her locks. Within twenty minutes, she'd stowed the thumb drive in her safety deposit box.

The morning dragged by. Pure discipline kept her focused on writing notes in her patients' charts. At noon she choked down two tacos and a Dr. Pepper from the nearby Taco Bell. *I hope they stay down.* Her stomach felt like she'd eaten Mexican jumping beans rather than tacos.

Charlie entered the station, greeted the officers she knew, and slipped past the detective division, hoping to avoid Ryan until after the meeting. When she arrived at Captain Strouper's office, he was waiting in his doorway.

"Glad you called me. We're all set up." He shook her hand as he pulled her into the room. He called over his shoulder to his secretary, "Annie, no calls," and closed the door.

A man stood and nodded to her, his gaze roaming over her like a CT Scan.

Two adjectives came to her mind to describe him: rugged and competent.

"Mike, this is Dr. Charlie Stone. She's the profiler I told you about. Charlie, this is Assistant Director in Charge, Mike Whatsley."

Charlie extended her hand, and Whatsley took it. She noted with pleasure that his handshake was brisk and respectful. After everyone sat, Whatsley focused his attention back on Charlie. He cocked his head in Captain Strouper's direction. "John here told me some incredible tales about you."

Strouper frowned. "Not tales. True accounts."

Ignoring the captain, he said, "You're quite a maverick. Checked on your file in Quantico. Quite impressive." He looked at the captain. "Top in her class." He smiled at her. "If you decide to move up in law enforcement, our Behavioral Analysis Unit is interested in taking your application."

"Thank you, sir." Charlie took the two CDs from her purse.

"Call me Mike." He glanced at the CDs. A furrow creased his brow. "The claim you're making against Special Agent Scott Horner is quite serious. It could ruin his career." He sat back and folded his hands in his lap. "He has high connections in the agency."

"So I've heard," Charlie said. "His behavior proves he's not suitable for a career in the FBI. I'm curious. If he has *high connections*, why did he end up in Huntsville, Alabama, and not someplace like D.C. or New York?"

"I wondered that, too," Whatsley said.

Charlie leaned forward. "And..."

"He requested Huntsville."

"Interesting," Strouper said.

Charlie sat back, her gaze shifting back and forth between her captain and the agent. "Especially since he moved next door to me."

Whatsley stiffened. "I didn't realize that he'd...."

Charlie interrupted his unfinished thought. "My theory is Scott spotted me while I was training in Quantico. There were times when I was running the trails that I felt watched, but I never caught anyone. He followed me to Huntsville, discovered the house next to me was for sale, and bought it. From that moment he has insinuated himself into my life under the guise of neighborliness and has caused problems in my relationship with Detective Ryan Roberts."

Tight-lipped, Whatsley scowled at her.

"Being a 'maverick,' I decided to have security lights and cameras installed during the day while everyone was at work and then set my trap."

Captain Strouper leaned his elbows on the desk and steepled his fingers. "Explain the trap to Mike."

Charlie related how she'd gathered items for charity to fill the bay of her garage, so she'd have an excuse to park in the driveway. Next, she described the incident with Scott regarding the chair.

"Last night, my dog woke me after a motion detector light flashed. When I looked outside, I could see the note on my car. I called my direct supervisor, Sergeant Joe Sparks. He came with a crime team to retrieve the note before it rained."

"I see, but I don't understand why you think *my* agent has been leaving these threatening notes?"

Captain Strouper opened his desk drawer and pulled out plastic bags. Each contained a note. After sorting them in the correct order, he handed them to the agent.

"As you can see, all the notes are similar. Our forensic team is convinced they were sent by the same person."

The agent took the bags and read each one. His frown deepened.

Charlie looked at the captain. Her stomach churned like a blender.

The captain shared a small smile and nodded.

"I can see why you would be concerned and frightened," Whatsley said. "These notes are a clear threat on your life, but why do you think *my* agent is responsible?"

Charlie handed one of the discs to Strouper. "Captain, I'll let you take it from here."

Strouper's large monitor sat on the credenza behind him. He placed the CD into a slot on the side. The grumbling that issued from the machine sounded as though the disk was being consumed rather than processed.

He clicked the appropriate icon on the monitor. When the video came up he rolled back his chair to watch.

A well-built male furtively moved toward Charlie's Honda. The outdoor light flashed on. The man stopped. He wore jeans but no shirt, and he had a head full of sandy blond hair. He rushed forward, placed a piece of paper under her wiper and turned to leave. The video showed a full-face shot of Scott before he hurried away.

Whatsley stood and leaned over the desk for a closer look. "John, run that again and pause it on the face shot."

The captain did. When he paused it, Scott's wide-eyed face filled the screen.

Charlie reached down into her purse and pulled out two 5x7 photos that matched the screen. "I had some photos printed for you." She handed one to each of the men.

Strouper took the photo and asked, "What happens now, Mike?"

"The shit hits the fan. Charlie, do you plan to press charges?"

Charlie looked at the captain.

He nodded.

"Yes, I do. Scott has cost this department resources and time. My friends and I have suffered much emotional trauma."

"I can't change your mind about this?" Whatsley asked. "A position at the BAU could be arranged."

Is he offering me a job to let this go?

The captain's voice hardened. "Are you bribing her so you can push this under the conference table in D.C. and avoid ruffling feathers?"

Charlie lifted her chin. "I'll file charges today. I'll be glad to cooperate with your investigation. Here's a copy of the security video."

Whatsley reached for the second case and scowled at it.

"What happens next?" Charlie asked.

CHAPTER 29

After Mike Whatsley left, Charlie sank back into her chair and exhaled. She noticed her internal shaking had worked its way to the outside.

Strouper sat back in his chair and studied her. "Quite a bribe. It could be a career builder for you. Sure you don't want to reconsider?"

Charlie didn't answer.

"I've known Mike a long time," he continued. "We went through the academy together and then went our separate ways after a few years. To be truthful, I'm surprised and a bit disappointed that Mike tried to convince you to let this whole affair go. Scott must be connected, big time."

"Does that mean he'll get away with stalking and terrorizing me?"

"Only if you don't press charges," Strouper said.

Charlie shook her head. "That can't happen. If it's not me, it'll be someone else."

Strouper stood. "I'd watch your back until he's in custody."

"Great! I turn the guy in with the evidence, and now my life is in more danger. When Scott finds out, he'll be freaking pissed and want to hurt me."

Strouper shrugged. "Let's hope not. Ryan asked to see you when we're through with this meeting."

She sighed and rose to her feet.

"Charlie, you're a natural detective. It took guts, grit, and integrity to let that BAU position go. If I had the funding for a full-time profiler, you'd have it for sure."

Charlie forced a smile and rubbed her stomach. *If I'm so great, why does my gut feel full of rocks?* She thanked the Captain for arranging the meeting, grabbed her purse, and left.

Ryan leaned against the wall opposite the door with his ankles and arms crossed.

Charlie stopped when she saw him, unsure of what to do.

"Joe told me you hauled his ass out of bed sometime after midnight because you found another note. What's going on?"

He means, why didn't you call me?

"Can we find a private place to talk?"

He straightened. "Sure."

They entered the conference room.

Ryan closed the door. "Coffee?" he asked.

"Your solution for all that burdens the world. No thanks. My stomach isn't up to the rotgut around here."

He grinned, walked over, and filled his cup. After taking a sip, he grimaced. He sat, wrapped his hands around the mug, and nodded.

Charlie told him all the information about the notes and everyone's suspicions. She explained that she had called Joe instead of him, so he couldn't be accused of any wrongdoing. "Joe is impartial."

"So it was Scott all along. I told you something wasn't right about him."

"I know. I thought you were jealous and it was clouding your judgment."

With an incredulous tone, he said, "Wouldn't you be jealous? Think about it. If a beautiful woman moved next door to me and tried to work her way between us, wouldn't you be concerned?"

Charlie nodded. Tears welled on the edge of her lashes.

Ryan handed her his handkerchief.

Charlie remembered the first time he'd handed her his handkerchief during the Huntress investigation. "Thanks."

"What's next?" Ryan sipped his coffee, scrunched his nose, and set it aside.

Does he mean with our relationship or the case? "I took today off. I'm filing charges when I leave here. What charges do you think they will file?"

"I suspect stalking in the first degree. It's a Class C felony," Ryan said. "His lawyer may try to plead it down to harassing communications, which is a Class B misdemeanor."

Charlie planted her fists on her hips. "Is that all?"

"I'm pretty sure he'll be brought before the FBI's Office of Professional Responsibility. They'll probably get him for misuse of his position. If he lies during his interrogation, they'll tack on a lack of candor charge. Who knows, he may have printed the notes on his office computer and used the Agency's car to deliver some of them. If so, the Agency will see it as misuse of their assets."

"Will they check his work computer?"

"Probably. I know our department will want to search his home and computer. Either way, his career with the FBI is a bust."

"Will he serve time?" Charlie asked.

Ryan frowned. "Probably not. He'll most likely get probation."

"That's not fair. Scott had us all scared silly," said Charlie. "Even worse, the guy lives next door to me."

"Until Scott is arrested, it might be best if you and Spanky stayed at my house for a bit."

She held up her hand. "Understand: I'm not moving in, just visiting."

"Either way, it'd make me feel better. I trust Scott about as far as I could toss a Tesla."

"If you had a Model S, you wouldn't toss it anywhere. It might get a scratch."

They both chuckled.

Charlie placed her hand on her forehead. "Dear Lord, what am I going to tell Marti? Will you help me explain it all?"

That afternoon, Charlie paced her living room, dreading the upcoming encounter. She wondered if the police cars and the forensic team would be gone before Marti arrived. Thirty minutes later, her doorbell chimed. Charlie was relieved it was Ryan.

She hugged him. The scent of his Polo cologne engulfed her when she rested her cheek against the textured surface of his sport coat. "What's going on over there?"

He ran a hand through his hair. "Let's wait until Marti arrives, and then I'll tell you both."

Charlie sensed it was serious by the grim set of his mouth.

"Hey," Marti called as she came up the walk. "What's going on at Scott's house? Did he get robbed or something?"

Charlie hugged Marti tight. "Something. Come in, we need to talk."

"Whoa!" Marti looked back and forth between Charlie and Ryan. "Did someone die?"

Only your dreams of a life with Scott, thought Charlie.

Once they were seated, Charlie told Marti about her trap and how she'd set it.

"So you caught the guy?" Marti's gaze skittered over to Ryan.

Charlie thought, *She's still convinced it's Ryan.* "Yes. I want you to see the video evidence." Charlie woke her laptop and swiveled it so Ryan and Marti could see the screen. She focused on Marti's reaction.

When the video started Marti slid forward in her chair, squinting at the screen. Charlie knew when the face shot occurred because Marti's jaw dropped and her eyes bulged.

"That looks like Scott!"

Ryan loosened his tie. "It is Scott. There will be more explanations later, Marti, but first I think you both need to see the inside of his house."

Marti's hand covered her throat. "It can't be true. He's an FBI agent."

Charlie said nothing as they followed Ryan to Scott's house. They all had to suit up and to wear gloves and booties.

Marti mumbled, "I don't see how y'all wear these suits. I'm smothering. I'm glad my position on the Sexual Assault Task Force doesn't require me to go to crime scenes."

Ryan nodded. "Have you been inside his house before?"

Marti frowned. "No. He always wanted to come to my house. I assumed he was messy or something."

Ryan said, "He's far from messy."

Charlie noticed how similar the layout of Scott's house was to hers. A giant flat-screen TV took up most of one wall, dominating the living room. A burgundy leather couch and recliner with an end table filled the rest of the space. The spotless kitchen opened into the breakfast nook, which held a small table with two chairs.

"The way he talked, he didn't have much furniture," Charlie said.

The dining room held a conference table with one high-backed chair on rollers. The surface was covered with papers.

Ryan put out an arm to stop them. "These files are related to FBI cases. Come this way."

They followed him into a small bedroom, similar to the one Charlie used as an office.

Charlie and Marti both gasped when they saw the inside.

Marti's hand covered her mouth. "Holy shit!" she said through her fingers.

All the walls were plastered with photos of Charlie.

Marti turned to look at Charlie. "These are all photos of you. The whole room is a damn Charlie shrine." Her eyes narrowed. "Were you seeing Scott on the side?"

The question hit Charlie like an emotional slap. She raised her hand to her cheek and met Marti's angry glare. "No! Don't you get it? He's been stalking me since Quantico." She walked across the room. "See? These photos were taken while I was running the trails."

Tears welled in Marti's eyes. "So you're saying he followed you here, bought the house next door, and wrote all those scary notes. That he loved you, not me?"

Charlie's frustration heated her face. "Marti! This. Is. Not. Love. It's some kind of sick obsession. The guy's dangerous."

Marti clenched her fists at her sides and screamed, "It's all about you! The great heroic Charlie Stone. You got the job as a community profiler. You saved the guy from the Huntress. You caught the Trainer. I'm sick of it!"

Stunned, Charlie took a step back.

Marti stormed past her and out of the house.

Charlie moved to follow her.

Ryan placed a restraining hand on her arm. "Let her go. She needs time to process all of this. It's a lot to absorb."

"Good Lord." Charlie looked up at Ryan. "She must have fallen for him harder than I realized. That wasn't the Marti I know and love."

CHAPTER 30

Charlie packed two suitcases and gave them to Ryan to put into her car. She followed with an armful of hanging clothes.

Glenda, her next-door neighbor, waved and yelled, "Charlie!"

Charlie handed Ryan the clothes and walked over to speak with her.

"What's going on over there?" She pointed at Scott's home.

Charlie gave a brief explanation. Glenda's expression shifted from open-mouthed shock to wide-eyed alarm.

"Are you moving out?' Glenda asked.

"No, I'm staying with a friend until it's safe."

"Do you want me to watch Spanky?"

"Thanks, but I'm taking her with me. I'd appreciate you watching the house."

After they gathered all of Spanky's supplies, Charlie put her on a leash and walked her to the car.

Ryan stood watching, his arm on the roof of his vehicle.

Charlie opened her car door. Spanky scrambled in, a doggie smile pasted on her face.

Ryan opened his door. "I'll follow you."

Charlie tossed and turned all night, examining each encounter with Scott. *How did I miss all those little clues? What if his shenanigans destroy my friendship with Marti?* She tried to lie still and not wake Ryan, but she couldn't.

She slipped out of bed and closed the bedroom door. She passed Spanky asleep on her bed, her paws twitching in a dream. She plopped on the sofa and put her head in her hands.

Ryan walked up behind her and placed his hand on her shoulder. She almost screamed.

"Whoa! It's me."

Her heart pounded in her temples. "Sorry."

He came around the couch and sat. "What's going on?"

Charlie grabbed a decorative pillow and hugged it. "I keep going over everything in my mind. There were times I felt watched at Quantico but I swear, I never saw Scott."

"He certainly saw you and has the photos to prove it."

Charlie rubbed her temples. "I'm still freaked over that room. I swear I never knew I was being stalked and photographed."

"I was as astonished as you. Nothing like seeing the woman you love plastered on the walls of another man's house. When I saw it, I knew this was some serious shit."

"Too bad Marti didn't see it the way you did. I can't believe she thought I'd see Scott on the side."

"Especially since you were the one who set her up with him."

"You have no idea how much I regret doing it."

Charlie crawled into Ryan's lap, buried her face in his neck, and cried.

CHAPTER 31

The next day, Charlie sat in her therapy room making notes in her latest patient's chart. Someone tapped on the door.

Charlie paused and looked up as Marti entered.

The serious look on Marti's face made her heart rate increase. *After that outburst yesterday, does she want to leave our business arrangement?*

"Marti, what's up?"

Pink-cheeked, Marti glanced down. "Do you have a minute?"

"Sure." Charlie signaled for her to take a seat.

Marti pulled her glasses off and polished them with the edge of her coral blouse. "First, I want to apologize for my behavior yesterday."

Charlie placed the chart on a nearby table. "I know it was a shock for you. It was for me, too. I promise you, I was not seeing Scott on the side. Just to make it clear, I didn't encourage him either. You of all people should know I love Ryan."

Marti placed her glasses on her face and then looked at her hands. "I know."

Thank goodness. Charlie said, "I owe you an apology for setting you up with an unstable person."

"He didn't act unstable. He sure had me fooled." Marti's face flushed an even brighter pink. "I guess I've been a bit jealous. Heck, I've been a lot jealous."

"Why?" Charlie asked confused. *Marti has always been supportive.*

"For one thing, you have Ryan in your life."

"I'm sure there's someone special out there for you," Charlie said.

"From your mouth to God's ears, as my grandmother used to say."

"Is there more?" Charlie asked.

Marti gripped her hands together. "Charlie, it's damn hard to follow in your footsteps. You're always doing something spectacular that places you in the headlines."

Charlie stiffened. "Marti, I don't seek headlines or the injuries and scars that came from trying to save someone's life."

Marti looked up. "I know all that on a logical level. It's why I treasure our friendship. These are my issues to work through, not yours. I guess I'll have to settle for being Robin to your Batman."

"Heck, Marti, you're not Robin, you're Wonder Woman. You don't follow in my footsteps, heck you've always forged your own path."

Marti chuckled, tears welling in her eyes.

"What's egged all this on? Scott?"

Marti shrugged. "Partly. I ran into Joyce on the stairwell the other day and well…"

Charlie leaned forward. "What did stir-the-pot Joyce have to say?"

"She asked me how it felt to be Midge to your Super Hero Barbie."

Charlie shot from her seat. "What!"

Marti cringed a bit.

Charlie paced. "Why is she always trying to cause dissention between us?"

"Maybe she's jealous. I know she's envious of you."

Charlie stopped and faced Marti. "Me? That woman makes twice as much money as I do."

"I think it's because…you're special. I've got an appointment with Harold Walter this week. I want to work through some of this stuff. I think parts of my feelings are related to transference from my perfect sister."

"Transference can be a powerful psychological phenomena. Are we good for now?" Charlie asked. "You're my best friend, and I don't want to lose you."

Marti smiled. "I feel the same way."

They stood and hugged. When they released, Marti said, "We may need to talk about this again, if that's okay?"

"Sure. Whatever it takes," Charlie said.

"Right now I need to discuss something else with you."

Charlie's relief shifted to anxiety. *What now?*

Marti sat down. "This is probably nothing."

Charlie nodded. "But…"

"I have a new client whose situation is triggering alarm bells."

"Then there's probably something weird going on. Marti, you have the best clinical intuition of anyone I know."

"Thanks." Marti adjusted her glasses on her face. "My patient's father raised her since the age of five. She saw him murder her mother and suspects she's buried someplace on their property."

"A mother buried somewhere on the property sounds like what happened to my patient, Rose. Did she say why she believes this?"

"She told me he came home from Bolivia when she was five. Her parents argued because her mom had gained some weight while he was overseas and he thought she'd been unfaithful. My patient reports her dad was 'very controlling.'"

"Sounds like Rose's dad." Charlie shifted her position and crossed one leg over the other. "Since you used *was* instead of *is*, can I assume he's deceased?

Marti nodded.

"We both know hyper-controlling men have been known to resort to violence," Charlie said.

"I saw her before lunch. She reports that the morning after she witnessed the murder, her mother was gone. The 'official story' was her mother left with another man. Dear Ole Dad informed her at breakfast she was now the woman of the house. He started sexually abusing her that night. When she turned fifteen, she gave birth to his child."

Charlie cringed.

Marti sat back in her seat. "She knows about our work on the Sexual Assault Task Force from the news coverage and is here to work through all that abuse."

Charlie sighed and shook her head. "Sounds like this could take a while to work through."

"Oh, yeah. To add to this poor woman's stress, she's worried about her son."

"How old is he?"

"Twenty-something. She said he and his father were like 'two peas in a pod.' Her father took Jared everywhere with him when he wasn't in school."

Something prickled in the back of Charlie's mind. "Does Jared know about his father?"

Marti sat back and frowned. "No. He was told his father left when he was a child. Jared knew him as his grandfather and called him Grumps."

Charlie thought about the old bluegrass song, "I'm My Own Grandpa."

"That'll be an issue someday, but it doesn't explain why she's so worried about her son," Charlie said.

"After his Grumps died, he's started acting strange and has become verbally and physically abusive toward her. She claims he hit her last week."

Charlie tapped her lip. "Did she call the police?"

Marti shook her head. "She was too afraid."

"Did she say anything about his strange behavior?"

"She's caught him having a conversation with her father as if he were sitting in the room. He's isolating himself in his room when he's home. He leaves, and she doesn't know where he is for hours."

Charlie thought a moment. "Does he tell her where he's been?"

"All he'll tell her is to 'mind her own damn business,'" Marti said.

"What's your game plan?" Charlie asked.

"Work on the abuse issues and try to help her get her son set up for mental health services."

Charlie nodded. "Sounds reasonable, although I suspect you'll have more success with the mother than getting her son hooked up for services."

"True. I wanted your opinion as to whether this client might be appropriate for our women's group dealing with sexual abuse. I mentioned her as a possible addition a while back."

Charlie tapped her lip again. "After some individual work, it sounds like she'd fit. When you feel she's ready for a group experience, we'll prep the group for her to join."

Marti rose and wiped her palms on her pants. "Again, I'm so sorry. The more I think about Scott, the more I remember little things that didn't quite seem right. I can't believe I missed all those little warning flags."

"I can. You were focused on his 'marble butt.'"

Marti chuckled. "He did have a fine ass."

CHAPTER 32

Charlie arrived home before Ryan. They had leftovers waiting in the fridge, so there was no reason to start cooking. In fact, she didn't know when he might arrive. His shift ended in a few minutes, but if he and Joe were next up to investigate a major crime, it could be hours before he would cross the threshold. Such was the life of a homicide detective.

Feeling antsy, Charlie scooped the Huntsville Times off the coffee table and started reading. The national headlines held several interesting stories. Paul Manafort, Trump's former campaign manager, pled guilty to several crimes and worked a deal to divulge his secrets to Special Counsel Robert Mueller about the Trump campaign.

Charlie looked at Spanky, who sat at her feet. "Do you have anything to confess?"

Spanky cocked her head.

The photos of the flooding in North Carolina from Hurricane Florence tore at her emotions. Desperate to find something positive, she moved toward the community section of the paper. A full-page ad, featuring a color photo of a Native American in a full-feather dress costume, caught her attention. The ad announced the upcoming United Cherokee Annual Festival and American Indian Pow Wow.

Spanky yipped and ran toward the door. The garage door rattled as it rose.

Ryan walked in and placed his mail on the kitchen counter. "How was your day?"

Charlie rose and placed the paper in the chair. "Delightful and uneventful."

They met midway across the living room and kissed. Spanky circled them, her tail wagging.

Ryan bent to pet the dog. "Hey girl, have you been protecting your mommy?"

Charlie chuckled. "She hasn't chewed any burglars' noses off today." She returned to the chair, reclaimed the paper, and settled in. "Did you know there's an Indian Pow Wow taking place in Huntsville this weekend?"

Ryan shook his head while slipping into his recliner with a groan. "Where is it?"

"Monte Sano State Park. Tribes from across the US and Canada will be attending."

"I wonder what happens at a Pow Wow?"

Charlie skimmed the ad "There will be Native-American arts and crafts, drummers, and dancers with costumes."

"Sounds like fun. Let's go." Ryan patted his lap. Spanky leaped, circled once, and settled down for a nap.

Charlie glanced over at the dog. "Traitor." She leaned over and passed Ryan part of the paper.

The microwave received a workout heating the leftovers from two previous meals.

"I'm glad you like leftovers," Charlie said as she filled a pair of glasses with ice from the fridge dispenser.

"It's like a small buffet. A bit of this and that." He took one plate of food out of the microwave and put in another.

Charlie filled the two glasses with sweet tea. "True, but it also reminds me of Thanksgiving dinner where you have a plate full of dabs of food. Kinda like an edible artist palette."

He cocked his head. "I can see the resemblance if I squint real hard in my mind's eye."

Charlie nudged him with her elbow.

He grinned.

"Anything new on the Marksman case?" she asked.

"Same type of bullet."

"I'm not surprised." She ran her hands through her hair. "I keep feeling like I'm overlooking something."

"You always feel that way when you're working a case," Ryan remarked.

They took their plates to the table and sat. Spanky trotted over, lay down, and placed her head on Ryan's foot.

Charlie glanced down and grinned. "Fuzzy traitor."

"See, I have the Spanky seal of approval."

She pointed her fork at Ryan. "You've been feeding her those bacon treats when I'm not looking, haven't you?"

He gave her a sheepish grin.

"I knew it!"

They ate in silence for a bit.

"Have you heard anything about Scott?" Charlie asked.

"I've heard he's returning to D.C. for an FBI investigation."

"What?" Charlie sat back in her chair. "I've pressed charges against him here. Didn't they serve the warrant and arrest him?"

"Yes." Ryan took a bite of green beans and chewed.

Charlie put down her fork. "Well, what happened?"

"Scott lawyered up, so he didn't answer any questions." He scowled. "Then someone bailed him out."

She slammed her hand down on the table causing the ice to jiggle in the glasses. "This is crap. Scott can't leave the state if he has a pending case, can he?"

Ryan shrugged. "I'm not sure what Scott can manage. I heard he left the jail escorted by his attorney and two FBI agents."

Charlie shook her head and fumed.

After dinner, they carried the dishes to the sink. Charlie turned on the water to rinse the dishes and realized Ryan had disappeared.

He returned to the kitchen after Charlie had loaded the dishes in the dishwasher and wiped the counters.

She gave him the stink eye. "Perfect timing, Ryan."

He picked her up in his arms.

Charlie squealed with surprise and wrapped her arms around his neck.

He carried her to the master bath and placed her on her feet.

"Oh, Ryan!"

Bubbles floated on the surface of the massive tub's steaming water. Candles flickered on every surface while soft music played.

Charlie gave Ryan an enthusiastic hug and kiss. "So this is where you disappeared to while I was cleaning the kitchen. I thought you were avoiding the dishes."

"Oh, ye of little faith." Ryan grinned and started massaging her shoulders.

Charlie closed her eyes and let her shoulders droop into a relaxed state.

"Better get undressed before the water cools." He touched his finger to her lips. "I'll be back with two glasses of wine."

Charlie slipped out of her clothes and placed a foot into the water. *Perfect,* she thought. She slid into the tub, immersing herself to the neck, and sighed. The sensation of the warm water and the tickle of the bubbles on her chin were delightful.

Ryan returned with two glasses of chardonnay. He handed one to Charlie and placed the other on a corner of the tub.

She sipped the wine and watched Ryan undress. She admired his broad shoulders, flat stomach, and legs, all sculpted at the police gym.

He definitely fits the "Detective Hottie" nickname Marti gave him.

Ryan eased into the tub opposite her and picked up his glass of wine.

"To us."

Charlie smiled and clinked glasses. "And to what comes after this luscious soak."

Ryan winked. "I'll drink to that, but why wait." He pulled her close, wrapping his legs around her in the wide tub. He kissed her at first with gentleness, and then with heat and passion.

Desire flooded her body. She pulled him closer returning his urgency.

His hand caressed her breast, a finger teasing her nipple.

She wanted more and wanted it now.

Charlie woke in the middle of the night, her mind struggling, to process the stream of ideas whirling past. When the final conclusion solidified in her mind, she reached over, shook Ryan awake, and turned on the bedside lamp.

"W-What? What's going on?" Ryan rolled over and squinted his bleary eyes as he raised a hand to block the light.

"I know where the Marksman may strike next," Charlie said.

Ryan sat up, the cover sliding down to reveal the chest she'd caressed a few hours earlier. He yawned. "Yeah? Do you get these blinding insights often at…," He looked at the clock, "…three o'clock in the morning?"

Ignoring the sarcasm, she explained the irresistible lure that the Pow Wow would have on the Marksman. "It's this Saturday. Can y'all pull something together in three days?"

Ryan yawned. "I'll discuss it with Joe after he has his first cup of coffee and a donut. He should be half pleasant by then."

CHAPTER 33

Charlie longed to stop and immerse herself in the pageantry of the Pow Wow. The costumes. The dancing. The chanting. The rhythmic beating of the drums reverberated in her chest like a second heartbeat.

"This is an impressive sight. So much color and movement!" she said to a woman standing near her. *Makes it hard to concentrate on spotting a possible sniper.*

The woman smiled, "I try to go to all the Pow Wows if they're close." She raised her chin. "I'm a quarter Creek."

Charlie stepped to her left and tripped. Tree roots stretched their gnarly toes across the sandy surface of Monte Sano. *Glad I wore my hiking boots.*

Joe Sparks huffed his way up a slight hill to join her. "Seen anything, Doc?"

"Not yet. You?"

"Nope. This is something. Sarah would love this."

"Bring her next time," Charlie said shading her eyes to check a nearby tree line.

"No way. One gander at all the jewelry and she'd whip out her credit card. I'd be payin' for months."

Charlie shook her head. "Don't you think Sarah deserves something pretty?"

"She's pretty enough without a bunch of jewelry."

Surprised, she stepped back and focused on Joe's face.

"Don't look at me that way."

She chuckled. *Sarah's right, he is a big, grumpy teddy bear.*

"Don't you go telling her I said it, either." Joe turned, grumbling something about women while he walked away.

The dancing continued without a break in the continuity. Without ever breaking the rhythm of the drums or the loud chanting, the men changed places with each other.

Something about it stirred her inside, making her want to dance and lose herself in the meditative pattern of the steps.

She saw a movement near the tree line. She stopped and stared. *Am I seeing things or am I paranoid? Who wouldn't be paranoid with a psychopath sniper on the loose, possibly aiming at any man, woman or child—even me?*

Two children darted from between the tree trunks holding colorful leaves and then sprinted toward their mothers. The women gathered them close before shooing them toward a group gathered nearby.

Charlie's shoulders lowered. She spotted one of the uniformed police officers patrolling nearby.

Joe and Ryan, who were wearing jeans to be less noticeable, were the only detectives present.

Charlie chuckled. *Joe looks like a walking fireplug with a crew cut. His very essence screams cop.*

The tribes had been warned the event might draw the sniper, but they refused to cancel the festivities.

An hour later Charlie felt dizzy. She knew the symptom. *Plummeting blood sugar.* The feeling both panicked and angered her.

She stopped at a food truck and bought a fry bread, fries, and a Coke. She knew she should eat more protein, but she couldn't resist the chance to try the fry bread. She took it to a nearby picnic table and sat. The position offered her a different viewpoint of the event.

A glint to her right caught her attention. She paused, trying to pinpoint the source.

Nothing. The shakiness brought on by the hypoglycemia was amplifying her hyper vigilant state. She unwrapped the beef-filled fry bread, ignoring the pickle on the side, took a bite, and chewed. She closed her eyes to enjoy the flavors.

A hand brushed against her hair and grazed her shoulder.

Charlie's eyes sprang open. She involuntarily inhaled some of her lunch down her windpipe. Choking, she stood and tangled her foot on the bench seat before falling sideways onto a pile of pine straw. She struggled to her hands and knees and coughed the final bit of food out of her windpipe. With tear-glazed eyes, she looked up.

Ryan reached down to help her rise. "I'm so sorry. I was going for your pickle. Didn't you hear me? Are you okay? Thought I'd have to do the Heimlich maneuver for a moment there."

Charlie grabbed the Coke and drank until she felt she could talk. Her voice came out raspy. "How could I hear you over all this noise?"

Her fry bread lay on the grass. The ants were already finding their way onto it.

Charlie glared at the ants and then turned the same look on Ryan.

"I, uh, will be back with another one."

Charlie munched her fries and tried to calm her racing heart.

Ten minutes later, Ryan returned. Instead of another fry bread, he'd brought her a fresh bison burger. "Thought you could use the protein."

"Thanks." She unwrapped it, handed Ryan the pickle, and took a bite. This time she savored the symphony of flavors: Fresh tomato, lettuce, and the smoky flavor of the grill.

"I'm beginning to think this is a waste of time," Ryan said. He threw a leg over the bench seat and sat before pilfering a fry.

Charlie shook her head. "Don't you feel it?"

He shrugged. "Feel what?"

"The building tension. The Marksman is here and waiting. I think he has a special target in mind."

He studied the fry. "All I feel is tired."

Charlie jabbed him. "Get something to eat. Your blood sugar is dropping. According to the schedule, there are special dances after lunch. There're so many people scattered across the dance area now, it would be hard to pick a target."

"You're probably right. I'll be back."

Charlie was wiping her mouth when he returned with two bison burgers, fries, and a Dr. Pepper.

After a quick glance to locate a trash receptacle, she stood and gathered her trash. "I'll look around while you eat." She dodged several yellow jackets that swarmed the trash.

She decided to venture out further from the dance area and stepped into a copse of trees. The shade dropped the temperature several degrees. From this rise she could see the entire dance area. She weaved between trunks, watching for poison ivy. The ground was carpeted with colorful leaves in an array of fall colors.

An internal sense of alarm zinged along her nerve endings. She stopped and looked up, only to be blinded by the sunlight filtering through the red and orange leaves of a Maple.

Shielding her eyes, she tried to blink away the spots and looked down to let her eyes recover. The leaves chattered as a light breeze danced among them.

A racket to her right froze her. Ducking low, she scanned the area as she backed behind a tree for cover. Waiting. Looking. Listening.

Is it him?

More noise erupted from behind some nearby bushes.

Charlie reached into her fanny pack for her Charter Arms five-shot. Her gaze remained glued to the area. She held the revolver pointed down at her side. *Don't get trigger-happy. It could be a kid running around up here.*

Two squirrels scampered into the clearing. One chased the other up a tree.

Sighing her relief, Charlie stowed her revolver. She shook from the rush of adrenaline and pressed her forehead against the tree to regain her composure.

Time to go back and check with Ryan. An eerie feeling of being watched tingled along her nerves as she hiked back the way she'd come.

Ryan was still at the table working on his second sandwich. The tension had dried her mouth. The icy Coke she'd left on the table felt good going down her raw throat.

He looked up, ketchup on his chin. "You see anything?"

She handed him a napkin and pointed at his chin. "Two squirrels."

Ryan wiped away the ketchup. "Were they carrying a sniper rifle?"

She laughed. "No, but one of them was armed with an acorn." She didn't mention the feeling of being watched. *He'll think I'm paranoid.*

CHAPTER 34

The Marksman looked down at the Pow Wow from a large oak tree. He'd only been there for ten minutes, enjoying his birds-eye view of all the dancing and chanting.

He rubbed his temples. The constant drumming had triggered a headache that pounded behind his eyes.

He'd never seen such fancy costumes. Many were covered with beading and feathers. *Too bad one of 'em will soon be covered with blood.*

He'd long admired deer heads, mounted and hung on the walls of some of his hunting buddies. He'd never be able to hang one in his small mobile home. *Damn things are too big and heavy.* He grinned. *Now, one of those feathered headdresses would work just fine. I know just the spot.*

His grandfather's voice said in his head. *"Don't need no crap hanging on your wall, boy. A sniper takes no trophies. He leaves no evidence. His kill count is private."*

The Marksman shook his head to stop the voice. *Grumps never kept trophies from his animal or human kills that I recall. When he killed a buck, we ate the meat. He sold the pelt and antlers for supplies. After he was discharged from the Marines, whenever he shot a human varmint, he made sure the body wouldn't be found.*

The Marksman knew where some of the graves were located. He'd helped to dig some of them.

His head pounded to the steady beat of the drums. He closed his eyes and rested against a branch, willing the pain to leave. *Time to get outta this tree. My ass hurts.*

He jerked to attention when he heard the rattle of leaves. He heard the woman coming long before he saw her.

Well, well. It's the woman I met at the shooting range. She may be a good shot, but she's no woodsman. Moves around like a Sasquatch.

He craned his neck to see further down the slope. *Is the dude she met for lunch that day with her?*

He waited a few moments to see if the guy would show. *Seems she's alone.* He licked his lips. *What I'd enjoy doing to her.* His groin ached and tingled. *I can drop out of this tree and pull her behind those bushes over there. With a knife to her throat, she'd be willing to do whatever I tell her. I might cut off a section of that purty, blonde hair and braid me a keychain as a souvenir.*

A sharp pain zinged across his vision.

Grumps bellowed in his head, *"Keep your mind on your goal and keep your pants zipped. That's not just any woman. She works with the cops."*

He held his head with both hands and took deep breaths to ease the throb.

The woman stopped and looked around.

He stiffened.

"If she sees you, you're gonna have to gut her and hide the body," Grumps said.

The Marksman grinned. *Not before I have some fun with her. Besides, I'm near invisible in this camouflage gear.*

She looked up, squinting.

He thought, *Oh hell!*

She blinked, shielded her eyes, and looked down.

He paused a moment to watch her reaction. *Don't think she saw me with the sun in her eyes. Otherwise, she'd be screaming and running.*

He went alert when he heard a ruckus from behind nearby bushes. *Is that the boyfriend?*

The woman ducked and hid behind a tree trunk.

Looking the wrong way, Hot Thang. He grinned. *I'm up here behind you. I see you got a gun.*

He had to control a chuckle when two squirrels chased each other into the open before running up a tree.

She leaned her head against a tree for a moment, put away her revolver, and left the way she'd come.

Silence fell. Even though the chanting and drums had stopped, they still filled his head.

The participants dispersed in different directions. Many headed for the food trucks, others to their campers and the restrooms.

Good time to climb down and get some water and a protein bar. After I eat, I'll set up. No need to hurry, what I'm looking to bag comes after lunch.

CHAPTER 35

Charlie looked up when a man's voice over the loudspeaker announced it was time to introduce each of the attending tribes.

The announcer said, "We are proud to have tribes from across the Southeast with us today. When your tribe is called, enter the center of the dance area, and you will have ten minutes to perform. When the next tribe is introduced, leave the dance area to make room. The tribes will be presented in the order listed in the program."

The chanting and drumming began again.

Charlie nudged Ryan. "Here we go."

They rose from the table. Ryan grabbed her arm and pulled her closer. "Don't get heroic on me. If you spot something, call me or yell for help."

Charlie nodded, and they separated.

"The Catawba Tribe," The MC said.

A group of several men in beaded buckskins and feather headdresses danced their way to the center of the area followed by some women wearing beaded buckskin dresses and carrying feather fans. The older men performed upright shuffling steps while a younger one bent and dipped in a more energetic version. Their beaded moccasins kicked up dust with each step.

Charlie looked at the handout she'd received when she entered the Pow Wow. Nine tribes were represented: Catawba, Chakchiuma, Cherokee, Chickasaw, Choctaw, Koasati, Muscogee Creek, Hitchiti, and Yamasee. *Thank goodness this is a smaller event.*

If it had been a week-long event with hundreds of tribes like some of the major Pow Wows out west, their task would be much more complicated.

When will he strike if he's here? What is he looking for in a target? She tapped her lip as she thought and scanned the area. *Think like a trophy hunter. He'll want it to be a famous tribe. Maybe one he studied during his Alabama history class.*

Charlie studied the list again. *The only tribes I can remember from my Alabama history class in high school are the Cherokee, Chickasaw, Choctaw, and Creek.*

She glanced around again and saw nothing unusual.

I was always fascinated with the Cherokee. She phoned Ryan.

"Roberts."

"I may be wrong, but I think if he's here, he may try to kill a member of the Cherokee tribe. They're the most famous in history due to the Trail of Tears."

"Roger that. I'll pass the word." Ryan disconnected.

Channel 31's news van pulled close to a food truck, and a female reporter and her cameraman exited. They started setting up a tripod close to the dance area.

The MC announced, "Will the Chakchiuma enter the dance area."

The Catawba danced to the edge while the next tribe entered. The chanting continued as the drummers exchanged places.

I wonder what they're chanting and if each tribe has their own chant? It sounds the same to me. Maybe there's a universal chant for a Pow Wow.

Charlie let her gaze go from one side to another, looking for anything out of place.

The MC announced over the relentless drums and chanting, "Will the Cherokee enter the dance area."

This may be it.

CHAPTER 36

The Marksman stretched, readying himself for the task at hand. His best estimate using the rangefinder was five hundred and ten yards, the longest one yet. He adjusted the scope. He knew this was an estimate, since he didn't know where exactly his target would be dancing.

"Don't forget to take the wind into account," murmured his grandfather's voice in his head.

"I always do, Grumps. I always do."

This was a downhill shot. He lay surrounded by bushes with his camo cloth covering him, in case someone happened by. He was grateful for the slightly cooler temperatures.

The drumming and chanting began anew.

An amplified voice announced, "The Catawba Tribe."

He focused down his scope on first one dancer, then another. He wasn't sure which Indian he wanted to kill yet, but he felt sure he'd know his target when he saw it.

Unlike his past kills, he hadn't been able to choose his target in advance and stalk them, since many of the tribal members drove in from out of town. Despite this, he couldn't pass up the opportunity to pop a Native American in full ceremonial dress.

The shuffling older men with their lined faces didn't interest him. Instead, he set his sights on the younger guy who wore a fancy costume with beading and feathers. He dipped and swirled while he held one of those feather fans.

Turkey feathers I bet. It'll be a difficult shot with him hopping around at this distance.

Grumps said, *"You can make it, boy, if he's the one you want."*

He put the crosshairs on the sweating dancer's face. *He looks like he's in a trance or something.*

He raised his head and took a deep breath. *None of this bunch is a worthy trophy.* He blew out the breath and resumed his position, while running through the escape plan in his mind. Grumps's truck was parked on a small dirt road down the hill behind him. He could escape out of the park the back way, and no one would be any the wiser. If necessary, he could hike out.

He raised his head and smiled when he saw the news van pull up.

"Well lookee here. I'll get some news coverage," he whispered. In his mind's eye he saw himself line up the shot and make the kill. It would air on the five o'clock evening news, where he could tape it with his Grumps's old VCR, and watch it whenever he liked.

"Get the stars out of your eyes, boy. You're here for one thing only. Make the kill."

The Marksman's face flushed hot.

The loudspeaker boomed. "Will the Chakchiuma enter the dance area?"

He got back into position and scoped the area. Gnats buzzed near his right ear.

The women wore long, full colorful dresses. The men's ceremonial costumes were less impressive than those of the previous group. He sighted on each member but didn't feel inspired to shoot. He shooed away the gnats and sighed.

"Don't you go getting impatient on me, boy. A good sniper has to stay alert and focused until the right opportunity arrives."

The Marksman rubbed his forehead and blinked a few times. Grabbing his bottle, he chugged down some water to take his focus off his frustration. Some of it dribbled down his chin. He wiped it off with his sleeve.

"It's gotta be something worthy, Grumps. The news folks are here."

"It's about the kill, not the glory. Get your head on straight."

"I could kill a policeman. There are at least four uniformed cops down there."

"Are your brains addled? They'll hunt you down for sure," Grumps said.

The announcer called the Cherokee tribe to the dance area.

"That's the Trail of Tears tribe." The Marksman remembered studying the tribe during his sophomore year in high school. "This is a tribe worth shooting." He shifted his position in order to shoot.

Six Cherokee female dancers shuffled into the ring. The younger ones wore jingle dresses in bright, bold colors. They danced vigorously, making their dresses chime to the beat. The two older women wore white buckskins with long, flowing fringe. All held feather fans.

"What's with the damn fans?" he mumbled.

Excitement ran like electricity through his veins when he spotted his trophy target.

He looks like a damn tom turkey with that spray of tail feathers all fanned out.

He set his crosshairs on the dancer's forehead. His finger tightened...

"Dammit man! Stay still," he grumbled under his breath.

"How many times do I have to tell you, anticipate your shot and let him move into the kill zone," Grumps said.

He was preparing to set his sight again when a young boy ran on to the dance area, a miniature of the dancer he'd been aiming to kill.

"A baby tom turkey. Ain't he cute." He shook his head. "Too bad I can't kill a kid."

"Why the hell not?" Grumps said.

Sweat broke out on his forehead. He'd never killed a child before.

"Do it!" Grumps commanded.

He set his crosshairs on the boy's forehead. *It's a smaller target.*

"Don't go gutless on me. Do it," Grumps said in his mind.

Damn, I need to check the range. He pulled out the laser rangefinder and aimed it at the kid's chest. *Five hundred and two yards.*

He made the adjustment to his scope and returned to his firing position.

"Oh, yeah. I've got you now."

A breeze kicked up. The ruffling leaves let light flash in his scope, blinding him. Blinking, he lowered his rifle to rub his eyes. When his vision cleared, he focused, drew a bead on his target, and pulled the trigger.

CHAPTER 37

The Cherokee shuffle-danced into the ring.

Charlie kept scanning the trees and the dance area, feeling inept in her attempts to spot the Marksman. "If he's there at all," she muttered to herself. Her heart pounded to the beat. *God, please don't let it happen.*

Four men followed the women. One man immediately caught her attention. He stood out drawing all eyes to him.

"That's the one," she said aloud. She sprinted to the edge of the dance area.

A small boy of about seven or eight ran to the principal dancer. His costume matched the man's. They danced together bobbing and weaving.

She searched the perimeter. The sun glinted off something in the line of trees to her left—the ones she'd walked through earlier. Charlie's senses tingled. Her gaze returned to the man and child. She blinked. *Was that a laser aimed at that child's buckskin shirt?*

"NO!" She raced onto the dance area and flung herself at the boy, clipping the principal dancer behind the knees and knocking him off his feet. She landed on her right knee. Searing pain shot up her leg. She stifled a scream, rolling as she tucked the child under her body.

The bullet hit the ground, showering them with dirt before ricocheting to shatter the glass window of a nearby food truck. The ceremonial drummers continued to pound, and chant.

Charlie rose on one elbow and pointed. "Shooter. Shooter. Get down!" she screamed.

A police officer that saw what was happening ran toward the musicians, and soon the drumming and chanting trailed off.

"Get down. Someone's shooting," Charlie yelled.

People scattered in every direction, screaming. A few dropped to the earth. Two officers attempted to herd as many people as possible behind the food trucks.

Charlie continued to shield the boy, murmuring words of comfort. She wondered if her racing heart gave away her panic.

The man she'd knocked down scooted closer. "That's my son." He pulled the boy into his embrace. "Thank you."

Charlie nodded. A spot burned on her back, waiting for a bullet to hit. She peeked to see what was happening.

The two remaining uniformed officers ran toward the wooded area with their guns drawn.

Ryan and Joe were already at the edge of the trees, bent low, using the trunks for cover. *Dear God, please keep them safe. Keep everyone safe.*

CHAPTER 38

The Marksman looked up. "Dammit!"

"How did you miss that shot, shit-for-brains?" Grumps asked.

"It was the woman. Now she's shielding the kid under her body." He wiped sweat from his face. "I ought to shoot the bitch where she lies. Damn busybody."

"Get going," said Grumps. *"You can kill her later."*

People pointed in his direction. The cops were running his way with their guns drawn.

No time to break it down. He rolled out from under the sheet and wadded it up and stuffed it and his water bottle into the backpack. He struggled into his backpack, turned on the safety, and grabbed the rifle. After a quick look around, he ran down the slope. Partway down his foot slipped on the pine straw. He yelped with surprise. Pain shot through his hip when he fell. He continued to slide down for several yards.

"Dammit to hell."

"Get your ass up," Grumps said.

He climbed to his feet, mumbling curses. He shouldered his rifle and half-limped, half-ran the rest of the way to Grumps's old truck. His hands shook while he placed the rifle on the passenger floorboard. He threw the pack behind the seat and climbed behind the wheel.

He turned the key.

The engine struggled.

He hit the steering wheel. "Start, dammit. Start!"

His heart pounded against his ribs.

He turned the key again.

The engine rumbled, coughed, then died.

He ground his teeth and pushed harder on the gas pedal.

"Don't flood it, you idiot," Grumps said.

The truck rumbled to life.

The Marksman shoved the gearshift into drive and punched the accelerator. The tires slipped on the dirt and gravel before gaining purchase.

The side mirror splintered as a bullet ricocheted off.

He ducked and rammed his foot harder on the accelerator. The truck bucked like a rodeo horse while it sped over the rutted back road. He felt relief when he spotted the paved park road that he knew led to Governors Drive. He skidded into the turn and adjusted to avoid a rollover. Once he gained control, he drove home, shaking like he was in a blizzard.

"You blew that one, boy," said Grumps.

He ignored the old man and drove on, gritting his teeth.

Some of his tension subsided when he eased down the gravel track to his mobile home.

"That was close, boy. You need to be more careful." Grumps said.

"I can't please you, can I? Nothing's ever good enough," yelled the Marksman.

He parked and opened his door. Fury turned to alarm when the crunch of tires on the gravel alerted him to an approaching vehicle.

"Did they follow me?"

Leaping from the truck, he ran to the passenger side and pulled his rifle from the floorboard. He rested it on the rail of the truck bed and sighted, waiting for the vehicle to appear.

"Damn cops."

A car pulled into the clearing.

Through the scope, he saw the round-eyed fear on his mother's face.

She skidded to a stop.

"Shit." He lowered the rifle.

She opened the door and stood. "What are you doing? Were you going to shoot me?"

Ignoring her, he grabbed his backpack from the truck, picked up the rifle and limped toward the trailer. He unlocked the door, walked to the kitchen, and grabbed a Mountain Dew from the fridge.

Grumps berated him in his head all the way to his room. He slammed the bedroom door and locked it.

The doorknob rattled.

He stared at it.

"Don't you open that door, it's none of that cunt's business."

His mother banged on his door. "Son, what's going on? What happened to the side mirror on the truck?"

He didn't answer. Grumps continued to scream in his head.

CHAPTER 39

Marti placed a glass of wine next to her favorite chair and eased into it with a sigh. She picked up *Inferno* by Dan Brown and thumbed to the bookmark before settling back. Two pages into chapter ten, the doorbell rang.

This was the delivery day for her new comforter set. She rushed to the door and peeked through the peephole. Nothing.

Hmmm. I bet the driver left it on the doorstep.

A rash of stolen deliveries in the neighborhood encouraged her to unlock the door to see if the box was on her doormat.

Pain erupted across her face. She hit the floor, and all went black.

Marti swam awake to throbbing pain. She blinked several times to clear her vision.

Scott Hornsby knelt in front of her. "Hello, Marti."

His breath stank of beer.

She jerked back and looked for a way to escape. *Tied to a chair in my own damn kitchen!*

He grinned, exposing perfect white teeth. "Sorry about punching you."

He doesn't look sorry. Marti shook her head to clear it, and immediately regretted it. Pain stabbed behind her eyes.

"Hon, I don't want to hurt you. I just need a bit of help."

Marti wanted to scream, but he'd tied a gag around her mouth. She pulled against her bonds to no avail.

"Struggle if you want. You're not going anywhere. Promise not to scream and I'll take the gag off so we can talk."

Marti nodded.

He removed the gag.

She screamed.

He backhanded her, knocking her and the chair to the floor.

The blow and the fall temporarily knocked the breath from her lungs.

"You stupid bitch."

She tasted blood and her cheek burned. Gasping, she struggled to breathe.

He replaced her and the chair to an upright position with no effort. After retying the gag, he said, "All I want is for you to call Charlie and ask her to come over. Is that so hard?"

Marti glared at him.

Scott ran a gentle finger down her cheek. "Sweet Marti. Be helpful. One quick call and I'll let you go. All I want is Charlie."

Bile rose up her throat. She willed it down and swallowed before shaking her head.

He punched her right side.

Pain knifed through her ribs. Her mouth opened as she struggled to breathe through the gag. Pure agony exploded across her side.

He smiled. "I hate that you're making me do this to you. If you'd just do as I say, this will stop."

She didn't answer.

Scott paced in front of her. "That idiot Ryan thinks he deserves Charlie, but he doesn't. He's nothing but a detective." He knelt in front of her. "I knew I loved her the first time I saw her running the trail at Quantico." He smiled and closed his eyes. "That gorgeous blonde hair was up in a ponytail that swished from side to side as she ran."

He stood and paced again. "We'll get married as soon as she comes to her senses. I need to get her away from that loser so I can help her to see the real me—the man who adores her."

He grabbed Marti by the shoulders and shook her. "Can't you see Charlie and I are meant to be together? Will you call her?"

Marti shook her head. A stinging pain crossed her cheek, and all went black again.

* * *

Marti sputtered. Water dripped down her throbbing face. Her bruised and swollen eyes had narrowed her field of vision.

"Welcome back, Marti. No need to suffer unnecessarily. I don't know why you keep making me hurt you." He caressed her breast.

She stiffened in the chair.

A grin spread across his face. "Have you ever noticed that Charlie has such full firm boobs? I can't wait until she's naked in my arms. I plan to own every inch of her."

Marti tried to pull away.

He squeezed her breast so hard tears stung her eyes.

He released her.

She gulped in air, trying to breathe through the pain and the soggy gag.

CHAPTER 40

Charlie lay in a cubicle of the ER. To her left, a nurse with blue scrubs was taking her pulse, blood pressure, and temperature. To the right, she saw a chair, a computer attached to the wall and a rolling stool.

When the nurse left, Charlie sat up and swung her legs over the side of the bed. While she waited for the doctor, she rubbed her swelling knee with trembling hands. *Adrenaline aftermath,* she thought. *I had to fall on my bum knee. Jeez, I hope I won't need surgery.* She moved her leg and winced. *Mom always said, 'No good deed goes unpunished.'*

She pondered her short career as a community forensic profiler. During her first case with the HPD, she had escaped while saving a victim from a female serial killer, and later she had survived an attack from the Trainer while releasing a kidnapped teen. For her heroic efforts, she'd received tiny scars from glass shards all over her back and mental scars that still gave her occasional nightmares. "Now I've been shot at, and I've screwed up my knee. I may not live through another case. To make matters worse, I'm talking to myself. These folks will think I'm bat-shit crazy." She glanced at the clock on the wall. *Is it only three? Feels like it should be six. I wish Ryan were here.*

She closed her eyes to avoid the glare from the bright fluorescent lights. *Thank goodness I didn't hurt the kid when I tackled him. He was spooked, but not as much as his dad.* She shook her head and smiled. *The boy seemed more upset that I broke some of the turkey feathers on his costume.*

The memory projected across Charlie's vision like a movie.

* * *

The child cried under her. The tearful father thanked her as he pulled the child into his arms. An older woman dressed in beaded buckskins helped Charlie to her feet and hugged her.

The paramedics and ambulances arrived. Ryan insisted she travel by ambulance to have her injured knee checked because he couldn't leave the crime scene. She endured a loud, bouncy ride to Huntsville Hospital's E.R., followed by a ride on a gurney through the hospital's halls.

Charlie shook her head and blinked. The overlay of events vanished. *Good grief! Now I have post-traumatic stress?*

A nurse in purple scrubs hustled into the room, followed by a white-coated doctor. His eyes were as green as the emerald coast of Gulf Shores on a sunny day.

Charlie thought, *Too good looking for his own good.*

"I'm Dr. Lovelady."

She bit her lower lip to keep from grinning. *You've got to be kidding.*

The doctor's eyes skimmed across the paperwork she'd filled out. He looked up. "I saw the footage of you tackling that kid on the news. Not often I get to see the injury-causing event before I see the patient. Good tackle. You could play for Auburn."

He had to ruin it. "I'm an Alabama fan."

He grinned. "I won't hold it against you."

He reached over and took her swollen knee in both hands. "This may hurt a bit."

Charlie winced and bit her lower lip once again to keep from crying out.

"I'm going to order an x-ray first and then decide if we need a CT scan."

He turned to the nurse. "Let's ice it."

He glanced through the paperwork again. "Do you have any problems with codeine?"

165

"Nope."

He scribbled something on the paper and handed it to the nurse. With two strides, he'd reached the rolling stool. He lowered himself onto the small round seat and typed the magic password that caused the computer to spring to life.

The nurse returned with an icepack wrapped in a white towel and placed it on her throbbing knee.

Charlie smiled. "Thanks."

The nurse nodded and left.

Dr. Lovelady rose causing the chair to scoot back toward the wall.

"I'll be back after I see the x-ray. The nurse will return with something to help with the pain."

Ten minutes later the nurse with purple scrubs returned and gave her a pill and some water.

Charlie rubbed her arms. "Can I have a blanket, please? It's chilly in here."

"Sure. I'll be right back."

Within minutes the nurse returned with a white blanket. "I got one out of the warmer. It should be toasty."

"Thanks."

Charlie lay down, arranged the icepack on her knee, and got as cozy as possible under the heated blanket. She soon fell asleep.

The jiggling of her bed woke her. A tall bearded man smiled down as he released the brakes on the bed.

"Good, you're awake. I'm Brad, I'm taking you for an x-ray."

Twenty minutes later she was back in the E.R. She settled down and managed to doze off again.

"Sleeping on the job!" Kate bustled in the door and stood with her thumbs hooked in her utility belt.

"They gave me some pain meds. I'm a bit loopy."

"You can't stay out of trouble, can you?" Kate asked.

Charlie shrugged. "I swear, I didn't think. The moment I saw the kid I knew he was the target."

Kate crossed her arms. "Uh, huh."

"Is Ryan mad at me? He told me not to do anything—"

"Stupid?" Kate offered with a frown.

Charlie laughed. "Those weren't his exact words."

"Not too much. Ryan's the one who called me. He tried to call Marti, but she didn't answer her cell, home, or work phone."

Charlie frowned. "Maybe she was in session with a client."

Kate shook her head. "I drove by, and her car wasn't there."

Alarm zinged up Charlie's spine. "That's strange. Marti's good about answering her phone. Did you leave a message?"

"Sure did. No reply."

Dr. Lovelady poked his head in the door. "The x-ray looks good. No broken bones. He left as quickly as he appeared.

"Whoa! He's hot." Kate fanned herself with a hand. "What's his name?"

"Dr. Lovelady."

"You're joking—right?"

"Nope."

Kate smiled and winked. "Good thing Ryan isn't here. He's even better looking than Scott."

Charlie winced as she adjusted her position and the ice pack. "Speaking of Scott, have you heard anything about him? Do they know where he went?"

"Last I heard he ditched his attorney after he was bailed out and slipped away from his FBI escort. Rumor is, someone in high places wants to question him," Kate said.

"Ryan thinks he'll get a slap and maybe probation," Charlie said.

"After he disappeared, Captain Strouper called a meeting. He's convinced his career with the Bureau is over."

Charlie ran her hand through her hair. "I hope so. What he did was serious in my opinion. Did you see his house?"

"Nope. But I saw the crime scene photos of the room." Kate winked again. "I never knew you were so photogenic."

Charlie looked over at Kate. "I'm not sure when I'll be released."

"I'm here for the duration. My kid's spending the night with a friend and I promised Ryan I'd make sure you'd get home safe and sound."

"Thanks, Kate. I'll need to go get my car. It's still on Monte Sano."

"No worries. Someone's already driven it back to Ryan's house."

"Great." Something niggled at the edge of Charlie's mind. "Will you try calling Marti again? I'm starting to worry."

CHAPTER 41

The Marksman fumed while cleaning his rifle in his room. His mother was busy in the kitchen. He could hear the slamming of cabinet doors and the rattling of dishes.

He'd watched the YouTube video of his missed shot twelve times. He shook his head. *The bitch knocked down Big Tom Turkey before she rolled on top of the kid.* His jaw ached from gritting his teeth.

He pointed the rifle at the screen. "My perfect shot ruined by you, bitch. I should've shot you in the woods after I made you suck my dick."

His grandfather's voice ranted in his mind. *"You didn't pull the trigger fast enough. It's your fault that you didn't make the shot."*

"The boy was dancing around. The sun was in my eyes. I did my best, Grumps."

"If that's the best you've got—"

"What about the others," the Marksman yelled. "I killed them all with one shot. Don't they count for something?"

"A sniper is only as good as his last shot."

"Son?"

His mother rattled the knob.

"What's going on in there? Who're you talking to in your room?" his mother asked.

"It's the TV, Ma."

"Dinner's almost ready."

"Ain't hungry. Eat without me."

Furious, he mumbled, "It's all that woman's fault. I should've known she was trouble the day I met her at the firing range. I'm gonna kill that bitch."

CHAPTER 42

Charlie rose from the wheelchair, limped over, and boosted herself up into Kate's blue Honda Odyssey. "Glad to be out of the E.R.," Charlie said before closing the van door.

"Marti didn't answer when I called," Kate said while buckling her seatbelt.

Charlie frowned. "That's not good."

"Maybe her phone ran out of juice?"

"A therapist who's on call 24/7 for emergencies always keeps a charged phone. Would you go on duty without a loaded gun?"

Kate adjusted her rearview mirror. "Only if I was Barney Fyffe. By the way, where am I taking you?"

"My house first, then Ryan's. I'm staying there until the Scott issue is resolved, whatever that means. I need some clothes, and I want to pick up my elastic knee brace. When we get there, we can try to call Marti again." Charlie clicked her seatbelt into place and grinned at Kate. "I would never have figured *you* to be a minivan kinda woman. I had you pegged as an SUV chick."

Kate winked. "This is my Mom Mobile, it suits my alter ego."

"You certainly don't look like a mom, wearing a bulletproof vest and a giant black belt with all that crap on it."

"Crap?" Kate glared over at Charlie. "I have you know, these are the tools of my trade."

"What tools?"

Kate checked her mirrors and pulled out. She drove with one hand while counting off the items on the fingers of her other. "I carry pepper spray, a Taser, my baton, an extra magazine, handcuffs, a flashlight, my radio, and of course, my 9 millimeter Glock."

"Good grief, how much does all that stuff weigh?" Charlie asked.

Kate stopped at a red light and looked at Charlie. "The equipment belt and the vest weigh about 30 to 45 pounds, depending on what I'm carrying."

Charlie felt her mouth drop open and closed it. "How do you ever run down a criminal carrying all that extra weight?"

Kate rolled her eyes. "It ain't easy."

Charlie looked at the broad leather belt. "How do you pee?"

Kate chuckled while she accelerated. "That ain't easy, either. I take the belt off first, which means you don't wait until the last minute to go, if you know what I mean. One of my friends on the force started using a 'Go Girl.' She bought it at Target."

"What the heck is a 'Go Girl?'"

"She showed it to me once. It's a lavender urination cup. You unzip your pants, slip it inside, do your thing, zip up, and then empty it into a toilet or wherever. You can rinse it in the sink."

Charlie laughed. "I bet it'd come in handy during a stakeout after drinking coffee to stay alert."

Within ten minutes they pulled onto Charlie's street. Kate pulled into the driveway, illuminating the word BITCH written in large red letters across the white garage door.

Kate looked at Charlie. "My, my. Have you been a bad girl and made enemies in this neighborhood?"

"I suspect it's Scott's handiwork." She sighed. "As if I don't have enough to do, now I'll have to paint my garage door. Let me grab a few things, then I suggest we go to Marti's place and check on her."

Charlie opened the van door and grabbed her purse before sliding out. She was limping toward her front door when Kate cut her off and drew her Glock.

"Stay behind me," Kate whispered. "I don't like this. Scott could be inside."

Charlie stopped and took out her keys. She followed Kate.

Kate stepped to one side of the front door and jerked her head toward the lock.

Charlie unlocked the door and crossed over to stand beside Kate. She whispered, "What's next?"

"Is the alarm set?"

Charlie nodded.

"I'll go in first. You turn off the alarm and wait outside until I clear the house."

"I have my pistol in my fanny pack," Charlie said.

"Keep it there for now." Kate flipped on the lights and disappeared into the house.

Charlie unzipped her fanny pack, just in case, and turned off the alarm. She strained trying to hear. Minutes passed like hours before she heard Kate yell it was clear.

Kate walked into the foyer, holstering her gun. "Where's Spanky?"

"At Ryan's house."

Kate leaned against the doorframe looking relieved. "Good, at least she's safe. Go get your stuff. I'll call Marti again."

Charlie hobbled toward her bedroom. She grabbed an overnight bag and folded some blouses, slacks, and underwear into it.

"Where is that knee brace?" She yanked open drawers and closed them without finding the contraption. She stopped and tapped her lips with her index finger while she tried to visualize where she'd last seen it. "I know!"

"Know what?" Kate asked, rounding the corner into the bedroom.

"Where my knee brace is hiding." She limped into the bathroom and knelt on her uninjured knee to look in the cabinet under the sink. "There it is."

Charlie pulled it out, dropped the lid down on the nearby commode and sat. She pulled up the leg of her jeans and unwrapped the ace bandage wrapped around her swollen knee. She pulled on the brace. "Much better. I hate those wrap-around bandages. I either get them too tight or too loose."

"Let's go. Now I'm getting worried about Marti." Kate ran her hands through her copper curls. "She's still not answering. She was dating Scott, right?"

"Oh, God! What if he's punishing me by hurting Marti? If he hurts her, I'll…I'll do something." Able to walk faster with the brace, Charlie followed Kate, who had her bag, to the door.

"Set the alarm. I'll meet you at my Mom Mobile."

After Charlie hoisted herself up to the seat, she asked, "Maybe we should call for back up or tell someone our suspicions?"

"Good idea. Ryan and Joe will be working the Marksman scene for several more hours. I hate to call it in before we know there's a real problem." She started the vehicle. "I'll call Sam. He has the unit at his house. He can meet us there. If we're wrong, there'll be no paperwork." She pulled out her phone and dialed Sam.

Charlie already felt better. Kate's partner, Sam, was a mountain of a man whose very presence made bad guys behave.

Kate explained the situation. She turned to Charlie, "Where does Marti live?"

Charlie gave her the address. "It's in Blossomwood, not far from the elementary school."

Kate tapped the address into her GPS as she repeated the address to Sam. "Okay, see you there in a few. I'm in the Mom Mobile." She disconnected and backed out. The word BITCH faded into the dusk behind them.

Charlie redialed both of Marti's numbers with no answer. Dread filled Charlie's gut. *Something's wrong.*

Ten minutes later Charlie pointed. "Sierra Boulevard, this is the street."

The GPS confirmed the turn.

"The house is about a block down the road on the left."

"Nice homes." Kate pushed a few buttons and canceled the Google Map directions.

Charlie sat straight, her heart pounding. "Oh, no!"

Kate glanced over at Charlie. "What?"

"Drive to the end of the street."

Kate drove along glancing left and right.

Charlie pointed. "Oh My God! That's Scott's truck parked at the end of the block."

"You sure?"

Charlie nodded. "He has a bumper sticker that says, *Back off or you will regret it!*"

Kate stopped and dialed the station. She loudly identified herself, so the Bluetooth would pick up her voice. When connected to the dispatcher, she read the license plate number and sat back to wait.

Charlie glanced over at her. "We can't sit here double parked and not draw attention. Go around the block and park short of Marti's house, where we can observe it."

"Good idea."

They rounded the block and Charlie pointed at an open space of curb. "Pull over and stop before he sees us." She ran her hands through her hair. "I can't believe all this is happening. He's more unhinged than I wanted to believe."

Kate pulled to the curb and turned off the vehicle.

The dispatcher came online and confirmed the truck was registered to Scott.

Kate disconnected and dialed Sam. "How long before you get here?"

Sam's deep booming voice shot from the vehicle's speaker. "Look behind you."

Sam pulled along the curb behind them. He'd left his headlights off.

"I don't know if this is a problem yet. Dispatch confirmed it is Scott's truck parked at the end of the street. Marti still isn't answering any of her phones."

"Unlock your doors. I'm coming up."

Sam left his car, slid open the van door, and climbed into the backseat.

Charlie and Kate shifted to see him better.

Charlie gawked. *Good grief, his shoulders almost fill the back seat.*

"Any ideas on how to approach this situation, *if* it is one?" Sam asked.

Charlie felt an unease elevating to panic churning in her gut. "Call the police."

Kate rolled her eyes. "Woman, we are the police."

"I mean *more* police. You know, back up." Fear raced through her body while she ran her hands through her hair again. "Better yet, ask Captain Strouper for advice, since Scott is still technically an FBI agent."

Kate frowned. "Last I heard he was suspended from duty pending further investigation, but I think you have a point. I'll call Strouper and let him make the decision."

Kate dialed and asked to speak to the captain, indicating it might be an emergency involving Special Agent Hornsby. When he was on the line, she gave a detailed synopsis, starting with the graffiti on Charlie's garage door.

The captain's voice filled the vehicle. "I'll phone my contact at the FBI. He's still their problem as much as ours. Sit tight until I call you. You'll have backup one way or another."

Kate said, "Yes, sir, we'll sit tight until you get back to us."

Charlie's panic rose like bile in her throat. Her imagination filled with all the awful things Scott could be doing to Marti. She threw her hands in the air. "He could be raping Marti or killing her while we're sitting out here waiting for the bureaucracy to make up their minds." She opened the passenger door and slid out.

"What the…" Sam slid his door open. Within a few steps, he grabbed the hobbling Charlie around the waist and picked her up like a doll.

Charlie squirmed, trying to get loose.

Sam plopped her down on the back seat. He closed the door, hopped in the front, and told Kate, "Engage the child locks."

"Yes, sir."

Sam turned to look at Charlie. "Woman! Are you crazy or something? I know she's your friend and all, but ringing the front doorbell will let him know we're here. Besides, he'd love to take you as a hostage."

Kate pointed her finger at Charlie. "He's right. You're the one he wants."

Charlie huffed. "Folks, I know I'm blonde but do I look stupid? I wasn't going to ring the doorbell for chrissakes. I was going to sneak around and peak in the windows."

"Haven't you done enough damage to that knee today?" Kate asked.

Kate's phone rang, and she answered.

"The FBI is sending a couple of agents to assist in this matter," Captain Strouper said.

She looked into the rearview mirror. "Looks like the reinforcements have arrived. That was fast. Thanks, Captain." She disconnected the call.

Charlie peered out the rear window. "That has to be them. They do *love* their black SUVs."

Two men in dark suits walked to the blue-and-white and glanced inside. They exchanged shrugs and proceeded to Kate's vehicle.

Kate powered down her window as the men approached.

The one with silver at his temples said, "Special Agents Brown and Henley."

Kate lifted her chin. "Officers Kate O'Cleary and Sam Nichols." She thumbed toward the rear. "Our part-time profiler, Dr. Charlie Stone."

Agent Brown looked toward the back window.

The window was tinted, so Charlie rolled it down and offered her hand.

Agent Brown shook it briefly. His brow furrowed, but his eyes twinkled. "So you're the subject of Scott Hornsby's fascination," he said. He shifted his attention back to Kate. "We've been partially briefed. Do we know who the hostage may be?"

Charlie explained that Marti, her friend and business partner, had dated Scott a few times and wasn't answering any of her phones. "His truck is parked at the end of the block."

"You sure?" S.A. Henley asked.

"We've run the plates," Kate said, her tone defensive.

"What's the plan?" Sam asked.

Agent Brown leaned lower to see Sam. "Let's try to get a visual first. We plan to circle the house and assess the situation." They left and crossed the street; each took a side of the house, disappearing into the deepening darkness.

Charlie rolled up her window. "See, they're going to peek into the windows."

Sam shook his head. "You're a trip."

Kate chuckled. "You don't know the half of it."

Ten minutes later the agents morphed out of the shadows and crossed the street.

"Did you see anything?" Kate asked.

"He's in there, and he has a dark-haired woman tied to a chair in the kitchen," Agent Brown said. "We need to approach this carefully to avoid a hostage situation."

Agent Henley added, "He never noticed us. He was too busy yelling, 'Call her,' in the woman's face."

Charlie's anxiety about Marti shifted to anger, rolling like lava through her veins. She lowered the window back down. With a tone sharp as a honed ax she asked, "Has he hurt her?"

"Yes, ma'am. She's roughed up a bit," said Agent Henley.

Agent Brown frowned at him. "Dr. Stone, calm down. We don't need to go about this half-cocked. Let's try this the easy way first. Does Scott know either of you officers?"

"He knows me from the SATF," Kate said.

"Good," said Agent Brown. You come with me. We'll take the front door. Officer Nichols, will you cover the back with my partner?"

"Sure thing." Sam exited the van and walked around the front to join the two agents, who eyed him.

Kate opened her door and stepped out.

Agent Henley who stood at six feet gazed up at Sam and down at Kate and said, "I got the better of the deal."

Sam chuckled. "Not so sure about that. Kate's a hell of a lot meaner."

Agent Brown nodded. "Let's go."

"What do you want me to do?" Charlie asked.

Agent Brown said, "Stay in the van and out of sight. We don't want Scott to see you. It could escalate matters."

CHAPTER 43

"Wake up, Marti. Time to make a phone call. Charlie's been calling you while you were out."

Scott moved the phone closer to her face. She realized the gag was gone.

She shook her head and waited for the next blow.

It came with a burning ache and a stream of cursing.

"Call her, cunt."

"No."

He grabbed her shoulders, his face inches from hers. "Don't make me torture you."

Marti lifted her chin. "What do you call this?"

A smirk settled on his face. "An appetizer." He walked over and pulled a knife from the block on the counter.

The doorbell rang.

Scott's face brightened. "It's Charlie. She's come to check on you." He pulled the gag up before he hurried past her toward the door.

Marti struggled to free herself.

Someone pounded on the door.

"Fuck!" Scott bellowed as he ran past her holding his gun. He fumbled with the lock on her rear kitchen door, cursing its existence. He ripped open the door, started outside and skidded to a halt on the porch.

A man she didn't recognize climbed the stairs.

Scott fired. The blast assaulted her ears and lit up the porch.

The man fell back into Sam's arms.

"Sam!" she mumbled through the gag.

Scott slammed the door shut and raced back toward the front of the house.

CHAPTER 44

Charlie peered out the window. The streetlights illuminated the team jogging toward the house.

Not good. Hope Scott doesn't spot them, Charlie thought. She lowered the window a bit, straining to hear what was happening.

Lights glowed in the windows of nearby homes, creating a false sense of serenity. A dog barked in the distance.

Agent Brown rang the bell. He hesitated and then knocked. "FBI!"

Seconds passed like hours to Charlie. *Why isn't he answering?*

He pounded on the door.

A shot resounded in the dark.

Charlie's hand covered her heart. "Oh, my God, who shot who?"

She heard shouts.

A door slammed.

Agent Brown leaped off the porch and peeled off to the left. Kate went right, pulling her Glock as she ran toward the rear of Marti's house.

Seconds after they'd disappeared into the darkness, Scott barreled out the front door, his Glock in hand. He sailed over the three steps and hit the sidewalk at a dead run, racing toward his truck. Once he reached it, he jumped inside and started it.

Charlie rolled up the window. "No!" She climbed into the front driver's seat, pain shooting through her right knee. "I can't believe this. He's going to get away."

Scott sped down the street.

"Thank you, Lord. Kate left the keys." Charlie started the engine. She shoved the lever into drive and jammed the pedal to the floor. In her peripheral vision, she saw Kate, Sam, and Agent Brown running onto the front lawn.

Two blocks down, Scott had turned left.

Charlie took her foot off the gas and slid around the corner in time to see him turn left again, two streets down.

Her phone rang.

She ignored it and turned right to follow him out of the neighborhood onto Governor's Drive.

Keeping her eye on Scott's truck, she fumbled her phone out of her fanny pack and swiped to answer.

"What the hell are you doing?" Kate screamed. "You're going to get yourself killed!"

"Chasing Scott. He's going west on Governor's Drive."

Scott swerved around a slower car, clipping the back bumper. The Lincoln pivoted, stopping part-way in the turning lane, facing the wrong way.

"Oh, shit!" Charlie dropped the phone in her lap. Using both hands, she veered the ungainly vehicle into the oncoming lane to avoid a collision. A red SUV's horn blared as it headed straight for her. She wrenched the wheel to bring the van back into the correct lane seconds before impact.

"You better not wreck my Mom Mobile!" Kate screeched.

Charlie exhaled and picked up the phone. "He's turning onto California. Can I get a little help here?"

"We're on our way. Henley's been shot. Sam is asking for backup. Stay on the line so you can report his location," Kate said.

Charlie hit the accelerator, closing the gap between them. She put the phone on speaker and slid it into the cup holder. "He's approaching the Maple Hill Cemetery. If he doesn't slow down, he's not going to make those curves."

Scott's brake lights glowed. He tried to make the curve but swerved into the oncoming lane.

Charlie jammed on the brakes.

A white Lexus jumped the curb to avoid him and smashed into a brick wall.

183

Scott adjusted his trajectory and fish-tailed down California.

"Scott caused a wreck at Eustis and California. Get some paramedics there. He's heading toward Five Points."

Charlie flinched. An older woman, her white hair barely visible above the steering wheel, eased out of the Star Market parking lot.

Scott careened around her on two wheels and raced on.

"He's heading toward the Interstate 565 entrance at Andrew Jackson Way and Oakwood Avenue," Charlie said.

Kate repeated the information over the police radio. "We have a car in the area."

Charlie had gained headway and was now six car lengths behind him. They sped past Mario's restaurant and were approaching a large church on the left. Charlie could see Oakwood Avenue ahead. Blue lights flashed to the right and left of the intersection. The traffic light shone green.

Scott swerved into the left lane to pass a truck pulling a trailer.

The light turned yellow.

Charlie slowed.

The officers stood behind the doors of their SUVs guns ready.

The light changed to red. Scott raced through the intersection and up the ramp.

Charlie flinched when she heard loud pops. *They must have put out spike strips.*

Scott lost control when his tires blew. He slid off the road to the right and skidded across the grass. The front end of the truck hit a chain link fence. He wrenched open the truck's door, leaped from the vehicle, and scaled the fence with monkey-like ease.

The nearest officer jumped from behind his unit and raced after him. One look at the officer's bulging waistline left Charlie little hope that he'd catch Scott.

Charlie turned right on Oakwood, yelling so Kate would hear. "He's wrecked at that on ramp near Oakwood and is on foot heading toward the Optimist Park."

Charlie heard sirens. "I hope he doesn't hole up in the gym and take hostages." She slowed and pulled over to watch.

Scott turned and spotted her. He changed course and sprinted in her direction.

Charlie fumbled to find the lock in the unfamiliar van.

He grabbed the driver's side handle and yanked open the door.

Heart thudding with panic, she rammed the van into reverse and hit the gas.

Scott clung to the door and its frame, one foot on the running board.

She juiced the gas.

He held on. "Stop, you bitch."

Determined to break his hold, she cranked the wheel hard right, sending the van into a circular slide.

He lost his footing and fell off, still grasping the door.

She hit the gas again.

He held on, while she dragged him across the pavement.

Charlie glanced in the rearview mirror and slammed on the brake. She'd missed ramming a car by inches. "Holy shit."

Scott lost his grip and rolled across the pavement.

Kate roared, "What the hell is going on? Don't you dare dent my van! It's paid for."

Scott cursed and rose to his hands and knees. He swayed when he stood.

Charlie shifted into drive and yelled, "You try that again buddy, and I'll run over your ass."

He lurched toward the open van door.

Charlie almost fell out of the van trying to pull it closed. This time she found the lock.

He tried the handle. Cursing, he banged his closed fist against the driver's window.

Kate bellowed, "What's that noise?"

"Scott is banging on the window with his fist."

Kate bellowed, "He's toast."

He moved around the front of the van, heading toward the passenger door.

Unsure if she'd locked *all* the doors, she gunned it, bouncing Scott off to the side.

She raced away, afraid he might pull his gun and shoot her.

She pulled into the Optimist Park lot and stopped. Her chest heaved like she'd been running a marathon. She couldn't stop shaking.

Scott stumbled to his feet and limped into the middle of Oakwood holding up his FBI shield.

The two cops were closing in, guns drawn, yelling, "Drop your weapon and place your hands on your head."

A black Camaro slid to a stop.

Scott staggered to the driver's door, his khaki pants bloody at the knees. He wrenched the door open, leaned in, and yanked the driver out.

The teenage boy that'd been driving fell, rolling on the pavement, and scrambled to his hands and knees. He looked up and stared, mouth agape, while Scott sped away in his car. Jumping to his feet, he yelled, "Hey! You can't do that. Gimme my car back." He chased after it, waving his arms.

The police officers stopped and put their hands on their knees, trying to catch their breaths.

Charlie picked up the phone and told Kate, "He stole a black Camaro and is heading east on Oakwood."

One officer ran back to his blue-and-white to join the pursuit. The other headed toward the spike strip to remove it from the entrance ramp.

"We're in pursuit," Kate said.

"I'll let y'all take over. I'm going back to Marti's. You can find me and your van there."

Kate yelled, "Oh, shit! He nearly hit that kid. Gotta go, Charlie."

CHAPTER 45

Charlie drove back to Marti's house, shaking with adrenaline. A light turned red, adding to her frustration. The pressure of her foot on the brake combined with the rushing energy in her bloodstream caused her leg to bounce. She tried to hold it steady with her trembling hand to no avail.

"Get a grip, Charlie, you've got to pull yourself together for Marti. Bless her heart, it's bad enough she's been terrorized in her home. Now she has an injured FBI agent on her back porch. Dear God, please let him be alive."

Ten minutes later, Charlie pulled onto Marti's street. Blue and red flashing lights bounced off the windows of the nearby homes. She pulled her Huntsville Police consultant badge from her fanny pack and looped it over her head. She pulled the keys from the ignition, slid out of the Odyssey leaving the driver's door open, and hobbled as fast as possible toward the sign-in station.

An attendant closed the back door of an ambulance and hopped into the cab. It took off with flashing lights and shrieking sirens.

Charlie covered her ears. *At least he's alive. If he weren't, the coroner's van would be leaving, instead of an ambulance.* She prayed for Agent Henley and his family while she trekked to the house.

Dennison was manning the sign-in station. She smiled when he looked up and waved. *Good, he'll catch me up on what's happening.*

She muttered, "Excuse me" and pushed her way through the crowd of curious neighbors.

When she cleared the spectators, she spotted Officer "No-Neck" Jackson, the brash young cop with the muscle-bound brain.

Dennison smiled. "I wondered when you'd show up. I hear your friend's been asking for you."

No Neck smirked. "Seems you've caused a lot of trouble." He rolled his massive shoulders. "Not surprised."

Dennison glared at his partner. "Back off."

No-Neck shrugged. "What? From what I've heard, she's the reason that nut came here in the first place."

Charlie tensed. She shot him a glare before taking the sign-in sheet to complete the process. "I don't have time for your foolishness, Jackson. My friend is hurt and needs me."

She limped toward the door. She'd intended to gather some information before facing Marti, but No-Neck had blown that option. She took in a deep breath to steady her nerves. *He's right. If Scott had never seen me at Quantico, he wouldn't have come to Huntsville, and none of this would've happened. All I need is more guilt.*

Inside, the strong smell of Scott's cologne assaulted her sensitive nose. *Did he come back? Surely not, the place is crawling with cops.* She walked further into the living room. A lamp lay broken beside Marti's favorite chair. An overturned glass of red wine stained a skewed oriental carpet.

She thought, *Oh Marti, what happened to you?*

She gathered her resolve and walked through the dining room into the kitchen.

Marti sat on a kitchen chair rubbing her wrists. A paramedic knelt in front of her cleaning the blood from her face.

"Oh my God!" Charlie's hands covered her mouth.

"Charlie!" Marti stood, caught her foot in the leg of the chair, and stumbled. The good-looking paramedic steadied her.

Charlie stepped forward, and they hugged and started crying.

Charlie sniffled, "Look who's the klutz now."

"Ow! Don't make me laugh. It hurts."

"Sorry. Let's both sit down. My knee is killing me."

Marti waved her hand in the paramedic's direction. "This is Brian. He's been taking good care of me."

"I see." Charlie winked at Marti, who blushed.

Brian said, "Marti is one lucky lady to be alive. She may have some broken ribs. Another ambulance is en route. She needs to be checked to rule out internal injuries, a concussion, and a possible torn retina."

Worried, Charlie eyed her friend. *She's putting on a good show, but what will happen after everyone leaves?*

Brian finished his ministrations. He noticed Charlie limping over to pull out a chair.

"I'll get that." He grabbed the chair and sat it beside Marti's. "How did you hurt your leg?"

Charlie sank into the chair with a sigh of relief. "I fell on my knee earlier today. They checked it out at the E.R. I'll live."

Marti frowned and pointed at Charlie, "This time." Her split, swollen lip eroded her enunciation. Brian pulled a second chair over and lifted Charlie's injured leg onto it. "It needs to be elevated. I'll be back." He walked out the back door, which stood open, allowing the night breeze to cleanse the smells of fear, blood, and Scott.

Charlie nudged Marti. "He's cute."

Marti flushed.

Brian returned with two cold packs. "Marti, hold this one on your face." He turned to Charlie. "This one's for your knee."

They accepted the cold packs. Brian said goodbye, giving Marti a parting wave.

"Can you catch me up on what happened here with Scott?" Charlie asked.

"Only if you'll help me understand how the FBI knew he was here," Marti said, gently probing her lip.

"Deal. You first, before your lip swells to the size of an orange."

Marti thought a moment. "I'd returned home from a meal at Little Rosie's. I was reading a book and enjoying a glass of wine when the doorbell rang. I got up and looked out the peephole and didn't see anyone."

"Why did you open the door if you couldn't see anyone?" Charlie asked, adjusting the icepack on her knee. "You're on me all the time about using the peephole on my door."

"Last I'd heard Scott was back in Washington getting his comeuppance. I was expecting a package from UPS. They ring the bell, leave the package, and disappear. My neighbor warned me some packages had been stolen from stoops. I didn't want it to happen to my new comforter set."

Charlie nodded. "Makes sense. What happened next?"

"I unlocked the door and opened it. Scott socked me in the face and knocked me out."

Charlie clenched her fists. "That asshole!"

"When I woke, I was here in the kitchen tied to this chair." She eyed the dinette set with distaste. "I think I'm going to donate this set and buy a new one. I'm not sure I can get past seeing myself tied to this chair."

Charlie reached over and massaged Marti's shoulder. "Whatever it takes. I'll go shopping with you if you like."

Tears welled in Marti's eyes. She wiped at them with her fingers. "He behaved like a madman. Charlie, I was so scared. He'd pace while he ranted about his undying love for you." Marti grabbed a tissue from the box on the table and blotted her eyes and blew her nose. "I'd hate to think what would've happened if you'd been here instead of me."

"Me, too. I'm so sorry. It's all my fault." Charlie reached for a tissue to mop her dripping nose.

Marti's swollen eyes widened a fraction. "Have you lost your mind? If it hadn't been you, it would've been someone else. I bet if they check his history, this has happened before. He's an obsessive personality." Marti moved her ice pack from one side of her face to the other. She shifted in her chair to better see Charlie. "Your turn. How did the FBI find out Scott was holding me hostage?"

Charlie started the tale with injuring her knee at the Pow Wow, which had led to the E.R. visit, where Kate had picked her up to take her home, where they had discovered the defaced garage door.

Marti's jaw dropped. "He spray-painted *bitch* on your garage door? That's so, so juvenile. I bet your neighbors will love that sight on the way to church in the morning."

190

"I'm sure." Charlie told her how she and Kate had kept calling her. "We suspected something was wrong when you didn't answer."

Marti winced when she shifted her position. "The something wrong was Scott."

"We drove over here to check on you. Kate and I called in Sam after I spotted Scott's truck parked down the block. Since Scott's still an FBI agent, we decided to contact Captain Strouper. His contact in the FBI sent the two agents. Special Agent Brown and Kate took the front door, while Special Agent Henley and Sam covered the back. I was told to stay in the van."

"Hard to believe you did, knowing you."

Charlie did her best to look offended. "Do you want to hear the rest of this story or not?"

Marti rolled her hand in a circle. "Go on."

"They knocked on the door. Shortly after, I heard the shots," Charlie said.

Marti started to tremble. She reached out to Charlie.

Charlie took her hand and squeezed. *It's icy cold. She's in shock.*

She struggled to her feet and hobbled into the living room to get the afghan draped over the back of the sofa. She returned to the kitchen and wrapped it around Marti's shoulders.

Marti looked up. "Thanks."

The butter yellow walls and white cabinets would usually cheer Charlie. Not tonight. Not when she could still smell the coppery scent of blood in the air. "Your turn."

Marti gulped and continued. "The doorbell rang. I could tell by the eager smile that lit Scott's face he thought it was you. I wanted to warn you, but he'd gagged me."

Charlie leaned toward her and patted her leg. "You did fine."

Marti took a deep breath. "Scott dashed back past me with his gun drawn. I didn't know what was happening. He threw open the back door and almost ran into..."

"Special Agent Henley."

Marti nodded. "Poor man. I think Scott panicked and fired. I saw the guy's eyes bulge with shock. He fell back into Sam's arms."

Charlie closed her eyes. "I hate you had to witness such a horrible thing." She squeezed her friend's hand again.

"Me, too. Scott whirled around and raced back toward the front door. Sam eased the agent down on the porch and tried to staunch the bleeding. That's when the second FBI guy showed up with Kate. The agent screamed instructions into his phone. Kate cut the rope binding me with a knife from the block. She handed me a kitchen towel and told me to help the man who was shot. I grabbed the towel and applied it to the wound. When I looked up, they were all running toward the front door." Marti grinned. "I could hear Kate scream all the way back to the porch, 'She took my van. I'm going to kill her if she wrecks it.' Did Scott get away?"

Charlie picked up the story describing her chase in Kate's Mom Mobile, Scott's erratic driving, the wrecks he'd caused, and his attempts to get in the van with her.

Marti put a hand over her mouth. She removed it and asked, "What happened next?"

"Scott limped into the middle of Oakwood, showed his badge, hauled some guy out of a black Camaro, and took off. That poor kid was cursing and chasing Scott down the road."

Marti laughed, tears dribbling down her face. Between gasps for air, she said, "Kate's going to kill you."

At that moment, Kate strode in the door, thumbs tucked in her belt. "You got that right! You left the driver's door open. I better not have a dead battery. I'm going to check my Mom Mobile tomorrow and if there's one scratch—"

Charlie held up both hands. "I'll pay for all repairs. Did you catch him?"

"No, we didn't," grumbled Sam, who stood in the doorway. "That fool was driving like a maniac. He caused at least three wrecks. Don't worry, ladies, we'll catch him."

Charlie rubbed her face with her hands. "I wouldn't count on it. He knows how to hide and how to work the system. I don't know who he's related to, but they have some power and influence with the FBI."

Kate's brow furrowed. "This means you both are still in danger."

Charlie winced and reapplied the icepack to her knee. "Maybe he'll glom on to someone else."

Marti moved her ice pack to the other side of her face. "Don't count on it."

"Crap! Your face." Kate took a step closer. "Does it hurt?"

By now, both of Marti's eyes were almost swollen shut. Her lower lip looked like a plastic surgeon had gone berserk with filler.

"Hell, yeah. Everything hurts. I don't want to know what it'll feel like tomorrow. I haven't looked in a mirror yet."

Kate patted her on the shoulder. "Steel yourself. It ain't pretty."

Marti sighed. "Damn."

Sam moved closer and reached down. He tilted Marti's face up with a gentle finger under her chin. "That shithead better hope they arrest him before I get my hands on him."

"You'll have to wait in line," said Ryan. He walked in and bent to kiss Charlie on the forehead. "Damn, Marti. Do you want me to take you to the hospital?"

The paramedic poked his head in the door. "Your chariot has arrived, my lady."

Charlie asked, "Did you catch the Marksman?"

Ryan hung his head. "Nope. He got away again. Let's go home. I'm beat. Um, sorry about the choice of words, Marti."

She waved it away.

A rap on the doorframe drew everyone's attention.

"Ma'am, I'm sorry I didn't have time to introduce myself earlier. I'm Special Agent Brown. It's going to be an hour or two before the crime scene crew is finished. Did Special Agent Horner enter your bedroom or bath?"

"I don't know. I only saw him in the kitchen, but there were periods I lost consciousness."

Charlie asked, "How's your partner?"

"He's in surgery."

The ambulance crew helped Marti onto a stretcher and rolled her out the front door.

Marti grabbed Charlie's hand. "My keys. They're in my purse."

"I'll get your purse, drive your car to the E.R., and wait with you."

CHAPTER 46

The Marksman paced his room. He curled his fingers in his hair, ready to scream. *Stop yellin' at me, Grumps. It wasn't my fault.*

His grandfather's voice dripped with contempt. *"You worthless whelp. After all your training, you let that little blonde bitch get the best of you?"*

He dropped to his knees. Holding his pounding head, he said, "I tried, Grumps. I really tried."

"You've got to kill her to even the score. She's your next trophy."

"Honey, you sure you don't want something to eat? I've put everything away and washed the dishes."

"I'm sure, Mom. My head hurts and I ain't hungry right now."

"I can make you a plate for later. You can pop it in the microwave when you're ready."

"That's fine. You do that," he said.

"Stupid little slut. Spreads her legs on command," Grumps said.

"Don't talk about my mother that way!" he screamed.

The door handle rattled. "Son, let me in. What's going on? Who're you yelling at?"

"Go away, Mom."

She banged on the door. "Let me in this minute!"

Grumps chuckled. *"You ought to kill her, too."*

The Marksman squeezed his head between his hands. "Noooo. Go away."

It was quiet for a few moments.

"I have to work a late shift tonight because someone's sick. I need the money to pay for my car repair. Hope you feel better tomorrow.

Your headache pills are in the bathroom, but you need to take them with food."

He heard the front door close. He stood and flung himself onto the bed.

"Don't be such a wuss, boy. Tomorrow you need to start following that woman you have the hots for and pick a time and a place. Do you think that pretty little thing is going to drop her cop boyfriend to give you a toss in the hay? A mama's boy like you? Shit, even if she did, you probably couldn't get it up."

The Marksman stood and walked to the door. He strode to the medicine cabinet and yanked it open. With trembling hands, he shook two pills into his palm. He paused and looked inside the bottle, estimating if he had enough to shut up his grandfather forever.

"Do it, boy. Do it. I'll take your worthless ass with me."

He closed the bottle and put it away. He ran some water into his palm and downed the two pills. He walked into the kitchen, grabbed another Mountain Dew from the fridge and a bag of Doritos from a cabinet. Tuning out his grandfather as best he could, he locked himself into his room.

CHAPTER 47

Charlie's relief was palatable when she arrived at Ryan's house. It was close to midnight, and she was in no mood for any more problems. She began her mental list. *Love on Spanky and feed her. Call the answering service.*

The garage door rattled down. Charlie eased in the kitchen door and tried to quiet Spanky, who whined and greeted her with tail-wagging exuberance.

She dialed her answering service.

Marie, one of the night operators, answered. "I saw you on TV. You took a bad spill. You want me to cancel Monday's appointments?"

"Cancel them for Monday and Tuesday. My knee needs to heal."

"Will do. You get better, Doc. Marti called ten minutes ago and canceled her folks for the rest of the week. What's going on with you two?"

"Long story, Marie. I'm tired. I plan to sleep in tomorrow and nurse my knee. Have a good night."

Ryan walked bare-chested into the kitchen. He ran his hand through his hair and yawned. "How's Marti?"

She yawned in response. "Three cracked ribs, a mild concussion, and multiple contusions. The good news is she has no major internal injuries. They're keeping her overnight for observation."

"Son-of-a-bitch almost killed her. I hate to blast your plans to smithereens, but Strouper wants us in a meeting Monday morning at nine."

She slumped further down her seat. *Pull it together, girl.* Steeling herself, she took a breath and stood.

"I need food, a hot shower, and Spanky kisses."

Ryan walked to her side. "How about my kisses?" He looked down at her with his kind, tired eyes. He wrapped her in his arms, his warmth seeping into her aching muscles.

The tension eased in her body. Her guard dropped, allowing her to sob.

Ryan held her while she wept. After she gained some control, he said, "It's been a helluva day."

She wiped her eyes with the heel of her hands. "I'm running on fumes. I'll feel better once I eat. Marti is the one who's had a horrible day. When I think of what Scott did to her, I could shred paper with my teeth."

Ryan cocked a brow. "An egg or toast? I can whip something up while you hit the shower."

Charlie managed a smile. "You're a prince. A fried egg, please." She grabbed a couple of chocolate almond kisses from the bowl in the center of the table.

He winked. "Are you supposed to be eating those?"

Charlie stood and winced. "This is insurance. I don't want to pass out from low blood sugar in the shower."

"Go ahead, Charlie. I'll start the egg."

"Thanks." She unwrapped the two chocolates and ate them as she hobbled her way to the bedroom. She couldn't undress fast enough, but her jeans weren't easy to shed with an injured knee. Once in the shower, she stood and let the hot water cascade over her aching body. The reality of her day washed over her. *I threw myself in front of a bullet, chased a maniac at high speeds through the streets of Huntsville in a Mom Mobile, and was almost kidnapped by Scott. Have I lost my freaking mind? I should've let the FBI and the police handle it. I'm not Super Woman. Scott managed to escape anyway so it was all for nothing.* She picked up the soap and realized she was crying. *Even worse, my best friend got beaten to a pulp because of me.*

Charlie scrubbed away the dirt and sweat, and then toweled off. She slipped on a robe and blow-dried her hair.

"Food!" Ryan yelled.

"Coming." She sat on a nearby stool and pulled on her knee brace.

Feeling at least human, she limped into the kitchen and took a seat.

Ryan had set the table. An egg with a slice of buttered toast sat in front of Charlie's place. A bouquet of colorful flowers in a vase occupied the middle next to the bowl of chocolates.

"Where did those beautiful flowers come from?"

Ryan winked. "The flower fairy heard you had a tough day."

Charlie stood and wrapped her arms around his neck and kissed him. "I do love you."

He grinned down at her. "That's convenient, because I love you, too."

Charlie sank back into her seat and crunched on her toast. "I was thinking in the shower."

"I think all the time." Ryan took a gulp of coffee, scrunched his face, and spit it back in the cup. "Hot!" He gulped some water.

She shook her head. "You weren't thinking just then. Didn't you see the steam rising?"

"Quit giving me grief, woman. I bought you flowers."

"I thought the flower fairy brought them," she said with a cheeky grin.

"Give you some chocolate and a hot shower, and you get sassy. Seriously, what were you contemplating in the shower?"

Charlie held up a finger and finished chewing a bite of egg. "My life is out of control."

"You've just noticed? You seem to draw stalkers, killers, and crazies to you like a magnet."

"Don't forget the ghost," she said, taking another bite.

"How could I forget *her*?" He shivered.

"I'm thinking about leaving my positions as profiler and consultant on the SATF."

Ryan paused, a slice of toast halfway to his mouth. He put it down and wiped his hands.

"You look upset," Charlie said.

"It's your decision. I can't say there haven't been times when I hadn't wished you'd resign. I worry." Ryan blushed. "On the other hand, you're so damned good at what you do. If you just didn't take so many chances, I'd feel better. What brought this up now?"

Charlie thought about his question while she chewed.

"Part of it's cumulative. The last straw was Marti. I put her in danger."

Ryan held up both hands. "Whoa! You didn't put her in danger. It's not your fault Scott's a nut case. You didn't ask him to move in next door. Besides, Marti was goo-goo eyed over him from the first time she saw him. What'd she call him?"

"Agent Marble Butt."

"You're running on adrenaline, emotion, and chocolate at the moment. Don't make any rash decisions. Give it a few days."

Charlie nodded. "You're right. What's this meeting about Monday morning?"

"The captain didn't say, and right now I don't care. I want to finish my coffee and love on my woman before I pass out from exhaustion."

CHAPTER 48

Monday morning, Charlie followed Ryan to the meeting at headquarters. She parked, opened the door, and prepared herself for the pain. It didn't help. She cringed when she stood.

Ryan walked over and took her arm. "Does it hurt worse today?"

"Yep. It's more swollen. I've never had my knee hurt like this before. When this meeting's over, I plan to go home, prop up my leg, and watch a chick flick."

"Sounds good to me. Can we have popcorn?" Marti shuffled toward them like someone who'd overdone it at the gym.

They hugged, while Ryan gently encircled them with his arms. Charlie asked. "How did you get here?"

"I Ubered."

Marti's face looked worse than Charlie felt. Both of her eyes looked like giant, purple grapes.

Ryan cocked his head. "If I didn't know better, I'd say you were the loser in a boxing match."

Marti giggled. "Don't make me laugh, it hurts worse than yesterday. I'm serious, Charlie; can I stay with you today? I don't want to be alone."

"Sure you can. I'll even make popcorn and let you choose the movie."

Ryan touched Marti's shoulder. "You're welcome to stay the night. I have a guest room."

Marti's eyes glazed with tears. "I'll think about it. I was so tired that I fell asleep, but I woke up terrified at three in the morning. Just knowing Scott's out there and he may come back loomed large in my mind during those wee hours."

"I know exactly what you're talking about." Charlie's heart ached to see her friend in this condition.

A puzzled look played on Ryan's face. "Marti, I'm happy to see you, but why are you here?"

"Captain Strouper called last night and asked me to come to a meeting, plus I need to make an official statement to the FBI." Marti glanced at Charlie. Special Agent Brown wants you to make one, too."

"Do we have to go to the FBI office?" Charlie asked.

Marti shook her head and looked like she regretted it. "They'll take our statements here, during the meeting." She steadied herself on Charlie's arm. "I need a favor."

"Name it," Charlie said.

"Will you take me to my eye appointment today after the meeting? It's to make sure I don't have a retinal tear," Marti said.

"No problem. After that, it's a movie and nap time."

Ryan took each of them by the arm to assist them inside.

Once they were in the meeting room, Charlie and Marti sank into chairs next to each other.

"I don't remember the conference room being this far," Charlie said.

"Me either. Thank God for elevators. Of course, I've never come here after being beaten by a lunatic," Marti said. "I wonder if they have a wheelchair around here. I wouldn't mind being wheeled out."

"How long are you taking off?" Charlie asked. "I'm taking two days."

"I'm taking the rest of the week. I'll reevaluate at that time. I stood naked in front of the mirror this morning. I looked like a black and blue punching bag. I don't want to scare my patients." Her hand rested on her side. "I never thought bruised ribs could hurt so much."

"I'm so sorry. I never—"

"Stop it! You're going to piss me off. This is *not* your fault. I'm the one who wanted a relationship with that nut. My picker must need adjustment because I didn't see him as dangerous."

Charlie winked. "It was the marble butt."

Marti chuckled. Her hand held her side. "Ow, my ribs. How could I be so swayed by a sexy butt?"

Captain Strouper came into the room. He stopped when he saw Marti's face. His smile dissolved into a thin-lipped grimace. "Marti, we have an APB out for Special Agent Hornsby."

Charlie's frustration fumed to the surface. She threw up her hands. "He's the *golden boy*. He threatened and stalked me, so what did the FBI do? They slapped his hand. Thousands of this department's dollars were spent trying to find out who was leaving those notes. The FBI did nothing. Now he's kidnapped and beaten Marti beyond recognition, written bitch on my garage door, tried to kidnap me, caused numerous car accidents, stolen a Camaro, and resisted arrest. The Feds will only slap his wrist again." She banged her fist on the table. "Who is Scott? The President's son?"

The captain crossed his arms. "Close. He's the step-son of a senator."

Marti and Charlie looked at each other, then back at the captain. "Which one?" Marti asked.

The Captain held up both hands. "All I can say is it's a powerful one from a state near D.C."

Charlie sputtered, "If...if that's the case, he'll never face charges. They'll sweep it under the Senate building."

Captain Strouper folded his long frame into the chair nearest the whiteboard. "Not if I have anything to say about it." He opened his notebook. "The first meeting this morning is about the Marksman. It should be short. The second is about Special Agent Hornsby."

Within minutes the chairs in the conference room were filled. Ryan sat next to Joe, across from Charlie.

Captain Strouper stood. "What do we have on our sniper? The mayor is calling me daily for updates."

Joe cleared his throat. "We now know the Marksman drives a light-blue older Ford pickup. The techs acquired molds of his tire tracks. They're still trying to find a match."

"Did anyone get the tag number?" the captain asked.

"No, sir." Joe fingered the handle of his coffee mug. "He'd rubbed mud on the plate. One of my men did shoot his passenger-side mirror, which should help to identify the truck when we locate it. I have an APB out for the vehicle. That pretty much covers what's new. We're still going over witness statements."

The captain nodded and turned to Charlie. "Thanks to Dr. Stone, he wasn't successful in claiming another victim. I understand you injured your knee during that well-televised leap."

"It wasn't the leap, Captain," said Charlie. "It was the landing. I'm not known for my grace."

Marti piped up. "That's the truth."

Several people chuckled.

The captain looked at her and cocked a brow. "How did you know who he planned to shoot?"

"Three things. First he'd want a famous tribe that had special costumes. It makes for a better trophy. Second, I thought I saw a laser dance across the kid's shirt, and third, I saw a flash of light from the woods."

Joe grumbled, "I didn't see any of that."

The captain closed his notebook. "If that's all we have on the Marksman, we'll take a break and reconvene about Agent Hornsby. Special Agent Brown is due to arrive in about fifteen minutes."

The room emptied except for Charlie and Marti.

Marti asked, "Any idea how long this next meeting will last?"

Charlie shrugged. "I'd lay odds it will take longer than the last one. I'm taking a potty break."

Marti sighed. "Me, too."

With much grunting and groaning, the two rose and tottered to the ladies' room.

Marti glared at the toilet.

"What's wrong? Charlie asked, peeping into the stall.

"It hurts to squat and bend."

Charlie muttered, "I'm going to kick Scott's balls up his throat and out his mouth the next time I see him. Back up, Marti."

Charlie took tissues and wiped the seat. She then laid down a tissue barrier. "You're good to go. No pun intended."

"Thanks."

They had finished and were washing their hands when Marti asked, "Does everyone know Scott's related to a senator?"

Charlie pulled towels from the dispenser and handed one to Marti. "I have no idea. My guess is the captain didn't know until recently."

They made it back to the conference room and settled with groans into their previous seats. A few minutes later, the captain's secretary arrived with two coffees, sweeteners, and creamers.

"I'm Annie. The captain asked me to bring you some coffee. He saw y'all on the way to the ladies' room and thought it might be a bit much for y'all to make it to the break room."

Charlie's eyes misted. "Thank you, Annie."

Moments later the captain returned, placing his mug of steaming black brew on the table.

"Thank you for the coffee," Charlie and Marti said in unison.

He waved a dismissive hand. "The least I can do."

Ryan walked in with a pad and was pulling out a chair when the captain cleared his throat.

Ryan looked over.

"Roberts, don't you have work to do? This isn't your case."

Ryan glanced at Charlie, then back at the captain. He opened his mouth to speak when the captain cocked a brow.

"Yes, sir."

He gave Charlie a look that conveyed, *Tell me everything later*, and left.

Two men in suits who looked somewhat familiar to Charlie took seats across from her.

Captain Strouper pointed at the tall one sporting a mustache, and said, "Frank Jakes. His partner is Smitty Hinkle. They're assigned to the Scott Hornsby case."

Hinkle was Kojack bald.

Kate rushed into the room, her face flushed. She ran her hands through her short copper curls and took a deep breath. "Ran up the steps." She looked at Marti. "I didn't think it was possible, Marti, but you look worse."

Marti shifted in her seat and grimaced. "I didn't think it could hurt worse than yesterday, but it does." Then she grinned. "Come see me in a few days, so you won't miss the full-color spectrum of the bruises."

Sam lumbered inside. "I don't know about Kate, but I'll pass on that offer."

They both took seats beside Charlie and Marti.

The last to arrive was Special Agent Brown with an agent he introduced as Agent Higgenbotham.

Before Agent Brown could sit, Charlie asked, "How is Henley?"

"It was touch and go for a while, but the doctor said he should make a full recovery. I understand I can thank the two of you"—he looked at Sam and then Marti—"for saving his life."

Sam nodded. "Just doing my job."

Captain Strouper rapped on the table with his knuckles. "Let's start this meeting." He opened his notebook.

Captain Strouper sat tall and informed Agent Brown, "Due to the trauma and injuries of *my consultants*, I will be present for the joint interviews by you and my investigators."

Brown's brow furrowed. "Our department would prefer to interview these ladies privately."

The captain raised his chin a tad. "Not happening."

The two men stared at each other for several moments before the agent relented.

Detective Frank Jakes turned on a recorder. "Unlike the FBI, we'll be recording these interviews."

Brown nodded to Higgenbotham, who pulled out a pad, prepared to take notes.

Detective Jakes took Marti through the whole sequence of events she'd experienced the night before.

Charlie had heard most of it, but today, Marti gave a blow-by-blow account of what Scott had done to her. Fiery, acid-churning fury made her feel ill.

When Detective Jakes completed his questions, Agent Brown took over. "Did Agent Hornsby rape you?"

"No. I was afraid he would when he was mauling my breast, but he didn't. Instead, he talked about the sexual things he planned to do to Charlie when he captured her."

"Did he strike you as unbalanced?"

Marti paused and looked up at the ceiling as though the answer would fall into her head. "Yes and no. It depends on your definition of unbalanced."

Agent Brown studied her. "To use a nonclinical term, do you think he's crazy?"

Charlie thought *He's trying to set up an insanity defense.*

Marti stared him down. "As a Licensed Professional Counselor with many years of experience, I think Scott suffers from an obsessive-compulsive personality disorder, not a mental illness like schizophrenia. His obsessions are toward people. In this instance, it was about Dr. Stone. His compulsion was to own and control her."

Agent Brown glared at Marti. "Surely he was too distraught to realize what he was doing."

Marti dismissed his remark with a wave of her hand. "Scott knew his actions were wrong. He even apologized before hitting me."

"Oh, what did he say?"

"'Sorry about this, Marti. I'd hoped I wouldn't have to hurt you.' Make no mistake; Scott knew exactly what he was doing when he forced his way into my home. He planned both my kidnapping and how to lure Dr. Stone to my house. What he didn't expect was my resistance."

Captain Strouper interrupted. "Any more questions?"

The agent's jaw muscle flexed. "I think that's enough—for now."

"Do we need a break before we do Dr. Stone's interview?" the captain asked.

Marti and Charlie looked at each other.

Charlie said, "Yes."

When they returned, Detectives Jakes and Hinkle had Charlie take them step-by-step, through the events of the evening before.

Agent Brown ran his left hand through his hair while the other agent took notes.

When his detectives finished, Captain Strouper turned the interview over to Agent Brown.

"What made you think Agent Hornsby planned to kidnap you last night?"

Charlie's jaw dropped. *Are you stupid?* She leaned forward. "He wrenched open the door on Kate's minivan and tried to get in. If I hadn't forced him to let go, you'd be searching for both of us."

He nodded. "Perhaps he only wanted the vehicle. After all, he only stole the Camaro. He didn't kidnap its owner."

Charlie glared at him. "He didn't have that poor guy's photos posted all over his walls."

"When did you first meet Agent Hornsby?"

Charlie sat back in her chair. "When he moved in next door."

With a stern look, he said, "You didn't meet him at Quantico?"

"No."

"When did you discover Agent Hornsby was the one writing you threatening notes?"

"I'd hired a local firm to install cameras around my home and in my car. This allowed me to film the event where he left the note on my windshield. The next morning I took the evidence to Captain Strouper. He set up a meeting with your boss. The exact date should be in the FBI's records. Your boss has a copy of the DVD."

With a sarcastic tone, Agent Brown said, "You're a trained professional. Didn't you realize Agent Hornsby had a crush on you?"

Charlie paused and chose her words carefully. "There's a distinct difference between a *crush* and an *obsession*. Many men have liked me over the years. Until Scott Hornsby, none of them stalked me, wrote me threatening notes, or used my face as their wallpaper. He seemed like a lonely guy, new to our area, which sought some connections. He played the role of a helpful neighbor who sometimes overstepped his boundaries."

"What do you mean by 'overstepped his boundaries?'"

Charlie searched through her memories. "For example, Ryan and I were at my house. We'd planned a quiet dinner together. Without calling or discussing it with us, Scott showed up at my door with a large pizza." She studied the agent's face. *This is so strange. He's not asking us any of the questions I expected.*

The detectives questioned Kate and Sam next. They both submitted copies of their written reports.

In the end, it was quite clear. Agent Scott Hornsby had gone on a rampage and had a long list of charges facing him, the most serious being the attempted murder of Special Agent Henley.

Agent Brown pulled his phone from his inside coat pocket. He read a message and frowned. After a quick glance around the table, he told Captain Strouper. "That's all for today." He wasted no time collecting his papers before both men exited the room.

After they left, Charlie and Marti looked at each other. Charlie said, "Did that line of questioning seem weird to you?"

Marti nodded. "Yep. We need to leave if I'm going to make my eye appointment."

CHAPTER 49

Two days later, Charlie decided she needed a waffle fix. She headed for her favorite Waffle House, the one near her home. The staff there knew her name and how she liked her waffle chunky with pecans and crisp like her bacon.

Fine misting rain confounded the multiple-wiper settings on Charlie's Honda. None of them cleared the windshield to her satisfaction. Thirty-five mile-per-hour wind gusts buffeted the car. She tightened her hold on the wheel and pulled into a spot close to the door. Once inside, she scanned the interior, a habit she'd acquired after she started dating Ryan.

"Welcome to Waffle House," several voices shouted. When Barbara and Cinda recognized her, they said in unison, "Hey, Charlie."

She returned their greeting.

Cinda asked, "You here for a pecan waffle?"

"I need to order something different from time to time to confuse you."

"That'll be the day." Barbara grinned.

Charlie walked past an older man who sat in the booth closest to the register. His cane occupied the opposite seat. It appeared he planned to nurse a cup of coffee and enjoy the company of the staff for a while. Since it was past breakfast and before lunch, there were no other diners. She chose the small middle booth next to the window overlooking the parking lot. Gusty winds gave the little flags in the Arby's parking lot next door a vigorous workout.

Cinda approached with a glass of water in one hand and a cup of coffee in the other, and placed them on the table. Rummaging in the pockets of her brown smock, she produced Splenda packets and creamers.

"You want your usual?"

"Yes, please."

"Okey-dokey." Cinda wrote the order on her yellow pad. She strode back behind the counter, where she stood staring at the cook. When the young, dark-haired man working the grill nodded, she bellowed, "Pull one bacon, well." She paused and then continued. "One pecan waffle, dark."

Charlie noticed Sue, one of the regular waitresses, wasn't working today. Instead, a new waitress worked the booths at the other end of the diner. The woman looked familiar for some reason, although nothing was outstanding about her appearance that should trigger Charlie to remember her. She was medium everything.

The unknown waitress walked over to the Touch Tone jukebox and chose some selections while eyeing Charlie.

How do I know her? Charlie doctored her coffee. *This is going to bother me until I figure it out.*

The song, "Help Me, Rhonda," bounced off the white tile and stainless steel walls. Charlie tapped her foot to the Beach Boys' tune while watching the roofing tiles on the Microtel Hotel and Suites flutter up and down as if waving a greeting.

Good grief. Maybe I should drive by my house to make sure I haven't lost any roofing tiles. Possible house repairs reminded her that she had to paint her garage door. Her neighbors wouldn't be happy about the red BITCH written across it.

The thought brought to mind one of the reasons for her comfort food cravings—Scott. Her earlier visit to check on Marti had added to her plummeting mood. Her friend looked like she'd gone several rounds with a professional boxer. In two days, her bruises had progressed from purple and black to the green and yellow stage.

Charlie crossed her legs under the table and winced as the pain in her knee reminded her that the Marksman was also at large. She sipped her coffee and tried to focus on the positive. *The kid at the Pow Wow didn't get shot. Marti doesn't have a torn retina.* She tried to find another positive. *Oh, yeah. I didn't wreck Kate's Mom Mobile. So, it's not all bad.*

The song ended, making it easier to think.

In her raspy voice, Barbara asked the older man, "You want a refill, Roy?"

He pushed the mug toward her. "Sure, I'll take a drop."

Cinda placed her order in front of her. The steam from the waffle was fragrant with the aromas of butter and pecans.

Charlie looked up and smiled her thanks.

Leaning over, Cinda peeked into her mug. "I'll bring you more coffee." She returned with the coffee pot and a container of syrup.

"I'll need sugar-free."

"That's new."

"Yeah, I know."

Only Marti and Ryan knew Charlie's secret, the one she hadn't quite accepted herself.

The waitress returned with a bottle of sugar-free syrup.

Charlie cut into the waffle and grinned while she sliced through chunks of pecans.

The next selection on the jukebox blared, "Hit the Road Jack," in Ray Charles's distinctive voice. Charlie sang along in her head but replaced the name Jack with Scott. Crunching into a bite of waffle, she closed her eyes to appreciate the taste and texture better. *Perfect.* The bacon was crisp and flavorful. She looked up to see the waitress she didn't know, staring at her with a worried expression.

The woman looked away and busied herself by clearing one of the booths in her section.

This annoyed Charlie. *Why is she staring at me?*

Cinda appeared at her booth. "Need anything?"

Charlie lowered her voice. "What's the new lady's name?"

"Lorraine. She seems nice enough. She's worked for the company for years. Transferred to this location a few weeks ago. Why?"

Charlie shrugged. "Just curious. Seems like I know her."

Cinda glanced over her shoulder at her coworker. "You'll probably figure it out in the middle of the night. That's what happens to me."

Charlie methodically worked her way through her meal, so she had a bit of both waffle and bacon to finish. Satisfied, she pushed away the plate. She could feel the endorphins flooding her body and lifting her mood.

Reaching for her empty plate, Cinda asked, "More coffee?"

"Sure, half a cup, please."

Cinda filled the mug and placed the yellow check on the table before leaving.

The air conditioner kicked on, eliciting a shiver from Charlie. *Why do they have the air on? It's October and raining to boot.* The receipt skittered toward the edge of the table before stopping. She stirred her brew and gazed out the window.

An old blue truck pulled into the Arby's lot. She noticed it because it circled until the driver's side was close to the diner with the truck facing Shields Road. Typically, only vehicles pulling trailers parked that way.

"Excuse me."

Charlie jumped. Her heart felt like it shot to her Adams apple and back down.

Lorraine blushed. "Sorry, I didn't mean to scare you. Barbara told me you're Charlie Stone."

"Yes?"

"I thought I recognized you. I see Miz Marti. I'm Lorraine Springle."

Charlie's muscles relaxed. She lowered her voice so the others wouldn't overhear. "I thought you looked familiar. I've seen you in the waiting room."

Lorraine moved closer and whispered, "I need to talk to you about my son."

"Oh?" The air turned off. Grateful for small miracles, Charlie circled the mug with her hands to warm them.

"He's not actin' right." She slid into the booth across from Charlie and whispered, "He locks himself in his room all the time."

"How old is he?" Charlie whispered.

"Twenty-two." She leaned closer. "I hear him in there talking to my father."

Charlie was confused. "Have you talked to Marti about this?"

"I've tried. Delores, your new office manager, told me she would be out until next week due to medical reasons."

"That's true."

"Would you consider seeing my son?"

"Maybe. Is your son willing to come in for therapy?"

Lorraine frowned and shrugged. "My father died several months ago. He was a sniper during the drug war in South America, detached from the Marines to a black ops unit. Got discharged early for mental reasons. He and my son were like peas in a pod." She held two of her fingers close together. "He's the one who taught Jared how to shoot."

Charlie tapped her lower lip with her finger. "That name sounds familiar."

"When Jared came home Saturday, the passenger-side mirror on my father's old truck was damaged." She leaned closer. "When I pulled in the drive, he aimed his rifle at me. I thought he'd shoot me right then and there."

Alarms clanged in Charlie's mind. *Joe mentioned an officer shot the passenger mirror on the Marksman's truck.* "What happened next?"

"When he saw it was me, he lowered the rifle. He stomped off into our trailer, locked himself into his bedroom, and refused to come out and eat. I don't know what happened afterward because I left for work."

Lorraine pushed herself out of the booth with a grunt and stood next to Charlie. Her voice trembling, she said, "I think Jared is the one shooting all those people."

The air conditioner kicked on again. The yellow check drifted off the edge of the table.

Charlie dove to catch it.

The window shattered. Shards sprayed Charlie and the table.

Lorraine cried out, clutching her chest as she fell backward. She hit the floor, moaning.

Everyone behind the counter started screaming.

Charlie froze. Her coffee burned its way back up her throat. Swallowing it back down, she slid out of the booth to the floor.

"Get down! Shots fired!" she screamed. She grabbed her purse and fumbled to find her phone.

The staff had already ducked behind the counter. The elderly man sat like a statue in the nearby booth.

One of the waitresses hissed, "Roy, get down, you old fool."

Charlie scrambled over to him on hands and knees. She pulled him out of the booth to the floor. "Get down!"

A second shot pierced the window and pinged off a waffle iron.

The acrid scent of urine stung Charlie's nose. A wet stain spread across the front of the man's pants.

Charlie pointed toward the metal door that led to the restrooms. "Crawl to the men's room and lock the door."

She found her phone and dialed 911 while she scooted back to Lorraine who lay in a pool of blood.

Roy was making steady progress toward the relative safety of the restrooms. He left a wet trail behind him like a snail.

"What's your emergency?" a female voice asked.

"There's an active shooter at the Waffle House located on Shields Road. One person is shot."

"Stay on the line with me until help arrives. Is the shooter in the building?"

"No, not yet." A round shattered the glass of the cooler. Charlie felt the cool breeze.

"I think it's the Marksman. One of the waitresses has been shot. She needs an ambulance."

"Where's the victim been shot?"

"In the chest. I think the bullet hit one of her lungs. She's still breathing, but I'm hearing sucking sounds and there's bloody foam around her mouth."

She flinched when a round hit the venting hood over the grill.

"An ambulance and paramedics have been dispatched. Is she the only victim?"

"So far. If help doesn't get here soon, we may all be goners."

Charlie had taken several first aid courses over the years. *Oh, God. What did that instructor say to do for a chest wound?* She glanced around and spotted the plastic wrap on a nearby counter. She crawled over and reached up to grab it.

A shot shattered the coffeepot splattering her with hot liquid.

"Shit!" She slung the hot liquid off her hand and nabbed the wrap.

Sirens blared in the distance. She scrambled back to Lorraine while a volley of shots peppered the diner. *Damn, he's trying to get us with ricochets.* Charlie shielded Lorraine with her body and prayed, *Please, God, make him stop*

The shots stopped.

She saw blue lights bouncing off the metallic surfaces. Grateful for the silence, she opened Lorraine's smock, ripped off some plastic wrap, and tightly covered the bullet holes, front and back by wrapping her like a sandwich.

Lorraine's breathing eased a bit.

"Are you there?" the operator asked.

"Yes. I think the shooter left. Help is here because I see flashing blue lights. Tell the officers I'm on the floor with the shooting victim. There is one customer in the men's room and at least four other staff members are somewhere in the back."

"Roger that."

Charlie took Lorraine's pulse. It was thready, but it was there. She rose and stepped away to give the paramedics room to work on Lorraine. The tall one looked up at her. "Did you put this plastic wrap over the wound?"

Charlie nodded, wondering if she'd done the right thing.

He gave her a thumbs up before starting an IV.

Charlie stepped outside and phoned Ryan. "I think the Marksman tried to shoot me at the Waffle House on Shields Road."

Silence.

"Ryan?"

"Are you okay?" he asked.

"Yeah, thanks to the bill falling to the floor."

"What? You're not making sense, Charlie."

She heard Joe say in the background, "Do women ever make sense?"

"Can you come?" she asked. Her insides felt like quivering jelly.

"Joe and I are on the way."

The ambulance backed to the door.

Charlie rushed to hold open the restaurant door for the gurney. Lorraine gained consciousness just before they loaded her inside. She took Charlie's hand and gave her an imploring look. "Stop... him."

"You want me to try to stop him if he's the one?" Charlie asked.

Lorraine nodded.

Twenty minutes later, Ryan and Joe pulled into the lot. Charlie's shaking had calmed, but she still needed a hug. She walked into Ryan's arms.

Joe exited and walked around the front of the car to reach them. "What the hell happened here?"

Charlie explained while wiping a tear from her lashes with a forefinger.

Joe shook his head. "Doc, you're a trouble magnet. I ain't saying it's your fault or nothin', but it sure finds you."

"Thanks, Joe. You know how to make a lady feel special." She pulled free of Ryan and stepped back. "I think I know who the Marksman may be. His name is Jared Springle. His mother told me she feared her son is the Marksman before she was shot. Run his name and get his address."

"I'll be damned!" Joe returned to the driver's seat and called in the request. A few minutes later he had the address. He stood and rested his forearm on the roof. "We're going to need back up for this one. Can't go in half-cocked."

Ryan and Charlie moved closer. Charlie pulled out her phone and put the address in Google maps. "This is out in Madison County."

Joe looked over at Ryan. "Guess we need to call Sheriff Jarvis." He grinned at Charlie. "He'll sure be happy to see you again, Doc."

The brief thunderstorm storm had passed leaving dripping trees and patches of blue peeking through the thinning clouds. Sheriff Jarvis and two Madison County deputies were in the parking lot of a deserted gas station when Joe and Ryan pulled in. Charlie followed and parked under the awning near the pumps.

Two large maps weighted with stones covered the hood of the Sheriff's car.

"Why are we meeting here?" Charlie asked Ryan.

"It's close to the location of the trailer," Ryan said.

When Charlie stepped out of her Honda, Jarvis grinned and took off his sunglasses. "Well, if it isn't the beautiful Dr. Stone."

Joe and Ryan stepped in front of her and walked toward the sheriff.

Joe looked over at Ryan. "Now, don't you go getting territorial and start pissing a circle around Doc."

"I can hear you back here," Charlie said.

Jarvis shook hands with the new arrivals, holding Charlie's a tad too long. He walked back to his vehicle and pointed. "We were looking at the maps, trying to get the lay of the land."

Charlie pulled her iPad out of her purse and opened Google Maps. "This doesn't look easy to me."

She placed the pad on the hood and pointed at the Google Earth version. "There's a long driveway that opens into a clearing. Looks like a mobile home to me. Is there any way to approach the place through the woods?"

Jarvis took off his hat, wiped his brow with his sleeve, and replaced it. "We were discussing this when you arrived. I drove by the entrance. It's a gravel drive, so he'll hear us coming."

Joe pulled on the collar of his shirt. "Do we know if he's in there?"

Jarvis shook his head.

Ryan stood with crossed arms. "We'll put a guard on his mother's room when she gets out of surgery. Don't know if he'll try to see her, but we'll be ready."

"Do you think he was trying to kill her?" Jarvis asked.

Charlie shook her head. "I think he was trying to kill me."

Jarvis rocked back on his heels. He adjusted his hat to see her better. "Why you?"

"She kept him from killing his intended victim at the Pow Wow in Huntsville," Ryan said.

"I was diving to catch a check that fell off the table when he shot. His mother was standing next to me." She tucked her hair behind one ear. "It was an accident. My headshot turned into her chest wound."

CHAPTER 50

The Marksman drove away with his system zinging with adrenaline and Grumps screaming in his mind.

"I should have waited. The wind was too high, and I had to shoot through the glass."

"Damn right you should have waited," Grumps bellowed.

"You're the one who kept saying I should kill the bitch," the Marksman whined.

He couldn't believe he'd shot the wrong person. He had the woman's head in his crosshairs when he pulled the trigger. A brown smock was all that appeared in the scope before the person fell. *Who in the hell did I shoot?*

Grumps yelled in his mind, *"You've gone plum crazy, boy? First, you miss. Then you shoot up the place like a complete amateur. What's wrong with you?"*

He drove home to change vehicles. *I need to leave town for a while. Lay low.*

The tires crunched the gravel as he eased down the drive. *Good, Mom's not here.*

He carried the rifle inside. Once there he grabbed a gym bag and began stuffing it with clothes. *My pills.* He walked into the bathroom and pulled the bottle out. *Not many left.* He gathered his toothbrush and all the other personal care items he'd need.

He returned to his bedroom and shoved the pill bottle into a side pocket of the bag. Everything else went in with the clothes. He grabbed another bag from the closet and filled it with ammunition and his cleaning kit. *My scrapbook. Can't leave it here. Mom might get nosy.* He tried to think of what else he might need.

Grumps said, *"You need cash, boy. Don't you have no sense?"*

He went into the kitchen and checked his mother's hiding places. He found only twenty bucks.

Grumps chuckled. *"You gonna need more than that, boy."*

"Shut up, old man!"

The Marksman pushed the door open to his mother's room and turned on the light.

Grumps said, *"Everything's neat as a pin, just the way I taught her."*

The Marksman opened drawers and pushed around the contents looking for money. *Nothing.* He found a cigar box on the top shelf in the closet. Inside were papers and cash. He grabbed a wad of twenties and was about to leave the box on the bed when he saw his name on a document. He sat and placed the box on his lap. He put the money down beside him and pulled out the paper.

It was his birth certificate. Jared Michael Springle. Mother: Lorraine Ann Springle. Father: Horace Michael Springle.

He blinked and reread his father's name. *Horace Michael Springle is Grumps's name.* He looked closer, trying to see if he'd missed seeing Jr. at the end. He hadn't. For a few moments he ran this new information around his brain. *Was Grumps my daddy?*

"Bout time you learned the truth, son. I sired you. You're mine."

His mind raced back to all those nights his grandfather had made him leave his mother's bed and locked him out of the bedroom. *You were fucking my mother? Your daughter?*

His mind filled with his grandfather's laughter. He rushed to the toilet and vomited his disgust.

CHAPTER 51

Charlie stood at the abandoned gas station and listened to the plan. Her role in this takedown was to help if a hostage situation occurred. A deputy would go by foot through the woods, to determine if Jared Springle, alleged to be the Marksman, was in the mobile home.

Deputy Johnny Spack volunteered. According to Sheriff Jarvis, he'd proved to be an expert woodsman and tracker in the past. Tall, lean, and tanned, he looked every bit the part.

Spack removed his hat and placed it on the seat of his patrol car. He turned off his mobile unit to avoid unexpected squawks.

After running both hands through his dark hair, he said, "Give me about twenty minutes." He loped to the gravel drive and disappeared from sight.

Charlie prayed for his safety and the safety of the team.

Jarvis sidled up to her. "Hey, that was quite a leap you made to save that kid at the Pow Wow. I didn't realize you were that athletic."

She shifted to her left. "Thanks."

He shifted closer and winked. "I haven't seen you around much lately."

"I've been busy." She looked over at Ryan, who was leaning over the map pointing at something.

"Too busy to have a cup of coffee sometime?" Jarvis smiled.

Charlie faced him. "Sheriff, I believe in maintaining good *professional* relationships with all law enforcement personnel, but I have a policy."

His grin widened. "Yeah, what's your policy?"

"I don't have coffee, meals, or any one-on-one contact with married men. It's the best way to avoid misunderstandings and offers nothing to feed the rumor mill."

Jarvis took a step back. "I wasn't suggesting anything—"

"Good." Charlie smiled. "Then we understand each other. Did I mention Ryan Roberts and I are dating?"

"Uh, no. That's great." He checked his watch. "Wonder what's keeping Johnny?" He walked toward Deputy Handle and started a conversation.

Charlie exhaled her relief. This wasn't her first encounter with his flirtations. His reputation with the ladies was known far and wide in Madison County. She couldn't imagine why his wife tolerated the situation.

Ten minutes later, Deputy Spack returned. He swiped cobwebs from his hair. "A male in his twenties is in the mobile home. There are two vehicles parked in the clearing, a white Toyota Corolla and a blue pickup with a broken passenger mirror."

"Did he spot you?" Jarvis asked.

"Nope. He was busy digging through drawers when I looked through the window. Got a shot of him with my phone." He reached into his shirt pocket and pulled out an iPhone.

Ryan waved Charlie forward. "Dr. Stone is the only one who's seen the guy."

She took the phone. All the others crowded around her. "That's Jared Springle." She handed the phone to the sheriff. Feeling boxed in by the tall men, she backed out of the crowd.

Jarvis frowned down at the photo. "How do you know this suspect?"

"He approached me at a local gun shop where I was target shooting. He asked for my casings." Charlie shifted to the left to get the emerging sun out of her eyes. "When I finished and was putting away my gear, he asked me to join him for a burger." She glanced over at Ryan. "I declined, but he followed me to the Waffle House on Shields Road. Ryan joined me for lunch that day. When Jared saw Ryan, he left. One of the waitresses told me he gave her the creeps."

Ryan cocked a brow. "Where did he rate on *your* creep meter?"

"A nine."

"What would be a ten?" Joe asked.

"The Trainer." She reached into her purse and donned her sunglasses to reduce the increasing glare. "Jared is Lorraine Springle's son. I've been thinking. I'm not sure he knows he shot his mother. If it's true, he may not try to show up at the hospital unless he sees it on the news."

"What do you mean? How could he not know?" asked Deputy Spack.

"You hunt, right?"

He nodded.

"When I'm peering down a scope, I'm limited in what I can see. Our suspect does clean headshots, and I believe I was his target. Like I said earlier, I ducked down to catch my check that blew off the table. All that would be in his scope when he fired was a brown smock. He shot Lorraine in the chest, which is where my head would have been. She fell immediately. I bet she was out of sight by the time he looked up. He knows he shot a waitress. He may not know it was his mother. Lorraine had just told me she feared he was the Marksman right before he shot her."

Jarvis crossed his arms and shifted back on his heels. "This guy may not be the Marksman. He shot his mother in the chest before shooting up the restaurant. Isn't this Marksman a one-shot wonder?"

"Yes, he's good," said Charlie. "Conditions weren't ideal with the earlier wind gusts.

Joe said, "I think Doc's right. The truck Spack described meets the description of the one used at the Pow Wow."

"I think he's mentally decompensating," said Charlie. "I'm not sure what's going on in his head, but I do know his grandfather died a short time before the Marksman murders started."

Jarvis nodded. "Either way it goes, he's a shooting suspect. Let's work out a plan to get him."

CHAPTER 52

The plan was simple. The two deputies would circle through the woods to approach the mobile home from the rear. If the suspect tried to bolt from the back door, they'd stop him.

Sheriff Jarvis, Ryan, and Joe would cover the front. Jarvis insisted on approaching the door. Ryan and Joe decided to take cover behind the vehicles in the clearing, ready to return fire if needed.

Charlie's role was to stay in the patrol car parked in the drive and wait, ready to pull into the clearing once the suspect was apprehended. Sheriff Jarvis wanted her close in case a negotiator was needed.

She eased down the drive in the patrol car, trying to make as little noise as possible. She could only see the front door of the mobile home through some branches but had an unobstructed view of the clearing. Her heart felt ready to jump out of her chest. She gripped the wheel and tried to control her breathing.

Sheriff Jarvis drew his gun and crept his way toward the mobile home. He bent low, climbed the three steps, and banged on the door with his fist. Stepping to the side, he yelled, "Madison County Sheriff's Department. Open up."

CHAPTER 53

Jared rose from his knees, wiped his mouth with some tissue and flushed the toilet. He didn't want to believe it. *My grandfather was my father? How did Mom stand it?*

He ran through his childhood memories of his mom telling him about his make-believe father and warning him not ever to discuss it with his grandfather. It would be their secret.

She lied to me. All these years, I've craved to know a man who didn't exist.

He remembered how his grandfather had acted like a father, and had taught him everything.

Grumps said, *"That's right, son. I taught you everything you need to survive. You can join the military like I did, and become a sniper like your old man."*

He covered his ears. Pain shot through his head.

"Grumps, how could you sleep with your own daughter?"

"I was never convinced she was mine to start with."

"That's sick!"

"No worse than what you wanted to do to the woman at the Pow Wow."

"She's not my daughter. It's different."

Grumps said, *"Pussy is pussy."*

Someone banged on the door.

"Madison County Sheriff's Department. Open up."

"Crap!" He rushed into his mom's room, grabbed the cash and birth certificate, then ran back to his room and shoved it all into his gym bag. He zipped it and the bag with the extra ammunition closed.

Grumps said, *"You'll have to sneak out the back and go through the woods."*

Jared loaded the magazine and readied his rifle. He grabbed the bags and moved toward the rear door. He unlocked it and eased it open.

"Madison County Sheriff's Department. Drop the gun and put your hands up."

He closed the door, locked it, and knelt to the side of the door to make less of a target.

"You're gonna to have to take them out, boy. Find out how many there are and kill them one by one."

The Marksman grabbed some nearby binoculars and scanned the woods behind the trailer. It took a moment before he spotted a deputy. The guy was leaning against a pine with his Glock drawn. "There's one. Now, where's your partner?"

The Marksman scanned the area to the right and found the second guy. He had a rifle and had chosen a safer position behind a tree.

"That one's a hunter. He knows what he's doing. The other cop is an easy target. Take him first," Grumps said.

The Marksman pushed open the window. Using his scope, he found the guy leaning against the tree. He centered the deputy's head in the crosshairs and pulled the trigger.

The deputy dropped to the ground.

"That's the way to do it, son. Go get another one."

The deputy with the rifle yelled, "Officer down! Officer down!"

CHAPTER 54

Charlie had the window down in the unit. She heard a pop and sat straight.

Spack yelled, "Officer down" twice.

Charlie picked up the radio and called in code 00, reporting an officer down and gave the location. "Ambulance needed."

She could see the men in front of the mobile home were fine. *He must have shot Deputy Handle.* She said a prayer for him and his family.

Another pop.

"He's trying to go out the back," yelled Ryan. He left the cover of the truck and sprinted toward the side of the trailer.

"No! Ryan, no." She climbed over the computer to the passenger seat, trying to see where he went.

Jarvis crawled over to the front door, reached over, and tried the knob.

Two pops.

Jarvis scrambled back.

Charlie snatched the binoculars off the seat.

The metal front door sported two bullet holes. If Jarvis had been two inches closer, the bullets would have gone through his body.

"Jared is trying to pick them off, so he can escape. I've got to do something before he kills someone else."

She remembered her promise to Lorraine to stop Jared if she could.

She opened the passenger door and crawled to the trunk and opened it. Inside she found a bullhorn. She grabbed it and crept to the front fender, staying out of the line of fire.

In the clearing, a round pinged off a fender close to Joe. He ducked even lower.

Charlie turned the bullhorn on. "Jared."

Silence.

"Jared, this is Dr. Stone. We met at the firing range. You need to stop shooting and put down your gun. No need for anyone else to get hurt."

No answer. No shooting.

"Jared, your mother is in surgery at Huntsville Hospital. Someone shot her in the chest at work."

An anguished wail from inside the mobile home filled the clearing.

CHAPTER 55

Jared dropped to his knees and wailed. He held his head with his hands and sobbed.

Grumps yelled in his head. *"Killed your bitch mother, and now you've killed a cop. You ain't worth shit. A worthless whelp."*

Jared's hands clawed at his ears. "Shut up, Grumps. Shut up. I can't stand it anymore."

"You might as well turn yourself in," Grumps said. *"Let's see what the guys in the jailhouse do with you. You're such a sissy, mama's boy. Stop crying."*

Jared rose to his hands and knees and crawled toward his rifle. "I gotta check on Mom. She needs me. Gotta get to the hospital."

Grumps chuckled. *"She's probably dead by now. Nothing you can do, boy. You done shot her dead."*

"Dr. Stone said she needs me," he said, rising to his feet. "Where're my keys?"

"The bitch is lying. She's trying to get you to come out," Grumps said. *"The minute you step out that door with a rifle, they'll fill you full of lead. You done killed a cop."*

"I'll surrender."

Grumps screamed, *"A good soldier never surrenders. You do that, boy, I'll yell in your head every minute of the day and night. You'll never get a decent night's sleep. You hear me?"*

Jared squeezed his eyes shut for several moments. When he opened them, he swiped away his tears.

He'd made his decision.

He pulled a wooden, olive green footlocker out of the closet. It belonged to his grandfather. Grumps's name was stenciled on the top along with his service number. He opened it and took out Grumps's Beretta M9 service pistol. He loaded a single round into the magazine of the pistol.

"Don't you do it, boy! You hear me? Stop!"

Jared put the pistol's muzzle into his mouth. "Goodbye, Grumps."

"Noooo!" Grumps screamed.

CHAPTER 56

Charlie flinched when she heard the shot inside the trailer. *That shot wasn't silenced.*

The realization hit her like a bullet to the chest.

"Oh, God, no!" She ran toward the door of the mobile home.

Scrambling to his feet, Joe yelled, "Doc! Get down, woman."

She clambered up the steps, where the Sheriff tackled her.

"Let me go. He's shot himself!"

"What?" Jarvis asked.

"For God's sake, call another ambulance," said Charlie. "That last shot came from a pistol."

"One's on the way. Hear the sirens?" asked the Sheriff. "I'll go check on the situation. You're staying here out of harm's way."

Ryan came and led her to safety. He locked her in the back of the squad car. "Sorry, honey. I have to make sure you stay safe."

It took them ten minutes to safely enter the trailer.

Ryan came out to the car and opened the door.

Charlie stood and waited to hear what she already knew in her heart.

"You were right. Jared Springle shot himself with a pistol. Officer Handle's dead, too." Ryan opened his arms.

Charlie walked into Ryan's arms and cried for all the victims and their families. She even cried for Jared, a young man she suspected suffered from his own psychological demons.

CHAPTER 57

Charlie stood outside room 236. Her gut was threatening to reacquaint her with breakfast. It had been two days since Lorraine's surgery and she hadn't been told her son was dead. *How do you tell a mother that her son committed suicide?*

Marti stood beside her and rubbed circles on Charlie's back.

"At least she's out of ICU," said Marti. "I checked with her physician this morning. He thinks she's stable enough to handle the news."

Charlie nodded. Her feet refused to move. Her mother had died in the room next to Lorraine's. The memories of those last days flooded her.

Marti took her by the elbow, breaking the string of recollections, and propelled her forward.

Lorraine lay pale and small in the bed with her eyes closed. No flowers brightened the room. The television was off.

"Lorraine," Marti said.

Charlie took Lorraine's cold hand in hers.

Lorraine opened her eyes and looked at Marti. "Oh, Miz Marti. Your face!"

"I'm fine. Give me a week. By then I should look close to normal."

"What happened?" Lorraine asked. "Were you in a car accident?"

Marti patted her arm. "It's a long story and nothing for you to worry about."

Lorraine looked over at Charlie. "That means it's none of my business." She paused and examined Charlie's face.

Charlie met her gaze.

Her eyes widened. "Jared's dead, isn't he?"

Charlie nodded.

Tears trickled down Lorraine's cheeks. "What happened?"

Charlie swallowed, trying to find her voice. "The police had him pinned in the mobile home. He killed a deputy. Before the detectives and sheriff's department could safely enter the trailer, he shot himself with your father's service pistol."

"Oh, God!" She put her hands over her face and sobbed.

Charlie and Marti both reached for the box of tissues.

Charlie stepped back and let Marti comfort the weeping woman since Lorraine was her client. She sat in a nearby chair and waited to answer the grieving mother's questions.

Twenty minutes later, Lorraine was ready for more information. Charlie took her through the events of the day that led to Jared, aka the Marksman, taking his life.

"So they're sure it was Jared who shot me?" Lorraine asked.

"Yes. Ballistics from Jared's rifle matched all the Marksman's kill shots. It also matched the attempted murder at the Pow Wow, as well as your shooting," Charlie said.

Lorraine's hand covered her mouth.

"I believe your son shot you by accident."

"What do you mean?"

Charlie shifted in her seat. "I think I was his target. If I hadn't tried to catch the check that blew off the table, I'd be dead now."

Lorraine's hand covered her wound.

Charlie sat forward. "I thought I heard your son yelling at someone called Grumps while he was inside the trailer."

Lorraine shifted in the bed and winced. "He called his father, Grumps. I've heard Jared talking to Horace when he'd locked himself in his room. It started after the old man died."

Charlie nodded. "So your son was hearing voices."

"I should've got him help years ago. Hell, I should've left and taken him with me." She shook her head. "That old man poisoned him with all his talk about when he was a sniper down in Bolivia, hunting drug lords. I didn't leave because I was too damned scared he'd kill me, and I had nowhere to go."

"You can't change the past, Lorraine," said Marti. "Right now you have enough pancakes on your stack to deal with today. You're tired. No more talking. I'll sit with you until you fall asleep. Dr. Stone and I will come back tomorrow and talk some more." Marti turned and nodded to Charlie.

Charlie took the cue and left. Once she was out of the room, she glanced at the room where her mother took her last breath and fled down the hall to the elevator.

"I hate hospitals! I'm tired of death!" She punched the button several times. When it opened, she rushed inside and poked the lobby button, ready to leave. She thought about all that had happened. Discovering that Scott was the note writer, his kidnapping of Marti, and his dangerous high-speed escape. Jared's suicide. She swiped a tear from under her lash. *I still miss you, Mom.*

Charlie had watched the news conference earlier today. The Mayor declared that the closure of the Marksman case would help to set the minds of the citizens of Huntsville at ease.

"One down and one to go," Charlie said to herself. The "one to go" sent her heart rate back up. Charlie stared at the changing floor numbers in the elevator, willing them to go faster. *All I want is to go home and hide*, she thought as the elevator door opened. *With Scott still on the loose, I feel like I've got a gun to my head.*

She hurried through the lobby to the parking garage, alert for danger. When she spotted the rear of her Honda, relief flooded her. *I'm going straight to bed and snuggle with Spanky until Ryan gets home. Tomorrow, I'll pull myself together.*

She opened the door, slipped into the seat, clicked the lock, and froze.

CHAPTER 58

A note sat under Charlie's wiper.

Her heart tap-danced against her ribs. She got out of the car and backed further into the space between the two vehicles. She looked around in a panic for Scott.

No one.

She willed her pulse to slow. *Is that footsteps?*

She could hear them coming closer and closer.

"My gun." She reached into her purse and grabbed it. No matter how tight she gripped the revolver she couldn't make her hands stop shaking.

A bearded man in blue jeans and an Alabama sweatshirt walked past without noticing her crouched in the shadows, her gun trained on him.

She released her breath and listened.

Nothing.

She straightened and opened her car door. After a quick glance around she put the revolver on the seat and reached for her phone. "Marti, where are you?"

"I'm still in Lorraine's room. Why?"

"There's a note on my car," Charlie said, still looking around.

"Crap. What do we do?"

"Stay there. I'm calling Ryan."

"Okay. Let me know what's happening," Marti said, her voice trembling.

Charlie sat in the car, locked the doors, and called Ryan.

Ten minutes later a police SUV pulled up behind her car.

Sighing with relief, Charlie opened her car door and stood to greet him.

The uniformed officer hitched up his wide belt. "I'm Officer Williams. I was told to stay with you until the rest arrive."

"Thanks, Officer. I feel better knowing you're here."

He peered around her to look at the note. "See you got another one. This FBI Agent is the hot topic at the precinct."

It wasn't long before Ryan's car turned the corner, tires squealing. He parked and strode over. His flexing jaw muscles relayed his level of tension.

Ryan shook Williams's hand. "Anything else happen before I got here?"

"Nope."

"Thanks, I've got it until my team gets here," Ryan said.

The officer nodded. "I'll drive around a bit and make sure this guy isn't hiding on another floor of the garage."

"Good idea." Ryan said.

The officer drove away.

"Why are you here?" Ryan asked with a clipped tone.

"Marti and I came to tell Lorraine about her son. Marti's still with her but I decided to leave and go home."

He eased past her to look at the note. "Well, hell. This asshole just won't quit."

They stood silent for a long moment staring at the folded note.

"We've learned a good bit more about the Marksman case," Ryan said.

Charlie rubbed her forehead. "Yeah? What?"

"We took a cadaver dog out to his place."

Charlie dropped her hand. "Dear, Lord, what did you find?"

"So far we've found five bodies. One of the graves is really old. It'll take a while to process it all," Ryan said.

"Good grief." Charlie rubbed her neck. "I hope it clears up some missing person cases. Maybe it will bring some family somewhere closure. Did y'all find any clues in the trailer?"

"Oh, yeah. The grandfather left a chest. Among other things we found a diary."

"What is it about killers and diaries?" Charlie asked.

He shrugged. "You're the shrink. It was more of a list of his kills. Who, when, where, and why he thought they deserved to die. Based on what he wrote, Lorraine's mother is probably in one of those graves."

"Why did he kill her?"

"He thought she screwed around on him while he was overseas. He wasn't convinced Lorraine was his kid."

Charlie rubbed her throbbing temples. "I'm glad Lorraine is Marti's patient. This will be a hard one to handle. The poor woman has been through some tough times. Imagine having that man for a father and then discovering your son is a serial killer."

"Joe found Horace Michael Springle's military records. He was a sniper during the drug war in South America. They discharged him for mental health reasons."

Charlie shook her head. "I'm not surprised about the discharge. I suspect Jared was psychotic and hearing his grandfather's voice in his head."

Ryan shrugged. "That's one theory. He was getting ready to run when we showed up. Had a bag packed with clothes, migraine pills, money, and his birth certificate."

Charlie leaned against the car and crossed her arms.

"You might find it interesting to know his grandfather is listed as his father on the birth certificate." Ryan cocked a brow. "What do you know about that situation?"

Charlie shrugged.

"That's what I thought. Glad you and Marti are dealing with all that stuff."

Charlie said nothing.

Ryan leaned against the car parked next to Charlie. He crossed his arms and ankles. "Our shooter had a scrapbook. Wrote Marksman on the front with a marker. He apparently liked the name the press gave him. Printed out any articles he'd found and taped them into it."

"I guess it's better than hanging people's heads on the wall," said Charlie. "Quantico would love to get their hands on his scrapbook and the diary to study."

"I heard you were offered a position with the FBI at the BAU," Ryan said. He ran a hand through his hair.

Charlie tilted her head. "I saw it more as a bribe."

"Are you going to take it? I wouldn't blame you. It's a great opportunity."

"Do you mean am I going to move to Washington?"

Ryan blushed.

"I agree it's a great opportunity offered for the wrong reasons. I can't drop the charges against Scott, and I don't expect Marti to either. Besides, Washington is too noisy and expensive and it doesn't have my favorite person there."

Ryan scrunched his brow. "Who's that?"

"You." Charlie walked into his arms and hugged him.

"Good to know," Ryan said. "You had me worried. A position with the FBI would be some people's dream."

"Would it be yours?" Charlie asked.

Ryan shook his head. "It's a whole new level of bureaucracy. I'd pretty much have to live the job. Not my thing. I don't like working as much as I do now. Besides, they can transfer you anywhere in the States on a whim."

Charlie grinned. "I guess we'll both stay in Huntsville."

Charlie leaned against him absorbing his warmth and enjoying the comforting fragrance of his Polo cologne.

He encircled her with his arms.

"Ryan, this whole mess has worn me down. I need a vacation. With Scott out there, I'm afraid to travel alone."

"I need to get away, too. My uncle owns a condo in Ft. Lauderdale. He'd let us use it for a week. It's still warm down there this time of year,"

"Can we take Spanky?"

"I'll ask. Uncle Steve takes his dog."

Squealing tires alerted them to an approaching vehicle.

Ryan released Charlie and stepped away. "Here's the crime scene van."

Holly climbed out of the van and grinned. "Charlie, is that besotted FBI agent sending you love notes again?"

Charlie held up her hands. "You tell me. I haven't touched it."

When the techs managed to get the note open and into an evidence bag, they gathered around to read it.

"IT'S NOT OVER UNTIL I SAY IT'S OVER. I'LL BE BACK FOR YOU, CHARLIE."

THE END

Made in the USA
Columbia, SC
14 April 2025

56644155R00137